'**Will pull readers in.**'
Kirkus Reviews

'**An intricate, historically rich tapestry.**
Fans of Holly Black and Sarah J. Maas will love this.'
School Library Journal

'**I couldn't stop reading** it,
and when I finished all I wanted was more.'
Daniel José Older

'Fast-paced . . . **a fresh take** on inclusive historical fantasy.'
NPR

'**A richly woven fantasy** . . . a clever, entertaining, thoughtful read.'
Shelf Awareness

'An **absolute feast** of imagination.
Complex, brooding, impossible to put down.'
Scott Reintgen

'Combining Yoruba myths, Shakespearean drama, a love triangle,
and a race-against time adventure, this fantasy debut
certainly **packs a punch**.'
Irish Examiner

'Williams's **fast-paced adventure** gallops apace . . . once
immersed in the world of Joan Sands, you're not going to want to leave.'
Tor.com

'A fun, quick read with diverse and queer characters
a reader will happily follow into battle.'
Historical Novel Society

SAINT-SEDUCING GOLD

◆ The Forge & Fracture Saga ◆

Brittany N. Williams

faber

First published in the US in 2024 by Amulet Books,
an imprint of Harry N. Abrams, Incorporated, New York.
First published in the UK in 2025
by Faber & Faber Limited
The Bindery,
51 Hatton Garden,
London EC1N 8HN
faber.co.uk

Printed by CPI Group (UK) Ltd, Croydon CR0 4YY

A CIP record for this book is available from the British Library

ISBN 978–0–571–38164–7

2 4 6 8 10 9 7 5 3 1

For Eric & Ericka, the coolest baby siblings
a chaotic older sister could want.

&

For every Black kid made to feel like you don't belong.
Ignore them, they're lying.

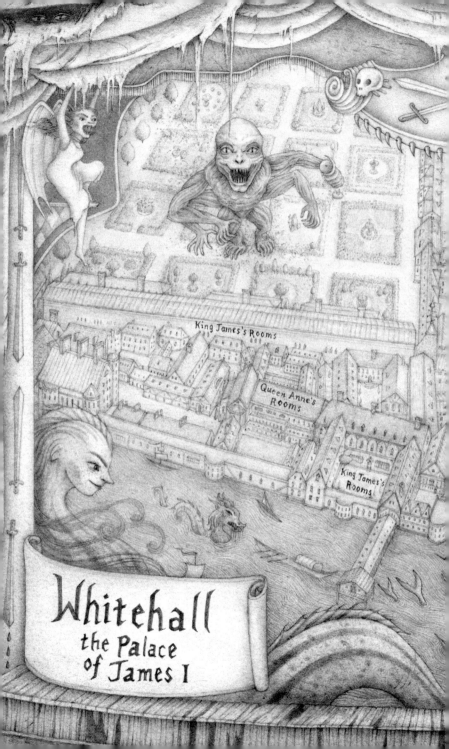

King James's Rooms

Queen Anne's Rooms

King James's Rooms

Whitehall
the Palace
of James I

Banqueting House

Lady Clifford's Rooms

DRAMATIS PERSONAE

The Sands Family

Joan – a teenage swordswoman blessed by Ogun

James – her twin brother and an actor blessed by Oya

Bess – her mother blessed by Elegua

Thomas – her father blessed by Yemoja

Nan – their maid

The King's Men

William Shakespeare – a playwright & actor blessed by Oshun

Richard Burbage – an actor

Augustine Phillips – an actor

Nicholas 'Nick' Tooley – an apprentice actor

Robert Armin – an actor

Rob Gough – an apprentice actor

The Fae

Titanea – queen of the fae

Robin Goodfellow – a powerful fae

Rose – Goodfellow's half-mortal daughter

Herne the Hunter – leader of the Wild Hunt

Various sirens, red caps, jacks-in-irons, goblins, hags and the like

The Royal Court

King James I –King of England

Philip Herbert – Earl of Montgomery & the king's favourite

Thomas Erskine – Earl of Fentoun & captain of the guard

Robert Cecil – Earl of Salisbury, Secretary of State & the king's spymaster

William Ceci – Viscount Cranborne & Cecil's son

Frances Cecil – Cecil's daughter

Catherine – Countess of Suffolk & the queen's lady-in-waiting

Penelope – Baroness Rich & the queen's lady-in-waiting

Lucy – Countess of Bedford & the queen's lady-in-waiting

Grace – a palace servant

Gregory – a royal footman

Various courtiers, servants & guards

SAINT-SEDUCING GOLD

• The Forge & Fracture Saga •

CHAPTER ONE
Fortunes Made & Marred

he queen is dead.

Joan Sands had expected Twelfth Night to go smoothly. She and her twin brother, James, would celebrate their birthday over a lovely morning meal with their family then spend the rest of the day at court with the King's Men. In the afternoon she'd help him and the rest of the players prepare for their royal performance. They'd pack up and end the evening eating royal delights, until Master Shakespeare and Master Burbage got drunk enough to take each other for an indecent turn on the dance floor. The day followed that exact pattern from the first time she'd attended the Feast of the Epiphany celebrations with the King's Men four years ago and every time since.

She'd been a fool to think the mayhem and bloodshed of last November wouldn't ripple chaos through this day and the royal court.

The queen is dead, and an imposter sits on her throne.

The breaking of the Pact between the Fae and the children of the Orisha released chaos upon mortal London. The only person with the knowledge of its sealing – Joan's godfather, Baba Ben – rotted in the Tower of London. Joan had killed Auberon, depriving the worst of the Fae of their leader; and Titanea, the Fae queen, had been killed by the explosion that decimated the House of Lords.

Or so they'd believed.

The quiet of the last two months seemed to prove they'd averted a greater crisis. But what did it mean now that Titanea was alive and wearing the face of the mortal queen of England?

More than that, she was the mastermind behind the broken Pact. She'd had Baba Ben arrested and imprisoned in the Tower of London. She'd orchestrated the explosion that had killed the true Queen Anne and so many others.

Titanea, who smiled as she lounged on England's throne and wore the form of its dead monarch.

Joan sat on the edge of her own gilded chair placed beside Titanea's on the highest scaffold. The rest of the royal guests spread out before their platform and along the sides of the hall; a sea of festive courtiers perched on row upon row of benches bordering the central playing space.

Joan had never felt more exposed in her life.

The warmth of Ogun's presence burned in her chest, the pulsing heat seeming to encourage her along with the persistent thrum of Bia, the sword she'd worn hidden around her wrist as a bracelet from the moment she'd laid hands on it. No other blade seemed so attuned to Joan's senses. Even now, its steady rhythm beat in harmony to Ogun's fire.

Titanea patted Joan's cheek. 'Do not make us regret our love for you, and remember you twice over are in our debt.'

Joan's heart raced at the memory, a shiver shooting down her spine as fear and regret overpowered even Ogun's burn. Her thoughts had been so overtaken first by her mistreatment at the hands of Queen Anne and her ladies and then at the queen's abrupt good grace, that Joan had offered her gratitude without hesitation.

Strike . . .

What a fool she'd been. Now the Fae queen held two chances to command Joan's absolute obedience to any request she may have. Two magical boons, which Titanea could use to compel her at any time to any purpose.

The potential in such unmitigated power was terrifying.

Strike.

Joan shook her head as if to dislodge the thought that she knew wasn't her own. She cut a look over her shoulder, certain that the women around them had heard every word. The queen's ladies faced away from the two of them, not a bit of attention paid to Joan. They twittered idle gossip like an obnoxious flock of birds, speaking eagerly to each other as if willed to do so by some force. A glance at Titanea's knowing smile told Joan they had been. None of them realised who they served in disguise, though Joan doubted they'd care so long as they continued to curry the monarch's favour.

She wondered if the difference mattered to her. She swallowed the uncomfortable lump in her throat when she couldn't give a simple answer even to herself.

Yes, Titanea had had Baba Ben arrested, but he was alive and unharmed – if she was to be believed. She'd caused the death of the true queen, but she'd also aided Joan in her greatest time of need. Titanea had given Joan the opportunity to rescue James by telling all under her command to stand down. Whatever dismay Joan felt over the loss of the true Queen Anne was hardly strong enough to drive an attack on its own, let alone when weighed against Titanea's aid.

Strike.

Ogun and Bia held no such doubts. The sword at her wrist pulsed so intensely that she feared Titanea could feel the vibrations. Her chest blazed with Ogun's pressure, the scorching heat urging her, driving her to attack the Fae queen though she'd done no harm in the time since the explosion.

Strike.

Ogun's command echoed firm and sure within her, but Joan didn't feel the Orisha's certainty. The doubt she held in her mind stayed her hand. She couldn't attack Titanea if any remained, refused to gamble with the lives of her loved ones. The stakes here loomed too high to allow any such errors.

Now. Strike now.

Joan took a shuddering breath, forcing the demand down and trying to calm the fire within her. Moving to murder Titanea now was not only unprovoked but rash and unwise. However much Bia and Ogun compelled her to attack, Joan knew she could not. She needed to be sure.

'Why have you done this?' Joan said, even as the insistent whispers raced through her mind.

Strike.

Titanea smiled indulgently and squeezed Joan's cheeks. 'Know us better and you will understand the why, dear Joan.'

Joan gritted her teeth but held the smile on her face. The vague response along with Ogun's pressing made her head swim. Joan hadn't expected a direct answer to her question, but Titanea's face held genuine affection. There was an advantage to be found in that. She only needed to press it.

'I would like to, Your Highness,' Joan said, exaggerating the deference in her voice. She cast her gaze down demurely. 'But your star lies so far above my own that we may find no more opportune moment to speak than this.' She frowned and lifted her eyes. 'A mere merchant's daughter could hardly hope to meet with Queen Anne once. Twice is unprecedented and I fear any more time together would be impossible.' The sad resignation she forced into the words would've made James proud.

Had her brother been in her place, he'd have cajoled a full confession out of Titanea as easily as breathing, but he stood with the actors in the tiring-room, the lot of them completely unaware of the queen's true identity. Joan prayed her own playing moved Titanea to make even a small admission, anything to help Joan plan her next action.

Strike.

Joan watched the Fae queen's expression shift from comprehension to dismay to a sudden sly satisfaction. She released Joan's face and leaned back on her throne. 'If it's time you want, dear Joan, then time you shall have.' She patted Joan's hand gently, her grin shooting apprehension through Joan's gut.

Strike!

The Orisha's voice screamed in Joan's head, and she found herself fighting against the familiar haze of Ogun's possession. Her vision darkened around the edges.

Strike!

She'd wavered for too long, and her indecision left her conflicted mind open for Ogun to overtake her. He'd attack where she wouldn't and damn them all to traitor's deaths.

She tried to resist but felt herself drifting, a numbness overwhelming her as her consciousness was shoved away from her physical body. Ogun pushed through and left her to see and feel with no control of her actions.

It played out in her head. She'd grab the front of Titanea's chemise, wrenching the Fae queen forwards as she called forth an iron blade.

One jab through the woman's throat would finish her with a wound she couldn't hope to heal.

A quick, clean kill before a room of spectators and an assured death for Joan and every single person she loved.

Her fingers twitched when the cool rush of iron flowed down her arm towards her palm. She breathed deeply, exerting all of her will to force the Orisha back. Her hands tingled with the effort, her movements nearly her own again. She shifted forwards just as someone seized her wrist. She spun and met Cecil's fierce gaze. Terror surged through her, slamming full awareness back into her body with a cold clarity.

'His Majesty the king approaches,' he said to Titanea, eyes slipping from Joan's face to her open palm, and then to her other hand still clasped within Titanea's. His scowl deepened. Did he know what she'd been about to do under Ogun's control?

'Cross me again and I'll see you burn, girl.'

The memory of the threat he'd hissed earlier in the hall rushed back into her mind. Even Cecil's own family wasn't free from his wrath. She passed the heads of Cecil's own in-laws, tarred and perched atop London Bridge as gruesome trophies, each time she crossed the Thames. If he'd seen her attempt . . .

Titanea raised one blonde eyebrow. 'We shall prepare space for the king.'

She snapped her fingers, and a flurry of activity burst around them. Two servants brought up another throne, larger and more ornate than the queen's, and placed it beside her. Her ladies scrambled to their feet, Lady Foul-Breath stumbling up from her cushion on the floor. Their idle chatter flooded Joan's ears. Lady Goose Neck attempted to shoulder Joan out of the way. Joan planted her feet and let the woman ricochet off her.

Cecil's nails dug into Joan's skin. 'Shall I return this child to her players?' He spoke the words lightly even as he attempted to draw blood with his hold.

Damn that man. But she was herself again and Ogun's voice had gone quiet.

'Your Highness,' Joan blurted, squeezing Titanea's hand even as she felt Cecil's grip on her other wrist tighten. 'If I might have your ear for one moment more.'

Cecil jerked her backwards. Joan stumbled, her attention on Titanea the only thing that allowed the weaker man to move her even slightly. The Fae queen scowled and laced her fingers through Joan's, holding fast.

'Have we dismissed her, Salisbury?' she said, her voice sharp with command.

Cecil paled.

'Oh my,' a voice said from behind them, their tone gleefully scandalised. 'It seems Lord Salisbury has soured Her Highness's happy mood.'

'You'd suppose that after his last failure nearly killed my queen, he'd tread more cautiously before her,' another replied.

Joan twisted over her shoulder to see the tall, pale form of King James ascending the stairs to the raised dais. Clusters of flickering candles on polished gold candelabras cast shifting light and shadow across his imposing form, playing over his sculpted blondee hair and beard. A striking young man barely older than Joan herself stood just behind the king, his equally flaxen hair secured with an ebony ribbon at his nape and pulled over one shoulder.

His gaze shifted from Joan's face to where Cecil held her wrist before sliding over to where Titanea's fingers intertwined with her own. A sly smile spread across the young man's face as he leaned towards the king. 'It seems this girl has caused some strife between our queen and Lord Salisbury. I'm surprised he has the temerity to so challenge Her Highness.'

'How impertinent,' the king grunted before dropping comfortably onto his throne. 'Erskine? Remind the Earl of Salisbury of his place.'

Cecil froze as a tall man approached from behind him, candlelight dancing over sharp features set in a pale but handsome face. His short fair hair was combed carefully to one side and brushed against his bushy blonde beard. He wore the crimson uniform of a yeoman guard, well-cut and bearing a host of medals and embellishments. A sword hung at his waist, shiny and well-made, but Joan could see the worn leather of the grip that spoke of its frequent use.

Erskine – for that must be his name – raised a bushy blonde eyebrow. 'I doubt the maid deserves such rough treatment.' A heavy Scottish accent coloured his deep voice, making the words sing. He placed one gloved hand casually on the hilt of his sword.

Cecil dropped Joan's wrist as if she'd burned him. She stumbled with the sudden release, and only Titanea tightening her grip kept her standing.

The young man slipped into place behind the king and leaned across the high back of the chair with an ease that spoke of comfort and frequency. A series of servants scurried around them, placing the brightly coloured standards bearing the royal Stuart crest all around the dais before disappearing discreetly.

King James's gaze swept over Joan. 'A blackamoor?' He raised an eyebrow. 'Is she so special?'

'She is indeed, my lord,' Titanea said, squeezing Joan's fingers again. 'After the loss of my dear Lady Clifford, I've found myself quite comforted by this girl's presence.' She sniffled, and one of her ladies dropped a delicate handkerchief into her other hand.

Joan fought the urge to snort as she watched the woman dab at dry eyes. The king smiled indulgently at Titanea, his expression gentle and affectionate.

'Of course, my queen,' he said. 'What would you have done with the girl?'

The queen is dead, and a Fae imposter sits on her throne.

Titanea cast a grateful look at the king, then turned to Joan, her expression sharp with glee. 'I want her as my lady-in-waiting.'

'What?' Joan blurted. Shock shoved any sense of propriety from Joan's mind as she boldly locked eyes with Titanea.

The Fae queen jerked her close to whisper in her ear. 'You wanted time, dear Joan, and time you shall have.'

Long live the queen.

itanea's request hung so heavily in the air, no one seemed to notice Joan's breach of etiquette.

'I want her as my lady-in-waiting.'

Joan cursed in her mind even as she appraised the opportunity Titanea had just given her.

Time indeed. The queen's ladies-in-waiting were members of the royal household, spending nearly every moment in the monarch's company. Joan needed answers from Titanea and hoped to secure the release of Baba Ben, and the Fae queen offered the perfect chance to achieve both.

But life at court would mean the loss of everything else she held dear. No lady-in-waiting could toil in a goldsmith's shop. No member of the queen's household could consort with the King's Men beyond hearing a play. She'd be leaving behind her friends, her family.

She'd be leaving behind Nick's suit.

Her heart thudded in her chest at the thought.

Cecil surged forwards, his pale, haggard face twisted in dismay. 'Your Majesty, I dare not to question the queen's judgement'—he bowed his head deeply to Titanea, who watched him with pursed lips—'but perhaps a less base choice would offer more comfort. My own daughter, Frances, is well-read and understands the intricacies of both the court and serving the crown.'

'That sounds exactly as if you are questioning the queen's judgement.' The young man standing just behind the throne draped himself across it to brush his fingers against the king's shoulders. 'Although I could be mistaken, Your Majesty. Lord Salisbury is so much more slippery than I.'

The king laughed, the sudden sound echoing out through the room. Cecil seemed to shrink at this, and the grin the young man sent back as he straightened was positively vicious.

Joan let herself enjoy Cecil's embarrassment. It was the least of what he deserved.

Cecil's gaze darted between the king and queen before he bowed his head. 'I mean no offence, Your Highness. The daughter of a mere merchant – even if he is a goldsmith – is not properly placed for such a high position. However, my daughter, Frances has the gentle breeding—'

'We do not want your daughter.' Titanea narrowed her eyes at him. 'We want Joan.'

The queen's ladies rushed to her side, Lady Goose Neck leading with Lady Foul-Breath and Lady Snort just behind her. Joan hadn't bothered to learn any of their true names and she let her mental rudeness stand in for admonishing their abhorrent behaviour towards her in real life.

'My lady, I must agree with Lord Salisbury.' Lady Goose Neck glared at Joan from just out of Titanea's view, a look that held nothing but venom and ill intent. The lady placed one pale hand on Titanea's shoulder and leaned close to the queen. 'Frances Cecil has grown to be quite a lovely young woman and, in my opinion—'

Titanea swatted her hand away, the casual flick of her fingers catching Lady Goose Neck's nose. 'Your opinion matters not, Catherine. Only our own. Joan Sands shall join our household and serve us.'

The woman squeaked at the hit before gathering herself to speak again.

'Silence,' the king said, his tone sharp. 'It seems during my queen's convalescence you have all forgotten your true places. Queen Anne has spoken, and she shall have exactly what she wishes.'

Cecil and the ladies bowed before the king as Titanea grinned, first at Cecil, then at Joan.

The queen's delicate, pale finger curled under Joan's chin and lifted her face. 'You *will* accept my offer, dear Joan, and become a member of my household. It will please me well.'

Joan felt a chill race up her spine as if icy-cold water washed over her whole body. Something frigid bubbled up in her throat, foreign and nearly choking her with its force. She could barely breathe around the crush of it. It felt like drowning while every bone in her body was being ground to dust. She tried to cough, to reach for her suddenly tight throat.

Titanea squeezed her hand tightly, her grip strong enough to hold Joan easily and pressed her thumb into Joan's chin. 'Say "yes," Joan,' she whispered so only they could hear as her gaze turned sharp, 'and the pain will stop.'

'Yes, Your Majesty. I shall do as you wish.' The words burst from Joan's lips in a rush of air.

Titanea nodded, and the icy force gripping Joan disappeared as suddenly as it had come, leaving her shivering and her teeth chattering. She tried not to curl in on herself as the fading pain rippled through her body. Titanea grabbed Joan's other hand to steady her as she shook.

She'd used one of the boons Joan owed to her. No doubt she'd have died if she hadn't agreed, ripped apart by the magic powering through her.

'You must acquaint yourself with losing, dear Joan,' Titanea said into her ear, 'before that stubborn need to win proves deadly.' She patted Joan's cheek and leaned away.

Joan grit her teeth as more shudders racked her body. The Fae queen held one more boon to wield at her pleasure. Joan feared its use.

'Lord Salisbury does make one valid point about Joan's station,' that same meddling, provoking young man behind the king said lightly, 'but one that is easily remedied should His Majesty choose to be generous.'

Titanea smiled brightly. 'Wise words, Lord Montgomery.'

Excitement slipped over King James' face as he stood. Cecil and Erskine stepped to one side of the throne, Erskine deliberately placing himself nearest the king. Titanea released Joan's hand and sat back as her courtiers surrounded her as if summoned. Joan blinked hard, her mind still stumbling through a haze of pain. Someone touched her arm. She turned to see the king's young man smiling at her. He beckoned her over to where he'd tucked himself behind both thrones.

'Come stand by me,' he said pleasantly, his hand outstretched.

Joan took it and slipped back into the half shadows alongside him. He wrapped her arm around his as King James raised his hands and a hush settled over the entire hall. All eyes looked to their monarch.

'When Jesus was born in Bethlehem of Judaea in the time of Herod the king, behold, Magi from the east came to Jerusalem, saying, "Where is the one that is born King of the Jews? We saw the star for him in the east, and are come to worship him."'

An excited murmur rippled through the crowd. The king's annual scripture recitation was only ever done in Latin or Greek. Tonight marked the first time His Majesty or any ruler had done it in plain English. King James tilted his head, basking in the excitement flowing over his subjects.

'He's very proud of this translation of the holy book,' the young man whispered to Joan. He patted her hand gently, his expression both kind and mischievous. 'Philip Herbert, gentleman of the bed-chamber and first Earl of Montgomery. But you, "dear Joan," may call me Philip.'

The name sparked a memory in Joan's mind, the barest bit of gossip traded between Shakespeare, Burbage, and Roz before a performance.

'You're the king's favourite,' she whispered back.

He raised an eyebrow. 'I am he, as it seems you are now the queen's. 'Tis a blessing and a burden. Tread carefully.'

The king spread his arms wide, and the room once again fell into silence.

'Today we celebrate the Epiphany and the arrival of those wise men who sought to venerate our Lord and saviour. We also celebrate the life of our dear queen, who survived a great blow to the crown and, in sustaining life, finds herself again able to blow the crown.'

Someone in the back of the hall gasped at the king's sudden shift from holy to base. Philip snorted beside Joan, and she bit her lip to stifle her laughter. The language of the scripture might be new, but King James's penchant for loosing bawdy jokes in the same breath remained unchanged from year to year.

The king laughed to himself at the scandalised reaction before silencing everyone once again. 'My lady has an announcement,' he said, then turned to sit again upon his throne.

Titanea, Joan thought, *Titanea has an announcement.*

Excited whispers passed among the courtiers as Queen Anne – just as blonde and pale and richly dressed as her husband – stepped up to address them. She lifted her hand, and the jewelled rings on each finger caught the light and sent it sparking in fragments throughout the room. Several people cooed in delight.

'Gentle friends, today is a day of great joy as we return to you alive and whole.' The crowd erupted into loud cheers. Titanea basked in their adoration, smiling benevolently before she silenced them with a wave. 'But it is also a day of extreme sadness as we mourn the loss of dear Lady Clifford, robbed of her youth in the explosion that was intended to sabotage the crown.' Here she pulled a handkerchief from her bosom and dabbed delicately at her eyes. She sniffled twice before she continued. 'While we will all miss Lady Clifford's sweet presence and youthful energy in our court, the time has come to name her replacement.'

Joan braced herself for what she knew came next.

Titanea dabbed at her false blue eyes again and sniffed a third time. 'In an effort to match Lady Clifford's exuberance and buoyant spirit, we have selected a young lady who, while not of noble blood, has impressed us greatly with her accomplishments. Mistress Joan Sands.'

The hall erupted in confusion at the queen's proclamation. Joan flinched even though she had expected the announcement. She searched the crowd for the King's Men but knew they were backstage packing up their properties and costumes. She wished she had them here now: Master Shakespeare to advise her on this sudden shift in her fortunes and Master Phillips to tell her more of Titanea.

James slipped out from behind the curtain that divided the playing space from their temporary backstage and tiring area. He still wore Hermia's white dress, styled wig clutched in his hands. Their eyes met across the vast room, and something he saw on her face shifted his expression from encouraging to horrified.

Joan hated that her confusion and dismay could be read so easily and at such a distance, but no one knew her better than her twin brother. He'd understand the smallest shifts in her demeanour where others saw nothing.

Or so she hoped. Life at court would be hell if she couldn't guard her thoughts.

She forced her lips into a more pleasant smile both to reassure her brother and to disguise her true feelings. She wished she could explain everything to him now; tell him about Titanea being alive and making Joan one of her ladies. Joan hoped he'd take the surprise well.

James's frown deepened.

Never mind.

She clutched her skirts with her free hand, putting all her anxiety into the movement no one would see. She shifted her gaze away from James – she couldn't watch him any longer. Somehow, the opinions of a crowd of strangers didn't trigger the same nerves in her that watching her brother's shifting expression did.

Another face in the sea of courtiers suddenly caught her eye. A tall girl about her age with pale brown skin and thick, curly black hair pulled back tightly stood among a cluster of people not twenty paces from the royal dais, familiar and infinitely welcome.

Rose.

Joan's heart skipped a beat. She hadn't seen Rose since she'd disappeared in the chaos of last November's explosion, dashing into the rubble to rescue Titanea, but Joan had thought about the beautiful girl nearly every day.

Philip tugged her back and Joan jerked to attention, feeling like she'd just come up from underwater.

'Now's not our time yet.' He shot another sly grin her way.

She turned, her gaze searching the crowd for that familiar face again. But Rose had disappeared into the sea of revellers. Joan wanted nothing more than to scour the entire hall for the other girl.

She was being foolish. Not only had Nick declared his intentions to court her, but it had also been months since she or any of them had heard from Rose.

Joan knew she should accept what that meant. As the half-Fae, half-mortal daughter of the powerful Robin Goodfellow, few forces could've stopped Rose from contacting Joan if she wanted. That she hadn't done so was message enough.

But Joan couldn't let the girl go.

'Your part approaches,' Philip said, catching Joan's attention as he patted her hand.

King James grinned. He glanced over his shoulder at Philip, who drew an ornate – and impractical – sword from behind the throne and winked at Joan. She recognised it, had seen it used in years prior when the king bestowed titles upon the favoured.

Oh.

Philip tugged her forwards as he presented the ceremonial blade to King James with a flourish, the two men's fingers tangling together briefly.

The king turned to Joan. 'Well, child, another's death proves a double blessing to you.'

'Kneel,' Philip whispered as he moved past her to stand behind the throne once more. He gestured towards the floor, smiling when she followed his direction.

King James raised the sword with one hand, his expression gleeful. 'I'd hoped to do another of these,' he mumbled to no one in particular.

'No other reason to linger so at court.' He lowered his blade, tapping the flat side against each of Joan's shoulders. 'From this day forth thou shalt be styled as' – he paused and Titanea leaned forwards to whisper into his ear – 'suo jure Baroness de Clifford. Rise, Lady Joan Sands, Baroness de Clifford.'

A gasp rushed over the crowd at the king's proclamation.

'Rise, *Lady* Joan,' Titanea said. 'This pleases us well.'

Joan straightened and met the queen's eye. She felt the heat of Ogun's presence blaze into awareness in her chest and did her best to tamp it down.

'My lord—' Cecil called out as he moved towards the king.

The king waved him off. 'Make it so, Salisbury.'

'But, Your Majesty, I must—'

'Make it so, my beagle,' King James said suddenly, his face a dark storm of rage. 'Do not question your sovereign liege.'

'I—' Cecil looked lost, as if the king's words had been a physical blow before his expression went blank. 'Your will is my own, Your Majesty. I shall see it done.' He bowed deeply.

'Your grace knows no bounds,' Titanea said as she stroked the king's arm gently and then turned to Joan. 'We shall call you to us in two days' time. But for now, do enjoy tonight's festivities, Lady Clifford. You are dismissed.'

CHAPTER THREE
Sweet Words & Low-crooked Curtsies

he king lifted his hand, silencing the room once more. 'Remove these stalls, for now we celebrate our most holy Lord with feasting, with dancing and with music!' He waved, and a rush of servants began to drag away benches and bring in tables, food and wine.

The royal musicians settled on the stage and struck up an easy pavane. Dancers found partners and took to the floor even as it was still being cleared. Philip stepped up to Titanea's throne, bowing deeply with a flourish of his cape.

'Your Highness' – he presented his hand to the queen – 'might you grace your humble servant with this evening's first dance?'

Titanea laughed brightly as she accepted. 'You are hardly *our* servant, Lord Montgomery.' She let him pull her to her feet and looped her arm through his. She glanced over at Joan. 'Dance and be merry, dear Joan, for you become ours in two days' time.'

A promise and a threat.

Joan curtsied, praying her sweaty hands didn't leave dark stains on her skirts and reveal her nerves to the world. Philip caught her eye as he led Titanea past.

'Keep your wits,' he mouthed. Then he was gone, guiding the queen down the wooden stairs and onto the dance floor. He moved with the smoothness of a practiced dancer, and Joan noticed how the king's eyes followed him intently but only sporadically checked in on the queen.

Joan set that information in her mind for later use and prepared to descend into the crowd herself. She'd been dismissed; there was no more need to stay in this vulnerable position. Besides, she needed to find James and the rest of the King's Men. The confusion muddling her thoughts might be resolved once she reached backstage and the comfort of her family of players.

'How old are you, girl?' the king said suddenly.

Joan started, sputtering with surprise before answering. 'I'm seventeen today, Your Majesty.'

'A child.' The king's eyes swept over her appraisingly, something in his gaze making her want to shrink until she could no longer be perceived. Then he waved her away with a flick of his wrist.

Joan curtsied again before tucking her shaking hands into the folds of her skirts. She felt eyes on her back as she headed towards the stairs leading down off the royal dais but didn't dare look back.

She just needed to find her players and all would be well. Or at least better . . .

She slipped around behind Cecil, trying to give the man a wide berth. He grabbed her arm before she could pass, jerking her towards him.

'You dare steal what rightfully belongs to your betters,' he sneered. 'You'll regret crossing me again, girl.'

Joan tugged away from him, using just enough strength to make the man stumble. 'You mistake me, Lord Salisbury. I can hardly "steal" something that was freely given.'

'Sneering jealousy isn't becoming on someone with such a sallow complexion,' Erskine said lightly as he stepped up behind Joan. 'It'll deepen your wrinkles.'

Cecil flinched away from the taller man before straightening again. He puffed out his chest. 'You lack-brained, light-footed bastard,' he spat.

Erskine laughed him off and stepped between Joan and Cecil, his hand once again on the hilt of his sword. He gestured for Joan to head down the wooden steps but kept his eyes locked on the other man. Erskine followed behind her and held her for a moment on the bottom step.

He glanced back at Cecil for a moment then shifted closer to Joan. 'Not even I can drive that man to such vexation. Quite the feat.'

'It's alarmingly simple,' Joan said, ''Tis merely my existence that enrages him.'

Erskine laughed again. 'He's an anxious social climber who's fallen out of favour. A dangerous thing, that.' He grabbed her shoulder just before she stepped back into the gathered crowd. 'Best fortify yourself before I throw you to the wolves.'

Joan thought of everything that had led her to this moment. Nothing could have prepared her for the chaos of two months ago, but perhaps that had prepared her for this. She'd find an advantage, she was sure of it.

There's only one choice. Forwards.

She lifted her chin and straightened her shoulders. 'Thank you, Lord Erskine.'

'It's Lord Fentoun, as of today, actually.' He gave her a playful wink. 'You're not the only one to have their status elevated. Though I doubt my new title will cause me nearly as much trouble.'

Joan chuckled to herself. This man seemed an ally – or as close to one as she could expect at court – as did Philip. She didn't know how far she could trust them yet, but they could at least share in their mutual dislike of Robert Cecil. For now, that might be enough.

He lifted her hand, dipping into a quick bow before a frown overtook his face. 'This bracelet you wear, is it styled after a sword?'

Shite.

'It is, my lord.' Joan's heart thundered in her chest. How much of Bia's true nature could this man sense? Was he Fae? Had she been discovered?

Would she be drawn into a fight in front of the whole court? The fingers of her right hand flexed as she calculated how quickly she could pull the blade.

Erskine straightened, turning her arm over to look more closely at Bia. 'The detail is exquisite. Is this of your father's making?' He glanced up, the smile on his face broad. 'I think I should like one for myself.'

'I'm afraid it was a gift,' she said, words rushing out of her in a relieved huff. 'Though I'm sure he could make you something just as lovely should you commission it.'

He nodded. 'That I shall, Lady Clifford.' He squeezed her hand and released it, turning to head up the stairs. He paused to lean back. 'Oh, and happy birthday.'

Joan watched him go, a matching smile shifting over her face. Even if this man didn't prove himself a true ally, she could count on his chivalry at least to offer some shield. And he didn't appear to be Fae.

She'd withheld her thanks all the same.

Joan sighed again, relief washing over her as Bia swung round her wrist. She was thankful that the secret remained intact. She descended the final step and was immediately engulfed in a sea of mincing courtiers. Lord Fentoun's presence had held them back but now they swarmed like a colony of ants on a bit of sugar.

'Congratulations to you, Lady Joan,' one woman said, the cloying smile on her face wide but not reaching her eyes.

A man stepped directly into Joan's path. 'How did you capture Her Majesty's attention, Lady Joan?'

She had neither the time nor the patience for being so waylaid. She clenched and unclenched her fist as she touched the fingers of her other hand to Bia's cold metal. Lord, that she could fight her way through this obstruction.

But if she couldn't attack, she could at least evade.

Joan twisted her body, slipping around the courtiers clamouring for her attention with ease. The simpering calls of 'Lady Joan! Lady Joan!' buffeted her from all angles but she ignored them. She clamped down on the frustrated scream building under the onslaught and forced her fingers away from the blade at her wrist. Here among the most powerful people in England and with all eyes on her was no place to pull a sword.

Someone grabbed her wrist and she jerked to a stop, prepared to defend herself as firmly and gently as she could. She might not be able to draw Bia here, but she'd make whoever threatened her now hurt. The cool rush of iron flowed down her arm to coat her hand.

'Joan Sands!'

Joan spun, hiding her palm in the folds of her skirts as she called the metal back into herself. Before her stood a boy about her age, a slim girl with matching angular features lurking just behind him. Both had dark brown hair that hung around pale faces, hers arranged in stiff ringlets and his in carefully placed clumps. They wore matching black garments made of expensive brocade woven with intricate patterns that could only be noticed up close.

The boy looked familiar and clearly knew her name, but Joan couldn't for the life of her place where they'd met.

'This is she, Frances, the girl I spoke of!' He grinned widely, hazel eyes crinkling with pleasure. 'I'd never forget the face of the angel who saved my life. I prayed I'd find you here tonight.'

Saved? When had she . . .

The memory hit her all at once. She'd followed a jack-in-irons halfway across London to a house on the Strand and saved a boy from being devoured in front of his father, Robert Cecil. Her actions that night revealed her abilities to the secretary of state and led to him demanding that she kill Auberon. Despite the fact that she'd saved his life, she wouldn't be surprised if Cecil's son hated her as much as his father did. And yet, he appeared happy to see her.

The girl she did not recognise but he'd called her 'Frances.' That and the shape of her face, so similar to the boy next to her, told Joan all she needed. This was Frances Cecil, Lord Salisbury's daughter and the one who'd been expecting to become Queen Anne's lady-in-waiting in Joan's stead.

'Lord Cecil, it is a pleasure to see you well.' She swept into a small curtsy. 'And a pleasure to meet you, Lady Cecil.'

William lifted her hand to his lips, his palm slick with sweat as he pressed a soft kiss against her knuckles. 'It's actually Lord Cranborne, but it would please me much for you to call me William.'

Joan heard the whispers begin all around them as the courtiers speculated on the nature of her relationship with William Cecil. She frowned, annoyance spiking at the sudden attention and their desire to make a scandal out of something as inane as the exchanging of names.

This is the way of court. My every move is fodder for their entertainment. How vexing.

'Shall we speak apart?' she said suddenly, gesturing away from the gossiping throng.

Whatever the Cecil siblings had in store, she doubted it would be worse than that bombardment of power-hungry courtiers.

Unless they were taking her to see their father.

William grinned and looped Joan's arm through his. 'Excellent idea. We'll take a turn around the room.'

'Yes, that should be private enough,' Frances said as she grabbed Joan's other arm. 'Go on, William.'

The three of them strode along the edge of the hall, moving silently until they skirted the dance floor. Joan spotted Philip guiding Titanea through the pavane's slow dance moves. She leaned heavily on his arm though no other sign of her weakness displayed itself.

How curious.

'Lord Cranborne—' She caught his frown from the corner of her eye and adjusted. 'William. I'm glad to see you are in good health and am happy to speak now that our environment is not so dangerous.'

He leaned close and lowered his voice. 'The court has its own dangers, though none so deadly as that monster you defeated on my behalf.' He grinned again at the secret that passed between them.

A quick laugh burst from Joan's lips before she could stop it, and she found herself smiling back. She appreciated his discretion.

'I'm well-acquainted with the latter, but I'm happy to have a friend well-versed in the former to guide me should I need it.'

William suddenly squeezed Joan's arm. 'I had hoped for months to become further acquainted with you.'

Something in his voice made her wary, a plaintive tone that she'd heard from admirers.

Her hand slipped up to grasp the engraved iron pendant hanging from the chain around her neck. She remembered Nicholas Tooley's warm smile and beautiful brown eyes, the way his brown cheeks had burned red as he'd given her the gift she now wore and declared that he intended to court her once his apprenticeship ended. She could feel her own cheeks heat up and the inside of her wrist tingled where he'd placed that soft kiss.

But even as the warmth of Nick's promise engulfed her, memories of another, of the girl made of magic and determination whose face and words Joan couldn't seem to forget.

Stop thinking of what's proper when you could have us both.

Her mind was split enough already, bouncing between two who captivated her far more fiercely than William Cecil ever could.

She prayed there was no cause to count the son of Robert Cecil in that number.

'My brother speaks of you incessantly,' Frances blurted. She plucked some imperfection from her gown. 'He's quite infatuated.'

William's face turned bright crimson, but he didn't let go of Joan's arm.

Damnation.

Of all the eyes to catch at court, how had her luck so run to have attracted this boy's?

'You flatter me, my lord,' she hedged, hoping to ease the sting of his sister's revelation and the inevitable rejection, 'but I—'

He turned to her and grabbed her hand tightly. 'Before you answer, consider this . . .' He squeezed, his nerves making his grip too strong.

Joan could weather it, but still . . .

'My father does not know of my affections towards you, nor will he'— his face turned ever redder, the crimson heat creeping from his cheeks to the tips of his ears—'unless you deny my suit.'

Joan felt as if his threat had stolen the very ground beneath her feet. His face seemed to brighten at her expression. She wanted to pummel him.

'William, what is this?' Frances hissed. She tugged at her brother's arm. 'This isn't how I advised you.'

William shook his sister off, keeping his eyes locked on Joan's. 'Joan, accept me and my father will hear nothing of it. Then, when I have devised a way for us to marry without sanction, I'll make you my wife. Is it not well done?'

'William, what are you doing?' Frances whispered. She glanced between William and Joan, her expression stricken. 'Lady Clifford, I—'

Joan jerked her hand back, but William only squeezed harder. 'Is it not well done, Joan?'

How dare you?

She ripped out of his grip, the strength of it making him stumble.

How dare you, you selfish, entitled parasite!

She wanted to shout the words in his face. She wanted to shove him away and strike him, to rail at him for having the audacity to threaten her into compliance.

But he only dared be so brazen because he knew the fear his father inspired. He knew the power Robert Cecil held over her and how easily he could destroy her with a word. And he would punish her for catching the heart of his precious son, no matter how she loathed William's attention.

She nearly regretted saving the boy's life. She could have avoided this violation if she'd simply let him be devoured that night.

'William, Frances?' Cecil's rasping voice broke through their tense silence. 'Is there something you needed from this girl?'

The siblings' faces paled as they spotted their father. A chill raced down Joan's spine. She could feel the man approaching from behind her but she dared not turn to meet his gaze. She fisted her hands at her sides as her fingers went numb and cold. Her eyes met William's.

What would he say in this moment? She'd neither agreed nor denied him.

He looked back expectantly. 'Well, Father, if you must know . . .' He paused here and raised an eyebrow as he stared at her.

He'd do it. He'd follow through with his threat and expose her to his father's wrath. If she said yes, she'd be surrendering to a tyrant, but if she said no . . .

Maybe she could buy herself time. Surely her new position as a member of Titanea's household offered Joan some protection from Cecil's menace and his son's too. She could acquiesce for two days, then tear William down as viciously as her station would allow.

But tonight, she needed to choose safety, no matter how it galled her.

'Yes,' she whispered, barely giving the word breath but exaggerating the shaping of it with her mouth. Cecil could neither see nor hear her but William would understand.

His eyes seemed to sparkle as cleared his throat and straightened his posture. 'Frances wanted to meet her.'

Frances started at her brother's casual implication and turned to gape at her father.

'You should know who stole your rightful place at the queen's side,' Cecil said, 'but enough. I must have a word with her myself.'

He stood close behind Joan now. She didn't move besides clenching her hands more tightly. Frances cast her eyes to the ground before she looped her arm through William's to drag him away. They whispered fiercely to each other as they disappeared into the crowd.

Cecil grabbed her suddenly, his grip on her arm hard enough to bruise as he dragged her back across the room. Joan let him pull her along but petulantly dropped her weight every few steps, forcing him to strain against her.

However petty and insignificant it may be, it offered her some satisfaction.

He manoeuvred the two of them along the edges of the hall and through a wooden door she'd never noticed in all her times here. It thudded shut behind them as they slipped out into a dimly lit room, a sparse scattering of candles casting long, flickering shadows along the drafty wood walls. Cecil rounded on Joan, his face twisted in a sneer.

This close to the vile man, Joan saw that his failure to prevent last November's explosion had affected him far more than she realised. Yes, the expensive black clothes that covered him neck to feet were tailored to perfection, but Joan could see where nervous sweat dampened the collar and sleeves. The dark bruises of exhaustion gave his gaze a skeletal look, and the bright sheen that overtook his wild eyes made him seem more wounded beast than man.

'I'm on to you, witch,' he spat, the words rushing over her in a wet spray of vitriol.

Joan jerked her arm out of his grip with an ease that sent him stumbling, and she was reminded of how similar to this man his son had proven to be. 'I've done nothing.'

His hand cracked across her face. Joan touched her fingers to her stinging cheek as her ears rang from the blow. She turned back to him slowly, rage bubbling up and clenching her throat.

She could knock him flat, could hit him hard enough to send him careening down the hall like a toy.

Yes, returning the insult would be so simple.

Their eyes met. A sudden fear flashed across his face as something in her expression shook him. It was gone just as quickly, replaced with a cold consideration, some master plan already taking shape in his calculating brain.

He stepped into her space. 'You cannot hope to outmanoeuvre me. Even now I'm leagues ahead of you.'

'As you were in November?' She couldn't resist the dig at his failure, letting every drop of her anger colour the words. 'Where was your great insight then, my lord?'

He swung at her again and she dodged him, her hands gripping the skirts of her borrowed blue gown as she slipped around his outstretched arm. She bolted back to the door and threw her weight into shoving it open.

'I'll enjoy crushing that fire in you, witch!' he shouted after her.

Cross me again and I'll see you burn, girl.

Joan didn't respond. She practically ran back to the main hall, that whispered vow of his dogging her heels. She needed to find James, find the company. Her brother, Master Phillips, Master Shakespeare and the rest needed to know things weren't as they seemed. They'd know what to do with every thought and trouble that plagued her mind now.

What a hellish birthday this was proving to be . . .

A chill wind whipped in through the tapestry-covered windows of the ramshackle Banqueting House at Whitehall Palace. Now that the benches and central stage had been moved away, the crowd of Twelfth Night revellers packed thickly onto the dance floor, their unfamiliar faces warped by twisting candlelight.

She was only half aware of who she bumped or nudged past in her rush. Her hands still shook and her cheek burned hot after the encounter with Cecil. That creeping fear he inspired in her nearly drowned out all other thoughts until not even the steady hum of Bia hanging round her wrist could calm her racing heart.

Why torture herself with thoughts of revenge against a man she had no power to oppose? She'd prefer to fall completely beneath his notice from now into eternity. Her life would be far safer that way.

Someone shouted from the other side of the room, and Joan spun to see Armin – the brilliant red hair framing his pale face and his short stature making him stand out even in this crowd – as he goaded Shakespeare and Burbage into downing their cups of wine. Surely James would be nearby.

She took a step towards them. Her head felt muddled and she wanted nothing more than to sit and gather herself. But the elder company members would soon be well-marinated and she wouldn't have long before they slipped into drunken incoherence.

Damnation.

With one final shake of her head, she turned and rushed towards where she could hear Armin's singing and Burbage's booming laugh piercing through the din of the crowd.

'What trouble have you found for yourself?'

Joan spun, one hand gripping her racing heart. Rose stood behind her, her black curls pulled back and pinned in an artless style that left them looking lifeless. She wore a crimson gown tailored perfectly to fit her tall form. Though there was rouge on her high cheekbones, her light brown face still looked pale.

Even so, she was every bit as beautiful as Joan remembered.

'Rose . . .'

Rose's eyes swept over her, pausing for a moment on Joan's cheek before she frowned. Joan reached out to grasp the girl's hand tightly, her eyes darting this way and that. She spotted a dark alcove that seemed to offer some privacy.

'Come on,' Joan said, tugging Rose along behind her.

They slipped through the crowd with ease as Joan struggled to still her racing heart. She knew Rose would feel the dampness of her nervous palms, but Joan wouldn't let go for fear the other girl would disappear again. She manoeuvred them into the dim corner of the hall tucked in the shadow between two sconces and a heavy hanging tapestry.

'Joan,' Rose said as they finally stopped, 'why were you talking with William—'

Joan pulled Rose into a deep kiss that sent tingles from the top of her head to the tips of her toes. Rose's hands slipped up to press against her cheeks. Joan slid her arms around Rose's back and squeezed, crushing their bodies together.

This burning fire was why no matter how long she'd been gone, Joan couldn't let her thoughts of Rose go.

Rose finally pulled away, breath rushed as she pressed her forehead to Joan's. 'Titanea's alive,' she blurted.

'I know, and she's who holds my godfather prisoner.' Joan leaned away, clasping one of Rose's hands in hers. 'How are you here?'

Rose snorted, her expression turning dark. 'To serve the qu-queen.' Her voice stumbled over the title, fear and anger colouring the word.

'She's had you close this whole time?'

'Yes, me and Zaza both. I wanted to find you and tell you, I swear it.'

Joan squeezed Rose's hand. 'No, I understand. I thought you'd grown tired of me.' How petty and insecure that thought felt now.

'Tired of you?' Rose started. 'Joan how could I . . . How could anyone grow tired of you? I—'

A sudden clamour erupted in the crowded room just beyond their quiet hideaway. It rippled over the gathered revellers, growing louder and louder as word of whatever was happening travelled closer.

Rose straightened, frowning as she shook her head. 'I have to go attend the queen,' she said. She touched her fingers to her forehead for a moment before pulling Joan in for another tight hug. 'I hate you'll be at her command but I'm happy to have you so close to me.'

Joan squeezed her back.

Rose pressed her lips against Joan's forehead one last time before disappearing into the crowd. Joan watched her go then slipped out of the darkness of the alcove.

'Joan, there you are.'

And immediately locked eyes with Nick Tooley, his face welcome as relief washed over her. Nick being here meant the other King's Men were likely nearby. His gaze darted out over the crowd, following the path Rose had taken before shifting back to Joan. He opened his mouth to say something, but Master Shakespeare burst from the throng of revellers and hurried towards her, James merely a step behind him.

Her brother reached her first. 'What troubles have you found?' he said, unknowingly echoing Rose as he grasped her hands.

Joan knew he spoke of the queen's proclamation and the new title but there was so much more.

'How can you encounter so much trouble in the two hours you've been out of my sight?' Shakespeare wailed. 'Your mother is going to kill me.'

She grimaced. 'I wish this was the sum total of my news.'

'I suppose we were due for a bit more excitement,' James said lightly, and Joan punched him hard in the arm.

Shakespeare paled. 'There's more?' She nodded, and he raked his hands down his face before huffing out an anxious breath. 'Of course there's more. Go to our room.' He gestured to Nick. 'Come, we'll fetch the others.'

The tall boy squeezed Joan's shoulder gently before he followed Shakespeare into the crowd to find the rest of their company. Joan reached for her brother and felt his fingers clasp around hers.

'From the look on your face,' James said, 'I can tell there's danger ahead. Should I expect to ruin another of my favourite shirts?' He sighed deeply as his face took on an exaggerated look of melancholy.

Joan snorted, the laugh bursting from her. 'You claim them all as your favourites.'

''Tis no fault of mine. Some of us show proper reverence and care to our wardrobes.'

She shook her head and dragged him towards their temporary tiring-room. A genuine smile slipped over her face as they wound their way through the crowd, skirting along the edges to avoid the countless eyes that followed her after the queen's announcement.

Yes, they had much to discuss. But even as Joan feared explaining the breadth of their troubles, the prospect of sharing the burden with her allies, her family of friends, finally allowed the tightness in her chest to unclench.

ames tucked the beautiful blue gown back into its
storage crate after helping Joan lace herself back into
her own juniper green dress. She'd felt lovely wearing
the expensive borrowed garment, but being back in her
own clothes was a welcome return. The dress made by
her godfather felt like a type of armour.

The King's Men used this side room to dress and store the company's
costumes and properties until they could be hauled back to the playhouse
in the morning. The wooden crates holding the tools of their trade sat
together in a corner, creating a perfect hidden nook for clandestine con-
versations. Here, away from the raucous celebrations in the main hall, they
had the security and privacy to speak freely. No one at court cared what
the players did with themselves once the performance was done, and Joan
was more than happy to use that to their advantage.

She pulled herself up onto one of the wooden crates as James
did the same across from her. She touched her fingertips to Bia, the
sword humming back softly. So much deception had come to light in

so brief a time. She wondered how to reveal these changes, how to deliver these discoveries with the gentleness due their shocking natures. But her exhausted mind could think of no more than to speak it plainly.

She only hoped they'd take it well.

'Congratulations, Joan,' Armin shouted as he burst into the room. His wine-heated cheeks glowed as red as his hair and beard in his pale face, though his eyes burned clear and alert. 'A baroness and lady to the queen, is there a better gift for a birthday?' He dropped to the floor and leaned back against a stack of crates.

Rob Gough slipped in after Armin with Nick close behind. Rob hopped up beside James, placing his hand near enough that their fingers could tangle together casually. Nick leaned his hips against Joan's crate. She could feel his weight pressed against her legs beneath her skirts. She wanted to lean into him but didn't dare at this moment.

Burbage stumbled in last, his stocky frame held up between Shakespeare and Phillips. 'Lady Joan Sands,' he bellowed as he shook the two men off and stumbled forwards. 'Now there's a thing to be wondered at.' He took another step, listing drunkenly to one side before collapsing on the last unclaimed crate. He stretched and sprawled out, eyes already slipping closed.

Phillips shook his head and settled into the space's only chair, his face as white as his hair and beard, his Fae glow stark in the candlelit room.

''Tis a provident change of fortunes that I don't understand.' Shakespeare frowned. He remained standing, his long fingers tugging at the point of his black beard, and his face pale but for the drunken flush colouring his cheeks. 'From what you told me of your last visit with the queen, she'd never be so generous to you.'

Joan felt her shoulders tense at the memory of having to sit through a performance of *Othello* at Queen Anne's feet while Her Majesty and her ladies poked at and belittled her.

'No, she wouldn't,' Joan said. 'The queen is not herself but Titanea in disguise.'

A cacophony of shouts echoed in the room as Joan shushed them frantically.

Shakespeare tugged at his hair. 'What do you mean she's alive?'

Joan understood their shock; she'd been just as unaware of the change. Although now that she looked back, the clues had all been there. Unlike before, today Queen Anne had welcomed her, had admonished the ladies who sought to ridicule her, had bade Joan sit beside her in a chair instead of on the floor. Zounds, she'd even requested the King's Men perform *A Midsummer Night's Dream*, the play that featured a lighter version of her, instead of one of Master Shakespeare's newer works.

'Who?' Master Burbage slipped in and out of sleep beside Shakespeare, his stocky form positioned to take up as much space as possible – whether he was conscious or no.

Joan pressed her thumb against the skin between her eyebrows, hoping to soothe the frustrated headache building there. 'Titanea.'

'She knows the queen?' He mumbled before pitching sideways.

He was useless like this.

Phillips groaned. 'She is the queen, you daft drunkard.'

He'd slumped in his chair and closed his eyes as soon as Joan had revealed that Titanea was alive.

'Nooo, the queen is Anne of Denmark. You know *that*, Augustine.'

Phillips stood suddenly. 'We'll get nowhere with you in this state.' He strode over to Burbage and kissed him square on the mouth.

'And this isn't a distraction at all,' Shakespeare muttered.

Phillips pulled away. 'Do you have your wits now, Richard?'

'Uh . . . yes.' Burbage blinked up at him, face slack but all signs of drunkenness gone. 'Have you always been able to do that?'

The older man snorted. 'Don't be too impressed, it won't last long.' He dropped back into his chair and waved a hand at Joan. 'Continue, Joan.'

'Titanea is alive and using her magic to pretend to be Queen Anne,' Joan said.

Armin snorted. 'No wonder she requested we perform *Midsummer*.'

'Are you going to offer something useful, or do I have to treat you too?' Phillips snapped.

Armin rolled his eyes. 'No, August. I hold my drink better and I'll not have your bushy mustache making me sneeze again.'

'The broken Pact has made way for this,' Phillips said abruptly.

Joan frowned. 'What do you mean, Master Phillips?'

'It's . . .' Phillips took a deep breath, seeming to steady himself before he spoke again. 'One of the rules of the Pact was that none of the Fae could take neither form nor shape of human royalty.'

James snorted. 'Well, that's surely out the window.'

'Did you know she was alive all this time, Master Phillips?' Joan said. She stared at his face as she awaited his answer, undecided over how she'd react to his answer.

He took another deep breath. 'I . . .' He paused to consider his words.

Phillips was Fae and therefore couldn't lie, but that didn't mean he couldn't conceal the truth. Their eyes met and he seemed to come to some decision.

'I thought her dead just as you did. Today I felt the pull of her presence, though even then it seemed so faint I thought it an illusion.' He leaned back in his seat and pursed his lips as if he'd tasted something sour. 'As queen, Titanea is connected to each of us. She is both a beacon and a lodestone.'

Burbage scrunched up his face. 'But why haven't you felt her until now if she's been alive all this time?'

'I think she needed to recover after the explosion,' Joan replied. 'Even in her disguise, she looked frail and weak.'

'Is this not a good thing?' Nick said. 'She helped Joan and Master Shakespeare get to James. She's our ally.'

Joan sighed. 'I don't know. She's the one who orchestrated Baba Ben's arrest.'

'Of course,' James said. 'With him out of the way, the Pact was sure to fall.'

Phillips rubbed his forehead wearily. 'And I'm sure she was behind the explosion at the House of Lords as well. She must've used her magic to exchange appearances with the true Queen Anne.'

'Harming herself and using the chaos of the disaster to steal one half of the throne.' Shakespeare snorted out a mirthless laugh. 'The plan's as brilliant as any I could write.'

Rob frowned. 'If the queen lies in a grave marked for Lady Clifford, what happened to the real girl? And how long did Titanea wear her face?' He glanced at Joan and raised an eyebrow. 'Have you never wondered any of this?'

'No . . . I . . .' Joan's mind raced. She'd known Titanea stood in place of the young Lady Clifford from her first encounter with the queen but she'd never considered what fate had befallen the real girl.

Shame rushed through her again. The feeling had sat in her stomach like a stone from the moment Titanea had revealed the depths of her deception. Shame for all she'd missed and the danger she may have brought because of it. For nearly attacking Titanea before the whole court and for being too afraid to trust Ogun's word. It felt blasphemous to question the Orisha's judgement. But she couldn't lose an ally – as she hoped the Fae queen still was – nor doom all she loved to a charge of treason.

The danger was supposed to be gone. There'd been no other attacks in the city since Joan had taken Auberon's head in combat. London felt as it always had, and Joan hoped that though the Pact remained broken, the loss of the Fae leaders had cooled any desire to move on the mortal realm. Even the presence of Ogun inside her had calmed; the roaring inferno that was her head Orisha had quieted to a warm smolder. Until today, when the burn of Ogun in her chest and the steady hum of Bia at her wrist, both aching for battle, had been so strong she could barely think of anything else.

But did that mean Titanea had to die? Joan couldn't be sure and she dared not make a move with anything less than absolute confidence.

She needed to be better. She need to slow down and focus before she missed any other details and made more mistakes.

Mistakes meant losing, and losing was as good as death.

She took another deep breath, forcing those dark feelings down for the time. 'I had not but I'll ask Titanea myself when I report to court in two days.'

'Two days?' James shouted. 'That's so soon.'

Joan met his eyes from across the room and felt an answering sadness rise within her. He was right, it was far too soon. Perhaps she could delay—

That icy magic surged through her body. She shivered and struggled to remain calm but it felt as if her very bones would dissolve.

This was the boon forcing her acquiescence again. How was it that the mere thought of disobedience triggered punishment?

Say 'yes,' Joan, and the pain will stop.

Titanea's command returned to her then through the chill and the ache.

'I must do as the queen orders,' she huffed out, the cold leaving her as she spoke the final word. She flexed her fingers. She'd clenched them so tightly that they'd locked. They clicked as she relaxed her hands, revealing the wrinkled fabric of her skirts.

From the corner of her eye she noticed Nick watching her, his face drawn with worry. Joan wanted to grab his hand but hesitated. Her clammy palms would reveal her struggle, then she'd have to explain—

He rubbed gentle circles along her back. She breathed slowly, relaxing at the soft touch. He turned to her, and the tension left his beautiful face as their eyes met. Her stomach flipped.

'We need Benjamin,' Shakespeare said suddenly, his gaze clear and all signs of drunkenness gone. 'Whatever her intentions, I think we'd all be safer with the Pact restored.' He tugged at his pointed beard and murmured to himself, as he did when unravelling some plot in his head.

This is what Joan had hoped for in bringing them what she knew. If anyone could figure out how to free Baba Ben, it was Master Shakespeare.

He snapped his fingers and turned to Joan. 'I have it. We'll need your mother's help, of course.' He mumbled something inaudible, shook his head, then leapt up. 'Yes, that's it! Joan, expect me at your house before dawn.' He rubbed his hands together. 'Prepare for an excursion.'

'Come, we shouldn't be away from the main hall for too long.' Phillips pushed himself up, a deep frown creasing his wrinkled face. He nodded them all towards the door. 'Someone is sure to have noticed our absence.'

Burbage stood and immediately pitched forwards, splaying across the ground. 'Think it wore off, August,' he said, his mouth contorted with his cheek pressed into the floor.

'I told you it wouldn't last long.' Phillips shook his head as he moved to pull the drunken man back up.

They filed out together, Phillips and Shakespeare bearing Burbage's weight between them with Armin right behind.

'Don't kiss me again,' Burbage slurred as he shoved at Phillips's mouth. 'I want to enjoy the rest of my night.'

Joan started to follow, but a hand on her shoulder held her back. She turned and locked eyes with Nick. The tall boy smiled at her, then nodded to someone else. Joan glanced in that direction and saw James and Rob lurking discreetly by the door, near enough to chaperone but well out of earshot.

'Joan,' Nick said softly as he took both her hands gently in his and kneeled before her. 'Your star has risen today, far above my own.' He paused, seeming to gather his thoughts.

Joan's heart raced in her chest, fearing what his next words would be.

'Everything is different now,' he said, eyes focused on their joined hands, 'but I have no plans to withdraw my suit. Unless you ask it of me.'

Her breath rushed out in a relieved huff. 'Do not withdraw.' She squeezed his hands. 'Please, don't withdraw.'

'Then I shall court the queen's lady,' he said, a bright smile breaking over his face and drawing forth her own. His expression turned serious. 'I had hoped that our battles would be done, but it seems that they are not.'

Joan sighed. 'I'm sorry, Nick. But you needn't—'

'No.' He pressed a kiss along her knuckles, then looked deeply into her eyes. 'Your fight is my fight, Joan Sands, and I swear to protect you with everything I have.'

Her heart skipped a beat, and she struggled to speak around the sudden lump in her throat. 'Nick, I-I'm the one who should be protecting you.'

'Just because you're stronger than me and better with a sword' – he ran his fingertip softly along the side of her face – 'and wield otherworldly magic doesn't mean I have no aid to offer you. Remember that, will you?'

Joan chuckled and leaned into his touch. 'Aye, I'll remember.'

'Excellent.' A genuine smile bloomed across his face, one that seemed to brighten the whole room. 'Shall we return to the viper's pit so that my lady might grace her humble servant with a dance?'

She laughed brightly and nodded. He stood, pulling her up with him and pressed a soft kiss to her forehead.

'We shall find some joy in this birthday yet.' He traced his fingers along her cheek again and then looped her arm through his.

They walked together to where Rob and James stood, then the four prepared to slip back out into the main hall.

'You know it's my birthday too,' James said, batting his eyes at Rob.

Rob grabbed his arm and tugged him close for a deep kiss. 'Happy birthday,' he cooed as he pulled away, leaving James dazed and pleased.

'How brazen,' Joan said, then easily dodged her brother's swing. 'Look how he blushes.'

She laughed heartily as James dove for her, sending her wiggling out of Nick's hold to hide behind the taller boy. The four of them could barely keep standing for laughing.

So much of her life had changed within the span of a half hour, but one thing had remained the same: Joan would always have people behind her, supporting her in whatever struggles were to come. That was one truth she could hold fast to.

CHAPTER FIVE
Interlude – Avalee Saunders & the Siren

onight was the first time Avalee Saunders heard the singing, although market chatter – and the sudden disappearance of two fishermen – had pointed to it starting the day before. Not many folks cared about the area along the Thames between London Bridge and the Tower. Avalee generally avoided it. Between the heads of traitors displayed on the bridge's Stone Gateway as gruesome trophies and the crown favouring executions carried out at the old castle, the seemingly quiet neighbourhood swarmed with restless spirits. They lurked, ready to latch on to anyone with an open heart or a conflicted mind.

Avalee was practiced enough to keep them at bay, but this was something different. She sent a quiet prayer up to her Orisha, Oshun, as she continued along the riverbank, following the chorus of voices singing their haunting melody. Beneath that, she could hear the Thames itself whispering to her, hissing warnings as its swift currents rushed past.

That unsettling hum had buzzed in her head briefly back in November before going quiet and then resuming fiercely yesterday morning. The noise of it had driven her here, clad in dark trousers and shirt with her thick black hair braided close to her head so any who saw her would assume she was a boy. She knew she should've spoken to her godmother before attempting something so foolish, but her curiosity and concern had outweighed her caution. She'd speak to Iya Bess when she could offer more than a feeling of something wrong. Still she crept along the darkness of the riverbank with a lantern and a knife, seeking danger and praying she wouldn't find it.

The sudden crunch of pebbles grinding together under fast footfalls sounded behind her. Avalee spun, and a man sprinted past her, his eyes wide and face bright with ecstasy. She rushed after him, noticing that the singing grew louder and louder as they moved east along the river. She gripped her lantern tightly in one hand and tried to keep up, but the man was far faster than she. The edges of the light kept him in her sights, but she was still too far behind to grab him.

Finally he stopped. Avalee caught up to him, casting the candle's full glow over him as he threw himself into the arms of a glowing woman lying half submerged in the water. This was one of the Fae – the light burning beneath her skin marked her so to Avalee's sight.

The air seemed to ripple over the Fae woman. Any rosiness her complexion held faded to a pale greenish grey as her dark hair shifted into a long fin that ran from the crown of her bald head down along her spine. Her arms disappeared, the smooth, muscular expanse of her torso showing that they'd only been an illusion. She slipped further out of the water, wrapping her long body around the man like a snake. Or an eel.

She nuzzled her sallow face against his as she continued to croon softly into his ear. The man appeared to be experiencing pure bliss, eyes closed, jaw slack and completely unaware of anything beyond the sweet song.

This was a siren. This was what terrorised these shores, feasting upon innocents before slithering back into the murky depths of the Thames.

The creature looked up suddenly and locked eyes with Avalee. Her lips spread into a wide grin, revealing a row of knife-sharp teeth as she stopped her song. The man she held blinked rapidly as if awaking from a dream and seemed to perceive the true nature of his paramour for the first time. His face contorted in horror as the siren twisted her neck around to stare him down. He sucked in a breath to scream, to fight, to beg – but her mouth opened impossibly wide and swallowed him down to his shoulders.

Avalee cried out, her lantern falling from her shaking hands and casting the creature and her prey into darkness. She dropped to her knees, hands scrabbling across the rocky shore to take up the light again, thankful that the flame hadn't been snuffed by her fumbling. Her fingers closed around the handle, swinging it around and catching the siren in its beam just as the creature's second row of teeth dragged the man's legs and feet into its gaping mouth. Her tongue swept across thin lips in satisfaction before her eyes locked on Avalee once again.

Run!

Avalee's feet moved before she'd finished the thought, and she raced back down the beach. The knife she clutched in her hand felt pitifully inadequate against something so formidable.

Whatever she'd thought she'd find at the river, it wasn't this.

A loud splash sounded behind her, and Avalee could feel the pulse of something dangerous swimming through the water towards her. She glanced over her shoulder and caught sight of the siren's dark shape slinking against the swift current with ease.

She'd never escape that thing like this. Her knife might not be enough to stop a siren but that wasn't the only trick she knew. She skidded to a stop, pebbles sliding away under her feet as she turned to the water and held up her hand.

Avalee wasn't sure this would work. She'd only ever used the powers granted to her by Oshun to move the river in superficial ways. This would require strength and focus. She prayed she had enough of both.

She concentrated on the water surrounding the long, slithering body of the siren and willed it to flow faster. For a moment nothing happened, then that small portion of the river rushed away, carrying the creature with it. The siren screeched and leapt up out of Avalee's trap, splashing back down into a calmer portion of the Thames.

But the success of Avalee's attempt made her bolder. She shifted her fingers, creating a spiral of water that lifted the siren up, suspending her long body over the river. The siren thrashed erratically as Avalee's hands shook with the effort of maintaining the water's shape. The creature shrieked and flung herself out of the column. She flopped down onto the shore with a squelching thud.

Avalee dropped her focus, letting the water fall back to normal. She raised her knife just as the creature surged towards her. She grunted as the siren's body slammed into hers, slick and heavy with muscle. The Fae reared back, and Avalee threw her arm in front of her face. She screeched as the siren's sharp teeth sank deep into her flesh, and she felt the warm gush of blood as the jaw locked on her.

But she refused to die like this.

She shifted the knife in her grip and jabbed it into the creature wherever she could reach. Eyes, jaw, neck, back – Avalee stabbed over and over. She managed to thrust her blade into a delicate fold at the side of the creature's neck, and the siren let go with a screech. She reared back, flopping onto the rocks and keening pitifully. Avalee waved a hand in the Fae's direction, sending a rush of dark river water washing over and dragging the creature away from her.

She scrambled to her feet, holding her wounded arm, and ran with all her might. She was sure the creature was still alive and that she wouldn't survive tangling with her again this night.

She needed to get clear of the river and tend her wound. Then, at first light, she needed to go find her godmother. Something evil had been unleashed on London once again and Avalee felt in her bones that Iya Bess and the other elders would know what to do about it.

CHAPTER SIX
Nature Must Obey Necessity

 don't like this. I don't like this at all.'

Joan watched her mother pace back and forth along the length of their sitting room. Mrs Sands had wrapped herself in a dressing gown, and her hair hung around her shoulders in small twists. Joan's father slumped on the sofa, brow furrowed and fingers rubbing steady circles on his temples. He hadn't bothered to fasten the lower ties on his trousers or put on stockings. The long ribbons hung loose at his bare calves.

Both their parents had been preparing for bed when Joan and James had returned from Whitehall with their news. Joan wasn't sure which disturbed them more: the Fae queen being alive, her role in Baba Ben's arrest or her demanding Joan become part of her court.

Joan wasn't sure which disturbed her more either.

Mr Sands ran his hand down his face. 'How much time do we have before you must report to the palace?'

'Two days.'

'Which is no time at all,' James said quietly from where he sat on the floor and leaned against the sofa. 'I can't believe you're a baroness.'

Joan rolled her eyes at him. 'That's the least troubling part of all this.'

'But still vitally important. You have a title now, which makes you an even larger target.' Her mother tugged her robe more tightly around herself. 'Especially to anyone who had hoped to claim a place at the queen's side.'

Joan felt a chill rush through her. She could fight more red caps or jacks-in-irons outright, but a conflict with a covetous lady or lord could never be settled with her sword. She sighed, her head falling into her hands. She knew next to nothing of the rules of court beyond not angering anyone above her rank. But who was above a baroness and queen's lady-in-waiting, and what did either of those titles even mean? Titanea had the ear of the king and the face of the queen. With her clear favour, what power had Joan gained to wield against her enemies at court? She thought of William Cecil pushing his suit and how she'd been helpless to do anything but accept.

Her head ached.

'Master Shakespeare has a plan to get Baba out of the Tower,' Joan said. 'He's coming here before dawn to take us. I think we should do it.'

Her mother crossed the room suddenly. 'Yes, Ben will restore that damned Pact and put a stop to all of this.' She lifted her hands, preparing to open a doorway. 'But we shouldn't wait. I'll retrieve Will now.'

'Bess . . .' her father said softly.

She shook her head. 'We're wasting time when we should act.'

'Bess, enough.' Mr Sands grabbed her wrist as she began tracing the door's shape into the air. 'We're all exhausted and nothing good will come of us this night.'

'Thomas, we have to move now,' her mother said, face stricken. 'Joan's departure will be upon us soon.' She held a hand against her belly. 'I could barely protect her at home; how can I hope to keep my daughter safe at court?'

Joan knew her mother's words weren't directed at her, but they still hit like a blow. She hadn't been the one who'd failed to protect the family. That shame belonged only to Joan.

The memory of James battered and barely conscious at the Fae's feet and the image of her mother pale and covered in blood from a near-mortal wound leapt into her mind once more. She clenched her fists, struggling to push down that surging fear and arrange the torrent of thoughts into something useful.

How could she hope to protect her family from so great a distance? She might hope that Titanea's favour might extend to the people Joan loved or she could use her position at the Fae queen's side to ensure that it did. Life at court was a small sacrifice for the safety of her family and friends. And maybe she would not have to reside there forever.

She gritted her teeth and braced herself for the pain of the boon's magic but it never came.

Relief flooded through her. There was some way around Titanea's commands, she just had to be clever enough to find them. When she thought of how the Fae she'd encountered could conceal and twist the truth without telling a single lie, such an evasion was a surety.

'I must go as she commands but . . .' She paused, carefully crafting her delicate statement. The wrong words would cost her dearly. '. . . I needn't stay.'

Nothing. The magic remained silent.

Encouraged, Joan continued and dared push further. 'I'll serve Titanea and hold her attention while you work with Baba to restore the Pact.'

All eyes turned to her, but her mother spoke, her words measured and expression stark. 'Joan, you shouldn't go at all.'

'But I must,' Joan shouted the words before her mind could repeat her mother's denial. 'And isn't it best to have me close to her? She's been an ally and clearly holds some affection for me. I can use that to our advantage.'

Her mother scowled. 'It's far too dangerous. You don't know what the loss of the Pact truly means or what Titanea is capable of.'

'And neither do you, Bess.' Joan's father stood, his expression gentle as he patted his wife's hand. 'You are not wrong, but neither is Joan. We need to think clearly, which we cannot do if we do not sleep.'

'Thomas—'

His hand cupped her cheek. 'No, Bess. We rest, then move when Will arrives,' he commanded firmly.

It wasn't a threat, but in this moment they all knew Thomas Sands was not to be argued with.

'Sleep, children.' He slipped Mrs Sands's hand into the crook of his arm. 'Come on, love, to bed with you.'

Mrs Sands sighed but allowed her husband to lead her up to their room.

Joan sighed as she dropped her head back onto the chair and closed her eyes. Their father was right. She did need to rest but too much had happened, the day's events and discoveries combining with her heavy thoughts. They raced through her troubled mind in an endless cacophony that staved off any hope of slumber.

'You heard Father, time for sleep.' James said pointedly. '*You* need to rest. You look like death, and if *I'm* saying that, you know it's dire indeed.'

Joan glared at him. 'That's cruel.'

'It's truth. Shall I fetch you a glass?'

Joan threw a cushion at him, ignoring his indignant yelp. He hurled it back and she caught it before it smacked her in the face. She tucked it behind her head with a smile.

'And you've the nerve to call me cruel,' he mumbled, his tone triggering a surge of guilt within her.

There were still things she hadn't told him, hadn't told anyone for fear of their worry. Perhaps she wouldn't need to. She could still resolve the William Cecil matter on her own, and they were no strangers to his father's dislike of her.

No, Titanea being alive, getting Baba to restore the Pact, and Joan being called to court were problems enough for now. Joan could deal with the rest herself.

She closed her eyes again and breathed deeply. Even if she didn't sleep, she could at least calm herself from the stresses and surprises of the day. Her scattered thoughts could prove just as dangerous as any hesitation.

'You know, I heard something quite interesting from our dear friend Nick,' James said, leaning against the back of her chair. 'That he plans on courting you.'

Joan's eyes snapped open, startled as much by his sudden closeness as the abrupt change of subject. 'He told you that?' She hadn't even heard her brother get up from the floor. Was she so distracted?

'No, but I overheard a bit of your conversation, and you've just con-firmed it.' He grinned widely. 'So, thank you for that.'

'James ...'

'Don't worry, I approve. And I'm sure Mother and Father will as well.'

Joan sat up, her hands tugging at her skirts. 'I told him yes but now that I think on it, perhaps it's too dangerous to—'

'Stop.' James held up a hand before heading for the stairs. 'Before you say anything else foolish, let's go to sleep. Father's right, your brain is addled. Next, you'll be back to wanting to marry Henry.'

'That would allow me to continue father's goldsmith work.'

'Or you could find a patron at court and get special permission to open your own shop.'

Joan froze halfway out of the chair and stared at her brother. 'What?'

'The thought never occurred to you as your sought to martyr yourself for us all?' He squinted at her then shook his head. 'You need to start considering yourself and what you want. You have a whole life before you once all this is settled.' He grabbed her hands and squeezed them firmly. 'Think on how you want to live it.'

You don't know that for sure, she thought but didn't dare give voice to the words.

'Let's get to sleep,' she said instead and followed her brother up the stairs.

The candles had been blown out in the hallway of the fourth floor where their parents slept, and only the gentle golden glow of the fireplace showed from under their closed door.

James doused the candles in their corridor on the fifth floor as Joan went into her own room.

'Joan,' he called just before she closed the door. 'Just because things are dangerous doesn't mean you shouldn't seek out happiness. No one wants you to destroy yourself in the name of protecting us.'

She smiled at her brother and nodded before slipping into her room. She closed the door and leaned back against it, her heart thumping loudly in her chest.

If she was honest with herself, danger wasn't the only reason she found herself suddenly worried about Nick's suit.

Whenever she gave herself the freedom to imagine her future, to picture herself at her happiest beyond this fight and the Pact and whatever other trouble she found herself in, she saw Nick so clearly beside her. But his wasn't the only face that sprang into her mind in those moments. Her feelings for both Nick and Rose burned so fiercely in her heart.

Joan knew her family would understand many unusual things, would never question her love for another girl. But what would they say to her wanting to be with them both? What would Nick say to her asking such a thing of him? Would he reject her outright? Would he resent her for thinking he was not enough – though that couldn't be further from the truth?

Joan couldn't be sure, and those questions bred a fear in her she wasn't ready to confront.

She shook her head and started preparing herself for bed, tying up her hair and removing her many outer garments. Finally, she slipped under the warmth of her thick blanket and fell asleep soon after her head touched the pillow.

Joan jerked awake, half fearing she'd see a blast of sunlight cutting through her window. But only the smoldering embers in her hearth glowed in the darkness.

How long had she been asleep? Had Master Shakespeare already come and they'd gone on to the Tower without her?

She needed to get downstairs before she was left behind.

She rolled out of bed, her addled brain struggling to coordinate the movements of a barely awake body. Her foot caught on one of the rugs on her floor and sent her stumbling into the door. She hit it hard enough to knock the breath from her lungs. Undeterred, she snatched at the handle and flung herself out into the hall.

The candles outside her room had been lit, which meant James had already risen. Why hadn't he woken her too?

She sprinted into the hall, feet thundering on the stairs as she raced down and past her parents' room. Light glowed from within the kitchen, where she could hear the faint sounds of Nan preparing for the day. The thought that Joan would disrupt the whole house with her noise struck her just as she hit the top of the next staircase and ran right into her father.

'Whoa!' he shouted. He wrapped an arm around her waist and braced his feet as he caught hold of the railing.

Master Shakespeare stood behind him, hands pressed against her father's back to steady him. A cluster of fabric pooled at his feet. 'It's nice to be received with such excitement, Joan, but I'd rather we all avoided broken necks.'

'If she'd waited but a moment,' her mother said from the darkness of the dining room beside them, 'she'd have known we were meeting up here.'

Joan felt her entire body go hot with embarrassment as her father set her back on her feet. He stepped around her and into the dining room where James was lighting the candles in the sconces along the wall. Master Shakespeare picked up the bundle of fabric and then patted her head as he moved past her. Joan followed, wishing she could sink into the floor.

She walked into the dining room and grabbed a taper to help her brother with his task. 'How did you wake before me?' she muttered to him.

He grinned at her. 'Simple, really. I never slept.'

'James . . .'

He snagged the candle from her, placing both in an empty holder before guiding her to the table. 'Nothing to be done for it now.'

Joan plopped down in a chair, her glare fixed on her brother as he sat opposite her. The three adults were already arranged around the table, their father at the head and Master Shakespeare and their mother on either side of him.

'I hope you've come with something productive, Will,' their mother said sharply.

Shakespeare sighed heavily. 'Such judgement before I've even spoken, Bess?'

'Enough, love.' Their father placed his hand over their mother's, and her tense posture relaxed just slightly.

Joan and James looked at each other, the same question passing silently between them. One neither dared to ask.

What conflict did their mother have with Master Shakespeare?

Shakespeare nodded to their father and cleared his throat. 'We need to get Benjamin out of the Tower immediately and with great discretion.' Here a smile spread across his face. 'I've secured the assistance of the washers who maintain the linens there. They are scheduled to service the Tower in one hour's time, and we shall enter with them, clothed in these garments. The laundryman was most accommodating with a little . . .' His grin turned wicked here ' . . . incentive.'

'You brazen flirt,' Joan's mother said.

He shrugged. 'Brazen but immensely effective.' He laid his bundle of cloth out over the table, revealing three utilitarian dresses and caps in brown and grey wool. 'Bess, James, Joan and I shall enter the Tower.'

Joan noticed for the first time that he wore an equally plain jerkin and trousers, nothing like the fine clothes he usually favoured. She found herself very glad to have him going along with them. Her mother needed to see a place before she could create one of her magical doorways. So, while she absolutely had to go to the Tower, she was was a terrible liar, and leaving all the talking to James was too heavy a burden.

'Bess, once we find where he's held, you can send him back here where Thomas waits. Then the four of us who remain shall depart the way we arrived to not arouse suspicion. When we've all returned here, we can decide the best place for Benjamin to hide as he works towards restoring the Pact.' He stepped back and spread his arms wide. 'Is it not well planned?'

James grinned. 'It's excellent, Master Shakespeare.' He grabbed one of the dresses, passing it to Joan as he took another for himself. 'We'll change now.'

'Well done, Will,' Mrs Sands said, rolling her eyes.

Shakespeare laughed. 'A high compliment from you, Bess.' He clapped his hands. 'Don your attire, we have a wagon to meet.'

CHAPTER SEVEN
A Matter Deep & Dangerous

he ride to the Tower felt both too quick and excruciatingly slow. They bumped along the roads in the open cart Shakespeare had procured. He and a gentleman named Dell sat in the front. Joan, James and their mother assembled in the back alongside Sarah and Kate, the two laundresses who worked for Dell. A lantern hung at the end of a long rod, lighting the road ahead of the mule that pulled them through the dark streets. Even still, the shadows seemed to loom too close.

'We're nearly there,' Shakespeare said suddenly, his whisper loud in the silence of the early morning.

The grey walls of the ancient structure came into view long before they reached its gates, and a malevolent energy seemed to circle the whole place.

Terrible things had happened to both the guilty and innocent in the Tower of London, and the spirits of those dead left a stain on the very air. Joan steeled herself against the onslaught. James shivered beside her, and she reached out to take his hand.

As a child of Oya, the Orisha of the dead, James could feel the ghosts of this place better than anyone else.

'You don't have to come in with us,' she whispered gently.

He shook his head. 'No, I'm fine.' He squeezed her hand and leaned close, dropping his voice so she could barely hear his words. 'Besides, we need someone besides Shakespeare who can lie well. You're shite at it and so is Mother.'

Joan rolled her eyes but didn't let go. Her brother cracking jokes brought some levity to the fraught atmosphere. She could almost forget that they were about to break someone out of the most secure prison in all of London.

They bumped across the drawbridge and approached the gates that would take them into the Tower. Two crimson-uniformed guards stood barring their entrance, the polearms they held as imposing as the glares on their faces.

'We're here for the linens,' Dell said firmly, his voice somehow balancing both a command and a request.

Joan glanced across the cart at her mother, who kept her eyes on the guards even with her head bowed.

The guard to the left frowned. 'You've got more than usual, Dell.'

'Many hands make light work,' Dell said with an unconcerned shrug.

'You've a need for this many?'

We're caught.

Joan's heart hammered in her chest. She nudged James and brought her hand up as if to adjust her cap, letting him glimpse Bia wrapped around her wrist. If they needed to fight their way out, she was ready.

She prayed it didn't come to that.

'By your leave, sir,' Shakespeare spoke up from the front of the cart, his voice pitched higher and more nasally than usual. 'If you'd like to be the one to help our employer gather the piss- and shite-stained linens from the prisoners here, I'm sure more 'an a few of us'd be happy to stay behind. If that would satisfy you, sir.'

James leaned forwards. 'Mister Dell, sir, I thought you said there was three times as much today as 'twere any other.' He'd made his voice high and rasping, his tone sounding perfectly feminine. 'Have you no need of us?'

'No use trying to get out of work, girl,' Shakespeare replied as he turned to glare at James. 'Not if this man'll let us through.'

James let his shoulders slump as he pointed at the guard. 'But he said—'

'Is he your boss?' Shakespeare turned back to the two blocking their entry. 'What say you, gentlemen?'

James leaned over the side of the cart suddenly and smiled at the men. ''Tis nasty work today. I'll not mind you taking up my part.'

The guard who hadn't spoken grinned at James, his pale face flushing red in the torchlight.

Damn you and your flirting, James.

'Don't listen to my sister,' Joan said as she slid up beside James. 'She thinks she need only smile and every man will do her bidding, just like her intended.' She didn't bother adjusting her voice because these men would never see her after today.

Or so she hoped.

Disappointment shifted over the man's face before he jumped to attention as his fellow glared at him.

'Go on, then,' the first guard said as he waved them through the gate.

Dell shook the reins, sending the mule and cart clunking along onto the grounds of the Tower of London. Joan and James collapsed back into its bed, silent as they rolled through to the other side.

'Are you whoring or working?' the first guard muttered.

James straightened. 'Me a whore?' He started to rise from the cart, but Joan grabbed him, jerking him back down.

'Shut up,' she hissed.

He had the decency to look ashamed.

Mrs Sands leaned up towards the front. 'Know you any subtlety, Will?'

'I fear I've never been acquainted with this "subtlety," for I always perform with every ounce of my passion,' Shakespeare replied, the slightest hint of venom in his voice.

Dell cracked the reins again. 'I can speak to that truth, madam.' A satisfied grin spread across his face.

'Spare me, I beg you,' her mother groaned as she shifted back into her seat with a scowl.

Joan shook her head as Shakespeare laughed.

Actors.

They clattered along a well-worn service path and rolled to a stop at the back side of one of the stone towers. A cacophony of roars and growls echoed from it as they unloaded themselves. Neither Dell nor the women reacted to the noise.

'That's the lions and tigers.' Shakespeare nodded towards the looming stone building. 'The royal menagerie.'

Dell pulled a lantern from the back of the cart, lighting it quickly and then handing it off to Shakespeare.

'The man you're looking for is kept in the top of that one,' he said, his brown face severe as the light cast harsh shadows over his wrinkles. He pointed to the tall structure across the dark expanse of the courtyard. 'You've one hour to get back here. Any more, and you doom us all.'

Shakespeare clasped the man's arm. 'Not a moment longer.'

Joan fell into step behind Shakespeare as he led them through the dark, her hand ready to draw the blade at her wrist should they need. They reached the far tower, which had a locked door at its base.

Without a word, her mother stepped forwards and laid her hand over the lock. It glowed deep red for a moment, then sprang open with the barest of creaks.

No door could keep a child of Elegua out, and her mother had thankfully been blessed by the keeper of keys.

The four of them slipped inside and up the spiralling stone stairs. They moved quickly to the top of the Tower, where there appeared a lone room with a heavy iron-and-wood door.

Joan marvelled at that. No metal answered the call of a child of Ogun as easily as iron – her godfather could manipulate it as easily as she herself. If this was all that held Baba prisoner, why had he not freed himself?

Mrs Sands touched the lock on this door and swung it open. She flinched as the hinges screeched and they all held still and silent in the hall.

'Robin?' A voice said from within the room. 'Is that you again?'

Joan felt hope bloom in her chest as her godfather called out to them. She rushed into the darkness of the room.

The walls were cold, tan stone and the space itself bare but for a small dresser and a low bed covered with thick blankets. And there, his tall form curled up on the windowsill and illuminated by moonlight, was Baba Ben. He was thinner than he should be, the shadows in his cheeks deep, and his shirt engulfed his form. His curls stuck out in dry bunches as if he'd often run his fingers through them.

He looked worn and tired but blessedly alive.

'Joan?' He turned, eyes widening as he took them all in. 'Joan?'

She ran to him as he scrambled from his seat and met her in the centre of the room, wrapping her up in his arms. 'Baba . . .'

'What are you doing here?' He pulled away and wiped at the tears that

Joan hadn't even felt wetting her cheeks. He looked over Joan's shoulder to the rest standing just inside the door. 'James? Bess? Will? How . . . ?'

Shakespeare grinned, looking incredibly pleased with himself. 'We're here to facilitate your escape, Benjamin.'

Joan's mother closed the door behind them. She laid her hand over the lock again and it clicked back into place.

'My escape?' Fear rippled across Baba's face. 'No.'

Joan grasped his hands, clutching them tightly when she noticed how icy cold they were. 'It's all right, Baba. We can hide you and protect you until we set things right again.'

'No,' he said harshly. 'It's better that I'm here.' He pulled away and stood, eyes going a bit wild. 'Who saw you? Who knows you've come?'

James reached out towards him, his voice placating. 'No one, Baba. Let us get you out of here.'

'No. As long as she knows I'm here in this prison, she'll leave Joan be.'

Joan flinched at the words. There was no need to ask what 'she' he meant. 'Is that why you've let this iron door hold you?' Guilt surged in her gut. Her godfather endured this prison for her sake.

'Aye.' Baba's expression softened when he noticed. 'You and I are the only two who could possibly stop her, but you know nothing of the Pact's rituals. That keeps you alive, and me remaining Titanea's prisoner keeps you safe.'

She opened her mouth to protest but he shushed her. 'I can bear all this if it keeps you safe, Joan.' He turned to the other two adults in the cell, his eyes pleading. 'You understand, Will? Bess?'

'Of course,' her mother said fiercely. She glanced at Joan for a moment. 'I think we might be able to do our work and restore the Pact from within these walls.' She glanced around. 'Now that I know this place I can make doors here as we need.'

Baba frowned and tugged at his hair nervously. 'That might be possible, if my jailer cooperates.'

'Who? Titanea?' James said.

Robin Goodfellow stepped from the air in front of the door, appearing between one blink and the next. 'Me,' they said flatly.

'You can help us get Baba out of here.' Hope bloomed in Joan's heart at the sight of the powerful Fae who'd helped her against Auberon.

Their soft brown skin and luxurious coils of white hair were just as she remembered. They were Rose's parent and Joan's ally. She hadn't seen Goodfellow in months, but their friendship in such a deadly time had been an immeasurable gift. If Goodfellow helped now, Baba Ben would have no reason to stay within this prison. Where Titanea's aid was uncertain, Goodfellow's was absolute.

But they offered only silence, refusing to meet Joan's gaze.

Oh.

Goodfellow's avoidance spoke volumes. They were under Titanea's control, and if the Fae queen wanted Baba in the Tower of London, then Goodfellow would use their considerable power to keep him there.

The betrayal brought tears to her eyes, though her anger dried them quickly. 'Do you serve her by choice?'

'She is my queen,' Goodfellow said, 'and she has my Rose.' A sudden pain overtook their face, so stark and bare Joan felt her own heart ache in response. 'I'm sorry, Iron Blade.'

Some instinct overtook her and through her anger she took special note of their answer. She knew how important understanding the exact words said were in deciphering Fae truth.

'Must you tell her all?' Joan said, doing her best to temper her voice. Emotion shifted across their face. 'All that I see.'

'And what do you see?'

'All that happens before my eyes.' They said the words slowly, deliberately, demanding she catch their intent.

And catch she did. They had to report everything they saw back to Titanea but they need not see everything. Her hope surged forth again.

Goodfellow might prove her ally yet.

Baba squeezed Joan's hands. 'Leave me – it's safer this way.'

She pulled him into a tight embrace, turning her face away from Goodfellow to whisper in her godfather's ear. 'I'll bring you your Ogun pot. We'll discover the rest once you have it. They'll keep our secrets if we're out of their sight.'

Joan forced a sad expression over her face and hoped Baba didn't react to her words. He pulled back and stared directly into her eyes, his gaze cautiously hopeful.

'We want you home,' she said.

He gave a wane smile. 'It cannot be. Go. All of you.'

Goodfellow stepped aside, leaving the path clear to the cell door. They moved over to Baba and placed a comforting hand on his shoulder.

'You won't see us again, Goodfellow,' Joan said pointedly.

They nodded, a small smile spreading across their face. 'I hope not.'

Shakespeare shuffled their group out into the hall and the cell door clanged shut behind them. But not even that heavy sound could douse the spark that flickered within Joan.

Perhaps everything would turn out well in the end despite their disadvantage. They had a way forwards. It wouldn't be easy, but it existed. That was enough for now.

CHAPTER EIGHT
The Rough Torrent of Occasion

hey met Dell, Sarah and Kate well before their hour was up and helped load the last of the soiled linens onto the cart. Joan scrambled up into the back alongside her brother and mother. The sky shifted to an airy blue as the sun crested the horizon behind them and the guards waved them back through the gate. James's admirer cast one last hopeful look at her brother before they rattled out of sight, bumping along the road away from the Tower.

The fear that filled Joan's mind as they'd arrived had no place to catch hold as they departed. Too many thoughts raced through her head along with a flood of hope.

She and Baba were safe so long as he stayed in his prison and she within Titanea's reach. Goodfellow served as his jailer; their loyalty to their queen and desire for their daughter's safety kept them obedient but not compliant. They would be watchful but not vigilant. The difference was subtle but Joan was confident they could do much within the sliver of opportunity that provided.

She'd retrieve Baba's Ogun pot from his shop and bring it to him in the Tower. The iron cauldron served as a physical representation of Baba's connection with Ogun. He didn't need it to hear the Orisha but having it nearby would let him commune much more intensely with Ogun and reseal the Pact.

Joan had her own pot that she worked far less than she should. She knew where it was and often went through the motions of keeping it clean when too much dust collected on it. But she didn't sit or pray with it nor just talk to it as her brother did with his Oya urn and her mother with her Elegua statue that sat guarding their front door. Maybe that's why Ogun spoke to her directly, because of her lax practices.

Although that could just be the nature of her connection with the Orisha, something as varied and personal within their community as any relationship.

Even still, she'd return Baba's pot to him. Now that her mother had seen the inside of his cell, nothing barred her magic from bringing them there.

They only needed to time their visits to fall within an opening Goodfellow might provide them. Though there was no way to plan such an opportunity. They needed to trust Goodfellow's discretion, and Joan absolutely did.

Their party split at Dell's laundry. Shakespeare offered his profuse thanks, kissing the man's cheek and whispering something in his ear that made him blush and throw his head back with laughter.

'A shameless flirt,' Joan's mother muttered. She glanced at James. 'Don't learn this habit from him.'

Joan snorted. 'Too late.' She grunted as her brother elbowed her.

Shakespeare passed a small purse that jangled heavily with coins to Dell before approaching Joan and her family. She watched Dell pass money along to his two workers before the three of them began unloading the soiled linens.

'Their secrecy is secured although Benjamin is not.' Shakespeare sighed, disappointment sweeping over his face.

Joan grabbed the tall man's hand. 'It was an excellent plan,' she said with a smile. 'And though it did not fall out as expected, we have reason to hope that it did indeed work.'

She beckoned them close, explaining quickly Goodfellow's subterfuge and her own plans for Baba's Ogun pot.

'Well done, Joan,' Shakespeare said. 'I'll send a message to my mother and see what she knows of the Pact. Bess, I'll inform you of anything I learn.' He patted Joan on the head affectionately and then headed north towards his home on Silver Street.

Joan and her family set off towards Goldsmith's Row, the sun fully rising by the time they turned onto the street. As they approached their house, Joan noticed the closed sign was still in the window of the shop, although the candles inside had been lit. Frowning, James swung the front door open, the bell jingling jauntily. Her father stood at the counter with an exhausted young woman slumped on the stool behind it.

'Avalee?' Her mother said quietly. She gestured at James and he closed and locked the door after them.

The girl looked up, her expression dazed and apologetic. 'I'm sorry to call on you so early, Iya Bess.' She wrung her hands together, glancing from Joan's father then back to Joan's mother. 'But it was urgent.'

Avalee was a familiar presence as a member of their Orisha community and one of Mrs Sands's godchildren. She was only a few years older than Joan and James and much taller. Her deep brown skin looked ashen, with dark circles bruising her tired-looking eyes. Her hair was arranged neatly, as were her black gown and grey woollen cloak, but the white bandages wrapping her left forearm were spotted with blood.

Joan frowned. 'What happened to you? Are you all right?'

Avalee jerked upright at the sound of Joan's voice and glanced hesitantly at Mrs Sands.

'Let's talk in my office,' Joan's father said. 'Joan, James, have Nan prepare your breakfast.'

The girl seemed to relax, but Joan felt outrage burn to life in her chest.

She could understand why the older girl didn't want to speak freely in front of her and James. Avalee had no idea what they'd been through, how many Joan had fought and killed just two months ago.

But Joan's parents knew. As she watched them lead Avalee up the stairs, Joan struggled to understand why they were leaving her out. Hurt raced through her, dousing the fire of her anger as she and James trudged past their father's closed office door.

'I, for one, am very happy to put on my own clothes,' James said suddenly. 'These muted colours do not suit me well.' He paused, a sly smile sliding over his face. 'Although I'm sure that guard would disagree. He seemed quite infatuated, attired as I was in these dull woman's weeds.'

Joan scowled at him, anger overleaping her hurt once again. 'How can you joke so now?'

'Why? Am I not allowed?'

'They're leaving us out. Aren't you furious?'

'No.'

She stomped her foot, feeling childish and not caring. 'Why not? We have every right to hear what happened to Avalee as they do.'

'And if you did hear, what would you do then?' He rolled his eyes at her, his quick answer cutting through her rage. 'You're already set to serve the Fae queen, how much more involved do you desire to be?'

As deeply as I need to be to keep you and everyone I love safe.

Joan clamped her mouth shut, holding the words in because as sure as she felt, she knew her brother was right. This wasn't her fight alone no matter how much the thought of her family and friends in danger terrified her. Attempting to shoulder every burden by herself helped no one. She needed to remember that.

She looked up at James to tell him as much, but he waved her off.

'Come on, you goose,' he said, climbing the stairs again. 'I have a colour combination I'd like you to try.'

Joan snorted and followed her brother the rest of the way up to their floor.

Joan had hoped when she sat down for breakfast, she'd feel more cheerful but as Nan placed sausage and bread before her, tension and trepidation crept along her entire body. Not even James's choice of a summer-sky blue dress with sunset-orange sleeves could stave off the foreboding feeling.

'It seems now is when I start regretting my lack of sleep,' James said glumly as he struggled to jab a sausage with his fork. The meat rolled away, skittering rebelliously across his plate.

Joan sighed. She wondered what was keeping her parents so long with Avalee but tried not to imagine what they spoke of. That mystery now caused her anxiety even as she suppressed the desire to know. She sighed again, pulling the soft middles out of the rolls and mashing them between her fingers before stuffing them in her mouth.

Her mother would normally disapprove of her mishandling of her food, but her mother wasn't there to admonish her for it.

'I've never been one to enjoy the theatre being closed,' James said as he sliced and stole half the sausage from Joan's plate, 'but I find myself desperately in need of a quiet day at home.'

Joan snorted and cut off her own small section of the meat before sliding the rest to her brother. 'I would prefer playmaking to whatever is surely in store for us.'

A loud banging echoed up from the front door downstairs. Nan nearly leapt out of her skin before she rushed for the stairs. Joan frowned at James as Nan disappeared down to the lower floors. It was too early for anyone calling on their father's goldsmithing services. His shop wouldn't be open for at least another two hours. That meant this was a personal call on their family, for good or for ill.

Joan tried not to let the wondering make her too nervous, but her already abysmal appetite completely disappeared, leaving her to pull the bread in her hands and drop it anxiously onto her plate. She shifted her focus to Bia and its gentle hum in case she needed to draw the blade quickly. Out of the corner of her eye, she noticed James tighten his grip on his dining knife. They were both ready for a fight, and Joan hated that this tension ruled their lives now.

The sound of doors opening and closing floated up to where they sat in the dining room before Avalee and a nauseous-looking Nan ascended the stairs. Mrs Sands hurried them along from behind, a sheaf of papers clutched in her hands.

'Nan, could you go to the kitchen and fetch some refreshments for Lord Salisbury?' Mrs Sands said tightly.

Joan's heart thundered to a stop.

'Yes, ma'am,' Nan said, and skittered off to do as she was told.

Cecil? Here? Why had he invaded her home again?

'Joan, love,' her mother said, her posture stiff as their eyes met. 'Lord Salisbury would like to speak with you in your father's office.'

Joan stood, wiping sweaty hands in the folds of her skirts. She glanced at her brother, who hadn't bothered hiding the horrified look on his own face. She was suddenly grateful that he'd insisted they change into their own clothes before breakfast, the familiar blue-and-orange gown offering some comfort as she descended the stairs.

Her father stood awkwardly outside his own office, the smile on his face at odds with his clenched fists and stiff posture. Two of Cecil's personal guards flanked the open door in crisp black uniforms, their pale faces coldly blank.

Joan moved towards the room, her father just beside her. One of the guards shoved his open palm against her father's chest, halting him midstep.

'It's fine,' Cecil's voice called from within. 'They both may enter.'

Searing rage burned through Joan at the man's audacity. Her father grabbed her hand and sent her a look that was both commiseration and warning. It didn't cool her rage but it helped her hide it, a relief because she knew there were some emotions she could not show this man.

They entered the office together to find Cecil standing behind her father's desk, shuffling through his papers. Joan felt her father tense beside her and squeezed his hand. After a long silence, Cecil held a blank sheet up to the candlelight. He hummed then finally looked up at them.

'Your daughter,' he said, sneering the word like a curse, 'through some craft or miracle, has been invited to join Her Majesty the queen's household.'

Mr Sands cleared his throat. 'Yes, Joan has informed us of her good fortune.'

'I'm sure she has. Just as I'm sure you know of her unusual skills. Although' – he cast an appraising look over her father – 'I believe that she may not be alone in these abilities.' He lifted the blank paper he held and tilted it towards the candle again, squinting as if he'd found something on the blank page. 'Interesting.'

Joan's heart raced. 'My lord, have you come all this way—'

'Speak not to me, girl.' Cecil turned his glare to her. 'You may have the queen's favour, but know this: If at any time I perceive you bear even the slightest threat to the royal family, I will end you immediately.'

Joan clenched her jaw, choking down the responses that threatened to fly from her lips. The last time she'd insulted Cecil, a slap had been her reward. Then she'd been able to escape into the palace's great hall and under the watchful eyes of the queen and a bevy of courtiers. Her sharp tongue would not be so protected here in her home.

It made her hate this man more than anything else. How dare he make her and her family feel unsafe here?

'That goes for all of you.' He brandished the paper he held. 'I can decipher some of these names.' He shifted it towards the light again. '"Avalee Saunders," "Rufus Thatch," "Benjamin Wick."' Here he paused, gaze considering. 'This last name I've seen somewhere before. These are your compatriots with similar abilities' – He sneered the word – 'I suppose.'

It was blank with not a single spot of ink upon the page. Her parents wouldn't have been so careless to leave those names where anyone outside of their community could find them. How had Cecil been able to glean any of that from empty paper? He angled it slightly away from the candle, and Joan could see the shadows of words reveal themselves, indentations left behind by her father's pen.

Of course that thrice-damned man would know how to uncover secrets from marks on a blank piece of paper. An icy chill overcame Joan as he folded it and tucked it within his black jerkin. She nearly looked to her father in her panic but fought the move with every fibre of her being.

If that page contained the remnants of what she thought, offering Cecil any confirmation of their importance would prove deadly. Her father's grip on her hand tightened, and that told her as much as if he'd spoken aloud.

Cecil potentially held the names of every Orisha worshipper in London. No one person could be expected to recall the names of every single member of their community, and Joan's parents had likely drafted the list in response to the danger Avalee encountered. That even some portion of it now laid in Cecil's hands put them all at risk.

Joan vowed not to let Cecil use it to harm any of their people. He wouldn't even have known of their unusual abilities if it hadn't been for her. As if she needed more reason to regret saving William Cecil's life . . .

Cecil pulled another stack of papers from his pocket, these neatly tied with crimson and gold ribbon, and tossed them onto the desk. 'Here are your orders, the details of your new title and the expectations of you as a member of the queen's household. Prepare yourself. I shall retrieve you on the ninth of January.' He strode around the desk and stood before Joan and her father.

'Indeed, my lord,' her father said, his voice as calm as the still waters of a lake, though Joan could sense a tempest raged within. 'Shall I see you to your carriage?'

Cecil lifted his chin as if to intimidate the taller man. He patted his chest where he'd stuffed their list. 'Do not give me cause to use this.'

He turned to the door, and Joan's father cast her a look before following after the secretary of state and his guards. She waited, heart thundering in her chest, until she heard the footfalls on the stairs give way to the jingling of the shop bell as the front door opened. Then she bolted from the room, skirts hiked nearly to her knees as she ran to tell her mother all that had transpired.

Her mother met her at the top of the stairs, face ashen as she clutched her chest.

'He deciphered the names on your list,' Joan panted. 'He knew how to read the remnants of father's writing on a blank page.'

Her mother nodded grimly. 'We need to warn everyone before he can make use of what he's learned.' She guided Joan up into the sitting room where James and Avalee knelt across from each other, papers spread out on the floor before them.

The originals to the one Cecil had discovered.

Joan nodded to her mother before moving to kneel beside Avalee. She took a paper from the older girl's trembling hand. Joan smiled at her frightened stare.

'It's OK,' Joan said with a confidence she didn't feel. She glanced at James and knew he saw through her feigned expression even though he kept quiet. She silently thanked him and forced a smile onto her face. 'What do you need me to do?'

oan's father eventually joined them in the sitting room, the shadow of guilt surrounding him a palpable thing. She'd seen James clasp his hand as they looked over a page together.

She hated for her father to blame himself when she'd been the reason Robert Cecil had invaded their home twice now. She wished she could repay the insults and threats he'd lobbed at her family but she doubted even one of the queen's ladies could wield such power.

Her mother flitted between them all, noting who among their list was also a child of Elegua.

She paused, hands crinkling the paper she held. 'We should have shared this with everyone in November,' she said abruptly.

'Mother.' Joan touched her mother's wrists. 'We thought there was no need because the threat was gone. But we can tell them now.'

Her mother nodded and unclenched her fists. Her expression remained tense but Joan accepted her small victory.

Despite the dark clouds of fear and shame that loomed over them, the family's plan came together rapidly after the secretary of state's departure.

Avalee, James and her parents would warn their community of both Cecil's stolen knowledge and the escalating Fae threat using her mother's doorways. Unlike Ogun, Elegua had spread his blessings to many within the city. Once word reached his children, they'd be able to pass it along using their doorway magic to move more swiftly than the wind.

Joan's role was to retrieve her godfather's Ogun pot from his workshop. She'd quickly offered to walk in order to reserve her mother's abilities for their messages – though her suggestion held another purpose.

She feared what she'd find at Baba's workshop since he had been arrested two months ago. She wasn't prepared to transport instantly into the wreckage of his life. The long walk would allow her to brace for whatever she found.

She rounded the corner of his street. His combined home and tailor's shop came into view. An open sign hung in the door's window and a warm light spilled out from behind the curtains. Something in her chest unclenched at the sight. Fear had kept her from coming to this place. The thought of the home her godfather maintained with such a fastidious eye for detail and cleanliness being left abandoned and in disarray had filled her with dread. Seeing it damaged would have made his absence so much more real. That possibility had dogged her steps even now, and she'd hesitated as she'd turned onto his street.

But everything was as it would have been if Baba had been there, and she knew she had Pearl to thank for that. Joan cautiously opened the front door, the bell above it cheerily announcing her arrival with a jangle.

'One moment, please,' a husky voice called out from behind a curtain that Joan knew led back into Baba Ben's main workspace. Soon after, a woman, hunched with age, stepped into the main room. She had deep brown skin and stark white hair neatly braided and pinned around her head, and her entire being shone with the glow that marked her as one of the Fae.

'Ah, Joan.' Her eyes softened. 'I've been hoping you'd come visit.' She held her arms out, and Joan leaned into her warm embrace.

Joan let herself enjoy Pearl's hug for a long moment before pulling away. 'They haven't tried to arrest you too, have they?'

'Oh, they have, child, but every time they're here, I get them so turned around they forget what they've come to do.' Pearl snorted out a laugh.

Joan grinned back at her. She should've known Pearl would use every bit of Fae magic she knew to keep Baba's home safe in his absence. The love those two shared was as deep as any bond between mother and son. Joan wondered if this was the first time they had ever been apart. The thought broke her heart even more.

'I need to retrieve Baba's . . .' Joan paused, reconsidering her words.

She knew Pearl would never intentionally betray Baba but Titanea might not give the old Fae woman a choice.

'I need to retrieve something,' she said simply.

Pearl nodded, her gaze conveying her understanding. She glanced at the door to the workshop before waving Joan back towards it. 'Go find what you're looking for.'

Joan heard the creak of the knob behind her and rushed through the curtain into the back room just as the bell announced a customer.

'Good day, ma'am,' Pearl said. 'How can I help?'

Joan lost the rest of the conversation as she moved through her god-father's workshop. Candles illuminated the large space brightly, a necessity for the delicate art of sewing, cutting and embroidering. That Pearl kept it so well lit in Baba's absence warmed Joan's heart and pained her in equal measure. A massive mirror trimmed in intricate swirls and twists of silver and gold leaned against one wall. Joan ran her fingers across the metal as she passed it and felt it sing to her softly. The Sandses had gifted the piece to Baba Ben two years ago; Joan's father had even let her do most of the metal detailing along it. She'd fashioned and refashioned the swirl of Ben's name that ran along its top about seven times before she was even mildly satisfied.

But the work had been worth it for the joyful look on Ben's face when they'd delivered it. Her chest felt tight, and she forced herself to keep moving.

She needed to be quick with her task. She shifted around his long worktables, covered in fabric and unfinished garments and organised in a loose H shape. Her skirts, too wide to pass easily, knocked a bolt of gold velvet to the floor. Joan cursed and knelt to pick it up.

'You'll find nothing here! Leave this place.' Pearl's angry voice carried into the workshop.

Joan felt the heat of Ogun's presence blaze to life in her chest as Pearl's body came flying through the curtain. She slammed into one of the tables, rolling across its top and dropping to the floor with a grunt. Her form shimmered and shrank, her face becoming wider and rounder as the tips of her ears elongated into sharp points. She locked suddenly emerald eyes – their true colour – with Joan, who still crouched behind another worktable.

'Run – that goblin doesn't know you're back here,' Pearl whispered as the curtain was ripped away from the doorway.

Joan glanced up as another short form stepped into the doorway, the top of its head barely clearing the height of the tables.

The creature shifted into the light, revealing pale blue skin stretched over a wiry frame and a head like a large toad with bulbous eyes perched on top. 'Your misplaced loyalty is disgusting,' it sneered in a flutelike voice.

'Leave this place,' Pearl said, pushing herself up to her feet. 'You'll find nothing you seek here.' She gave Joan a pointed look before she moved out of sight.

The creature laughed like the clanging of bells. 'I followed the girl here. You'd die to protect a mortal?'

There was the skittering of feet on the rush-strewn floor and Pearl disappeared completely from Joan's sight. Pearl shrieked. Fabric tumbled to the floor as the goblin slammed her down on one of the tables. Something squelched and Pearl cried out again.

Joan flicked her wrist. Bia launched from her arm, enlarging to full size. She snatched the sword from the air as she leapt to her feet. 'Get out of my godfather's shop.'

The goblin looked up from where it crouched half atop Pearl and sneered at Joan.

'Release Pearl and leave this place, as she said.' Joan sent iron flowing from her fingertips and down along the sword. She stepped closer, touching the sharp edge against the creature's neck. 'The next point I press won't be with words.'

She doubted this Fae would still want to fight when Joan already held it at such a disadvantage. If the creature surrendered and let them be, Joan wouldn't follow after it.

The goblin's gaze shifted along the blade then locked on Joan. A long tongue shot out, tasting the air as the rest of its head turned to follow. It was much smaller than Joan, its frame lean and wiry, but something about the creature—

It batted Joan's sword away and dove for her. Joan stumbled back as the impossibly heavy weight of the creature rammed into her chest. The goblin's long fingers stretched towards Joan's throat. Joan blocked them, flipping Bia to slice across its arms. It leaned back and Bia cut through empty air. The creature wrapped its legs around Joan's waist, throwing its weight backwards and flinging her across the room.

Joan slammed against the opposite wall. Something popped in her shoulder, the sudden pain shattering her focus.

'Joan!' Pearl called.

She looked up and raised her forearm, coating it in iron just as the goblin clawed at her face. Its hand caught Joan's metal-covered wrist. The scent of burnt flesh filled the air. She ducked her head to the side as the goblin's other claw scratched along her temple. Joan flinched but sent iron over her palm. She grabbed the creature's wrist, its skin scorching beneath her touch. The horrid stench intensified, but Joan tightened her grip as the goblin screeched and thrashed. Grunting, she hurled it across the room with all her strength.

Joan pushed herself upright, panting and gasping, but the goblin was on her again. They both tumbled backwards and slammed against Baba Ben's enormous mirror. The glass shattered. Shards rained down over them as they grappled. Joan lost her grip on Bia and the sword clattered across the floor.

The goblin's hands seemed to be everywhere at once, its speed incredible. It was all Joan could do to bat each strike away and keep her wounds shallow. Bia was too far away to grab, but if she could get a hand against the mirror's metal frame, she could run this beast through. She stretched her fingers towards one side, barely reaching the cool steel before she had to block another hit. She stretched for it again and felt the slightest chill as she came closer the edge of the frame.

She couldn't hope to manipulate the metal without touching it, but she still strained for it. Joan felt something inside her snap taut then stretch just that little bit further. Her head ached with the pressure of it, but she felt if she just pushed a little harder, *something* would happen.

Suddenly, a tiny sliver of the metal mirror wavered and reached back towards her. It wrapped around her fingertip as heat built in Joan's chest.

The goblin clawed at Joan's throat. She grabbed its wrist again to stop the creature from ripping her whole neck open. The warmth disappeared as Joan lost her focus and the mirror went back to normal. All at once she felt the hot trickle of blood along her neck, her face and her arms, everywhere the goblin had attacked her.

She glimpsed Bia on the floor and well out of her reach before she had to bat away another attack. No matter. She only needed enough of an opening to form her machete and she could end this.

Joan coated her fist in iron and struck the goblin across the face. She let the metal flow down along the same hand to form a blade and flip it in her grip to stab into the creature's side. The goblin caught Joan's wrist mid-swing and, looking directly into her eyes, wrenched her arm forwards with one hand.

Joan screamed as her shoulder was jerked out of the socket. The pain shoved everything else from her mind and the iron slipped back into her palm. The creature lifted Joan's arm, sending searing bolts through her whole body. The goblin's wide mouth spread into a smile. It drew its other hand back, claws extended. It gasped, eyes going wide, as Bia's iron-coated blade jabbed through its stomach.

Joan looked up to see Pearl standing behind the goblin, face twisted in pain as she held the sword in both hands. This was just the distraction Joan needed.

She slapped her other hand against the mirror's metal frame and felt it leap forwards at her touch. The steel and gold flowed down around them in slithering tendrils that wrapped around the goblin, tying it and ripping the creature up and away from Joan. She leaned back as the goblin's thrashing body was dragged over her head and bound tightly against the mirror's empty wooden back.

Gasping, Joan scrambled to her feet. Bia's hilt stuck out from where it had been stabbed through the goblin's back. She grabbed it and felt the sword hiss in rage. A matching emotion welled up inside her, the throbbing pain in her shoulder feeding the flame.

How dare this creature destroy her godfather's shop? How dare it attack them so? How dare it make her bleed?

Joan grunted and used all her strength to drive the sword upward, rending flesh and bone and dense muscle as she split the goblin in half.

She stepped back, taking in the bloody, bisceted corpse suspended against the warped and ruined mirror that she'd once put so much love into creating.

'Well, I doubt I could polish that out,' Pearl said as she stepped up beside Joan. She was wrapping clean muslin around her hands, which looked red and raw as her form shifted back to that of a glowing old woman. 'Get what you've come for, child, and be on your way. I'll take care of things here, as I always have.'

Joan glanced at the woman, the Fae, and felt the absolute truth in her words. 'Thank you.' She looked at the mirror again, an ache filling her heart at having to desecrate something so beautiful and made with such love. 'But I must ask you one favour before I go.'

'Of course, child. What is it?'

Joan gestured to the arm hanging limp and too long at her side. 'Could you help me set my shoulder?'

CHAPTER TEN
Sleek O'er Your Rugged Looks

earl cleaned Joan up as best she could before she left. Joan just needed to look unsullied enough to get home without drawing undue attention and have her father look after her injuries. Her whole right side throbbed from her dislocated and reset shoulder, but she'd managed to retrieve Baba Ben's iron Ogun pot and its contents.

Joan had shrunken the tools and slipped them into one of her pockets. The heavy pot she'd tucked under her good arm. It looked no different from any other large cooking cauldron and she was thankfully strong enough to carry it despite its great weight. None of it would've been a burden if that thrice-damned goblin hadn't gotten so many hits on her.

The only thing that hurt worse than her sword arm was her pride. She clenched her jaw then released it when she felt her teeth grind together, the muscles aching from the tension.

How could she have let her guard down, left herself so vulnerable? The Joan who today was nearly felled by a goblin would've died at the hands of Auberon. Something had changed since she'd rescued her brother two months ago, and that knowledge filled her with fear and loathing. She couldn't protect anyone like this.

Joan slipped inside the house, locking the door behind herself before drawing the curtains over the windows. She shrugged off her heavy cloak and let it fall in a heap at her feet. She sighed, relieved to have its weight off her aching shoulder. The sound of voices carried from her father's workshop, and she managed to limp her way there. Her family went quiet as they saw her, James's mouth open midsentence.

Her mother leapt from her stool and rushed over to Joan, hands fluttering helplessly from her face to her arms and back again. 'What happened to you?'

'A goblin attacked me at Baba Ben's.' Joan put the pot down gently on the floor and let herself be fussed over. 'I managed to kill it, but not easily.'

Her parents exchanged worried glances.

The city had been quiet, without any such supernatural happenings since November's events, but it was beyond clear now that the Fae had only been biding their time. Avalee's encounter and now Joan's stood as proof. They were all in danger once again. Unless Baba Ben was able to reinstate the Pact.

Joan wondered about that call Master Phillips had mentioned. Had Titanea's recovery triggered this sudden resurgence of violence and, if it had, what did that say of the Fae queen's true intentions in the mortal realm? Joan vowed to discover it at court.

'Father,' she said as her mother pulled her collar aside to inspect her bruised shoulder, 'we should tell everyone we know to always carry an iron weapon. I can forge some after a little rest.'

Her mother made a noise of protest. 'You need more than a little rest, love.'

'That goblin followed me to Baba's,' Joan said tightly. The thought of being watched, of being followed, made her angry. 'We can't let ourselves be surprised again.'

I can't let myself be surprised again.

She turned to James. 'We should tell the King's Men to so arm themselves and get some protections for Nan.'

'Stop pushing yourself so hard,' her mother said. 'You've retrieved Ben's pot, let that be enough for now.'

Her father sighed, his eyes suddenly shiny in the candlelight. 'An excellent plan, Joan, but first let's take care of these injuries.' He kneeled in front her, ignoring his wife's betrayed look, and gently took hold of Joan's arm. She hissed in pain. 'I'll fetch my salve from my office.'

'And I'll get you something else to wear.' James said. He gave a quick salute, then raced up the stairs ahead of their father, taking them two at a time.

Joan was sure she looked a fright. Her hair stuck out from its formerly neat braids, smudges of now brown blood stained the top of her chemise and a dark bruise was starting to form on the side of her face. Her cloak had hidden the worst of it on the long walk home and honestly, she was surprised she didn't look worse. She'd almost died, after all.

Her mother sighed and averted her gaze. 'I didn't want you drawn into any more fights.'

'A futile hope, it seems,' Joan said, shrugging then flinching as she shifted her arm again. 'But I can handle myself.'

'Yes, I know you can fight,' her mother said sharply, 'but you are a child.'

Joan frowned as the frustration she'd felt when Avalee arrived returned. 'I'm one of the few people with the power to effectively fight the Fae. If I step aside, who will protect you?'

'It should be me, or your father, or Ben! It shouldn't be you, none of this should fall on you!' Tears pooled in the corners of her mother's eyes, threatening to fall at any moment. 'I am your mother, and I am supposed to keep you safe. Do you have any idea what it was like having both of my children facing death while I could do nothing but bleed?'

Joan remembered that moment, remembered running off to save her kidnapped brother bereft of her magic, remembered having to leave her mother bleeding in her bedroom, remembered praying that this wouldn't be the end of her family. So much of that day had been burned into her mind, but the image of her mother pale and covered in crimson always seemed to leap to the forefront.

How could her mother not have felt that same catastrophic fear?

She felt the clawing anger leave her as she grasped her mother's hand. Her fingers were icy to the touch. Joan felt something in her break, and she threw herself into her mother's arms. Her shoulder throbbed at the sudden collision, but she ignored it.

'I won't lose you,' Mrs Sands said. She squeezed Joan tightly, careful to avoid putting more pressure on her injury.

Joan let herself be wrapped up in her mother's warmth, the smell of the jasmine oil her mother used in her hair washing over her. 'Keeping me from the fight won't do that.' She pulled back, feeling tears well in her own eyes. 'Besides, the trouble seems to keep finding me no matter what I do.'

'My sweet girl,' her mother blurted around a laugh. 'I love you so very much.'

She pulled her mother close again. 'I love you too, Mother. You raised a fighter. No matter what this world has in store for me, I promise I won't go down easily.'

Joan hoped the words, the only vow she'd let herself make, would bring her mother comfort through the dangers that lay ahead.

'Ah . . . May I . . .' James waited at the bottom of the stairs, his feet shuffling awkwardly as he clutched a fresh chemise and the orange dress that matched Joan's sleeves.

Nan stood just behind him with a rag and a basin of water. She paled when she saw Joan and pressed her lips into a thin, straight line. Joan's mother waved them over and the three set to making Joan look presentable again. For her part, Joan allowed herself to be moved and shifted, thankful to let her mind drift to nothingness as they worked. She didn't want to think back to her fight with the goblin, or ahead to what her time at the royal court might bring. She didn't want to consider the names Cecil might recover from the papers he stole, or how his son might press his suit. For now she only wanted to exist in her family home surrounded by the comforting sound of their voices and the smell of her father's forge. Things that wouldn't be hers after tomorrow. Before long she felt Nan tightening the lacing at the back of her dress as James and her mother carefully tied the sleeve onto her injured arm.

Knock. Knock. Knock.

They all looked up at the curt rapping on the front door. Joan's mother frowned before slowly moving to open it. She waved Nan upstairs then nudged Joan and James behind her as she stepped forwards. Joan slipped her fingers around Bia and allowed the sword to uncurl from her wrist and grow to its true size. She held it at the ready, moving in front of her brother as their mother pulled the door open just enough to peek out.

'Is this the residence of . . . wait . . .' a soft voice said full of confusion. 'Bess Sands?'

Joan's mother's posture relaxed. 'Jessica Beckley? What are you doing here?'

'I'm here to prepare a wardrobe for Her Majesty's new lady-in-waiting. You mean that Joan Sands is YOUR Joan? How did you manage that?'

'Well, that's a secret.' Her mother stepped back, swinging the door open wide. 'Won't you come in?'

A slim woman just a little older than Joan's mother stepped into the shop followed by a young girl hauling a heavy bag. The woman's coily black hair was tucked and pinned atop her head haphazardly, and her rich brown complexion was perfect. Even her few wrinkles managed to only enhance her beauty. She unclasped her heavy black cloak and dropped it into the girl's arms without glancing at her, revealing an immaculate, intricately patterned burgundy-and-tan gown.

The girl grunted with the sudden weight of the cloak and stumbled a bit, her cheeks and the tip of her nose burning bright red on her extremely pale face. Her light brown hair had been hastily pulled up and tucked in place with several straight pins.

Joan quickly shifted her hand behind her back, using her full skirts to hide Bia as she shrank and curled the sword back into a bracelet. She glanced at James, who shrugged before they moved as one to help the struggling girl. She gave them a grateful look as they took the heavy bag and cloak from her.

'Bess, I can't believe your daughter is going to be serving the queen herself,' the woman – Mistress Beckley – said before catching sight of Joan. 'Is this her? I haven't seen you since you were a tiny thing.' She wrapped her long fingers around Joan's chin and turned her face left then right. 'You've grown to be quite lovely, but I wouldn't expect any less from Thomas's child. Though your mother might have done something with your hair.' She turned Joan's face again, staring at scratch along her temple. 'Or with that ghastly wound.'

We hadn't time to fix it after I got my arse beat by a goblin.

'Poor thing.' Mistress Beckley patted Joan's cheek. 'Were I your mother I'd never let you be seen in such a sad state.' The woman finally spotted James standing just next to them and grabbed him with a half coo, half shout. 'And your son! Why he's the very image of his handsome father.'

James gave her an empty smile. 'I am my mother's son.' His face shifted to confusion. 'Though I'm afraid my father's never made mention of you. I wonder at that.'

'Oh,' she said, looking lost for a moment before collecting herself. 'Well, that shall be remedied today. Go fetch him, will you?'

James raised an eyebrow but turned and bolted up the stairs, screaming 'Father!' as he disappeared onto the next floor.

Joan heard her mother snort and caught her eye over Mistress Beckley's shoulder. Mrs Sands's face scrunched up in disgust before shifting to blankly pleasant as Mistress Beckley turned to look at her.

'My husband's beauty aside, I assume you're here to get Joan's measurements, Jessica?' Mrs Sands gestured to Joan. 'We don't want to keep you from your duties.'

Mistress Beckley sniffed delicately before snapping her fingers. 'Lily, bring me my tape. And make sure you use your best handwriting with the notes this time – no more of that juvenile scrawl.'

'Yes, Mistress Beckley,' the pale girl said. She grabbed the bag out of Joan's hands and struggled to set it gently on the floor. Then she opened it and rifled through for the items that had been requested.

'Lord, Lord.' Mistress Beckley rolled her eyes. 'My last apprentice was much more competent, but the way this girl's father begged me to take her on. "You're the best there is, Jessica! Lily can study under no one else!" Such caterwauling, I couldn't rightfully say no.'

Joan met her mother's eyes then ducked her head so no one would see the grin that burst across her face at Mrs Sands's sour expression. They both knew Baba Ben was by and far the best tailor in London. Mistress Beckley likely knew it as well. Joan would be glad once her godfather was free to practice his trade again and could put this woman in her place.

Until then, she let herself be poked and prodded for the new wardrobe she apparently needed at the palace. The experience was mostly pleasant, aside from the moments when she had to lift her injured arm. Though Mistress Beckley was far too focused on gossip to notice Joan flinching.

'Now, while you're at court you must convince the queen to find you a proper husband,' she said, draping a bit of black velvet across Joan's chest. 'In my experience, love matches often result in ill-suited marriages.' She nodded in satisfaction and tossed the fabric to Lily, who scribbled something down.

Joan knew where the seamstress's insult had been aimed and resisted the urge to look at her mother.

'Your parents and I were playfellows when we were younger. Did you know that, child?' She measured from Joan's chin to her chest and nodded again. 'Three layers, Lily. It was always agreed that between me and your mother I was the lovelier one. Even Thomas thought so.'

Joan highly doubted that but kept her mouth shut. Perhaps if she didn't engage, the woman might complete her tasks sooner and leave.

'It's a wonder he hasn't come down to say hello yet,' she said, glancing up the stairs wistfully.

It's a wonder my mother hasn't thrown you out on your arse.

One glance at her mother showed she was barely holding her temper, her hands curled around the edge of the workbench like claws. That Joan's father found reason to remain occupied upstairs until Mistress Beckley left was no surprise at all.

CHAPTER ELEVEN

The Author & the Instrument

hat night, Joan's mother opened a doorway directly into Baba Ben's cell. Joan carried her godfather's heavy Ogun pot, his tools placed carefully and safely within her pocket. Their covert manner of entry tonight made the morning's discretion unnecessary.

As she and her mother stepped through into the prison, Baba Ben rushed to her side. He took the cauldron from beneath her arm with a smile. He held it reverently, pressing a kiss to its rim before placing it on the floor with great care.

'I didn't expect you back here so soon,' Goodfellow said quietly.

Joan spun to see the Fae standing in front of the closed cell door, their gaze turned pointedly away. If the moment hadn't been so serious, Joan might have laughed at their ploy. Obedience to the letter but not the intent was certainly still obedience.

Trust Goodfellow to think of such a simple circumvention.

'I'll give you as much time as I can,' they said then faded into the air.

'Robin is doing their best,' Baba said suddenly, laying a hand on Joan's shoulder. 'Please don't blame them for this.'

She nodded to her godfather. 'I know and I don't.'

Goodfellow was her ally, had stood beside her against Auberon and revealed all their secrets to help Joan gain Titanea's help when she needed it. Even now, under their queen's thumb, they were finding ways to help Joan and her family at enormous risk.

What greater proof of their friendship did she need?

'Joan—' Baba Ben frowned, his eyes narrowing as he noticed the long red scratch at her temple. 'Who did this to you?'

She touched the mark, the wound already half healed thanks to her father's salve, and swallowed against the lump of shame in her throat. How could she tell her godfather that she'd barely been able to complete the task she'd promised?

She clenched her jaw, looking at a spot over his shoulder as she spoke. 'I was attacked by a goblin at your house. I killed it, but it dislocated my shoulder and knocked me about pretty badly.' She felt her face burn with the confession and wondered what her godfather would think of her weakness. 'Pearl is safe but we – I broke your mirror,' she finished quietly.

'What? The mirror? Joan—' Baba's voice caught in his throat as he shifted his gaze to her shoulder. 'A mirror can be replaced. I'm just glad that you're safe.'

Joan felt her mother come up on her other side. 'She's all right now. Thomas took care of her shoulder.' She looked to the door then back to them both. 'Come, we don't have much time.'

'It's fine, Baba,' Joan said, uncomfortable with her godfather fussing over her injuries. 'It only barely hurts when I move my arm.'

Ben rolled his eyes. 'Only when you move your arm? And how often have you needed to do that?' He shook his head but pulled away from her to look into his large cauldron.

'With Father's salve I'll be well by morning.' She reached into her pocket and withdrew the bundle wrapped with white fabric, hoping to shift the conversation away from herself. 'I have your tools. I shrunk them to transport them safely but they're all here.'

He hurried to take the items from her. Unwrapping them, he let out a tiny hum of pleasure. 'Excellently done, Joan. I'll keep them this way for now.' He turned away from her to place them back into the pot.

Joan glanced away to give him this moment of privacy, but in the silence questions crept into her head.

'Baba, couldn't you speak to Ogun without your pot?'

'Not with so specific a question.' He gestured to the pot in front of him. 'For this I needed to come to him directly.'

She nodded, her fingers twitching anxiously. 'Has he ever spoken to you when you haven't reached out?'

They both turned to her then, frowning.

'Joan, what are you talking about?' her mother asked.

Joan felt herself stiffen, wondering suddenly if she'd confessed some horrible impropriety. She'd never been the most diligent with her practices and forgot far more than she should have. Baba knew that. Her mother knew that. She hoped they wouldn't feel too ashamed of her.

She rubbed her chest, hand instinctively pressing against the place where she'd usually feel Ogun's burning presence. If there was anyone she could – she *should* – discuss such things with, it was her godfather. He was there to guide her spiritual growth and help her mature in her relationship with Ogun and all the Orisha. There was no need for fear.

And yet . . .

'Joan,' he said slowly, 'what—'

A sudden heaviness engulfed the room, the air going thick with pressure. Baba's posture changed, his back straightened and he towered over Joan, power rolling off him in waves.

'You are still afraid,' he said in a deep voice both his own and not his own, echoing with a sound she'd only ever heard in her head. 'We cannot move forwards so long as fear stills your blade.'

This wasn't Baba speaking. This was Ogun. The Orisha had come down to possess Baba's body, using him to communicate with them directly.

Her mother's grip tightened on her shoulder. 'Welcome, Ogun.'

Ogun nodded regally, the graceful move foreign in Baba's body. He glanced at Joan, the soft warmth she was used to seeing in her godfather's gaze replaced by a burning intensity.

'This one,' he said, touching a hand to his – Baba's – chest, 'has a question.'

She took a deep breath, steadying herself even as her stomach seemed to leap and flip anxiously. 'Yes.' She wiped a sweaty hand on her skirts. 'How do we restore the Pact made between you and the Fae?'

'With blade and blood, you have the tools you need.' He didn't blink as he spoke, his unnerving gaze fixed on Joan. 'But I cannot tell you how to use them.'

Joan bristled as anger burst through her. 'Why not?' she blurted even as her mother hissed her name in warning. 'Why speak in riddles when we so desperately need your help?'

'Man's work and spirit's work are two separate realms. I know my part, you must discover yours.'

Her rage cooled immediately as something like despair clawed its way into her throat. 'What?'

If the Orisha wouldn't give them the answer of how to restore the Pact, then all hope was truly lost.

'I was the forge, not its crafter. The fire knows not what it shapes at the hands of the smith. That child of mine who sealed the Pact is who you must seek to know the how.' His lips quirked up in a half smile. 'Remember that fire within you when you face our enemies, child.' And then he was gone.

Baba slumped forwards as Ogun's presence left his body and the air in the room lightened. Joan rushed forwards to steady him, grasping his arms as he sucked in deep breaths of air.

'What—' Her godfather swallowed thickly as he tried to collect himself. 'What did Ogun say of the Pact?'

Joan blinked helplessly at her mother as the two of them guided Baba over to the room's tiny bed.

'Not all are aware of what happens when they are possessed,' she said quickly over Baba's head. She helped him sit and knelt in front of him. 'Ogun says he cannot help us. We have to contact the one who forged the Pact in the first place.'

Baba choked out a laugh, void of any mirth, as he dropped his head into his hands. 'A child of Ogun from nearly two thousand years ago. He might have at least told us where to begin, given us a name.'

Joan hugged her godfather then and felt her mother wrap her arms around them both as the weight of their uncertain task stretched over them.

CHAPTER TWELVE
Interlude – The Price of the Hunt

rlene Whyman lay in bed, racked with pain as the plague wreaked havoc on her body. The corpses of her husband and father lay in the corner, a blanket thrown over them. The plague had killed them not long after the royal guard boarded up their home – and the family inside it – a fortnight ago.

Her mother shook beside her as another tremor hit her. Arlene reached for her hand in the darkness.

The two of them would join the men soon. All Arlene could hope was that they would all be reunited in heaven. She wrapped her aching fingers around her mother's, the fevered heat rolling off both their bodies excruciating.

'Yes,' her mother whispered suddenly, 'yes, I'll give anything.'

Arlene tried to turn her head to look, her swollen neck making the move near impossible.

'Anything. Anything you ask. Please.'

Her mother's hand twitched in her grip, and Arlene tangled their fingers together in worry. A sound, like the rush of air from exhausted lungs, came from where the men's corpses lay. She turned that way and watched shadows slink out from beneath the heavy blanket as some phantom wind danced along its edges.

Fear clenched her, making her cough hard enough to bring up blood.

'Please,' her mother whispered desperately into the dark, 'let me suffer this no more.'

Arlene squeezed her hand, struggling twice before she managed to croak out 'Mother . . .'

Someone suddenly stood over their bed, the hood of their black cloak engulfing their face in shadow. Arlene shrank back as much as she could on weak muscles.

How had this person entered their home? The royal guard had ensured there was no way out or in, no salvation nor escape.

'You'll give anything?' the figure whispered, and Arlene felt they looked to her even though she couldn't see their eyes. 'Do you swear?'

More shadows flowed from the corners of the room and seemed to gather around this stranger. Arlene swore she heard voices hissing 'Swear, swear' over and over again.

Surely this was nothing more than the imaginings of her mind on the brink of death.

'I swear it,' her mother said resolutely.

The sound of a bell seemed to ring far off and clear, and suddenly Arlene could breathe easily. She sat up in bed, all the pain abandoning her body in an instant. She looked down at her hands. The rotted black flesh that had overtaken her fingers and wrists had given way to healthy pink flesh, as whole as it had been before this disease had taken hold of their family. She touched her neck and felt the smooth skin of her throat. No sores, no swelling.

'Arlene?' Her mother sat up beside her, looking just as healthy and flushed as Arlene felt.

She dove into her mother's arms as tears sprang to her eyes. 'Mother, what miracle has blessed us so?'

'No miracle. But a promise.'

She and her mother both turned to see the cloaked stranger looming still. The shadows gathered around the figure, churning and writhing as if waiting for something. Her mother's arms tightened around her.

'You swore you'd give anything to stop the pain,' the stranger said, their voice echoing in the oddest ways, 'to be healed.'

A moan sounded from over near her husband's body, and his plague-blackened hand flopped out from beneath the blanket, carried somehow by a slinking sliver of darkness. Arlene whimpered and tucked herself closer to her mother.

What demon work was this?

The stranger seemed to smile, though she could see no face within their hood. 'You swore you'd give anything, and so we collect our due.'

A hissing laughter echoed through their tiny home, growing louder and louder with each passing moment.

'Mother,' Arlene whispered, true fear stealing her breath. 'What have you done?'

The stranger extended a hand gloved in some tanned hide. 'Come.'

Arlene felt her mother let her go and reach for the stranger. Shadows swirled along both their arms as their fingers touched. Her mother rose from the bed, as healthy as Arlene had ever seen her.

'Mother, what have you done?' She trembled as the darkness continued to grow, creeping from every corner to circle her mother and the cloaked stranger.

They caressed her mother's cheek gently. 'You shall join us and be free of this mortal pain.'

'Yes,' her mother whispered, leaning into the touch. 'Yes, please.'

The stranger took her shoulders, turning her to face Arlene where she still sat huddled on the bed. 'But first you must give us our due.'

'You would take her soul?' Arlene blurted, the fear holding her making her bold.

The laughter grew even louder, ringing in her ears clamourously enough to rattle them.

'No, child,' the stranger said. 'To join the Wild Hunt, she must feast.' The hood fell back suddenly, revealing a woman's face, pale brownish grey run through with veins of blue and black. Two great horns extended out from either side of her forehead, draped with bits of flesh, some dry and some bloody. 'And once she does, she shall ride with us for eternity.' She turned pure black eyes to Arlene and grinned.

Her mother's head dropped forwards as a shudder passed through her whole body. Slowly, she looked up again, and Arlene screamed as darkness overtook the woman's gaze. Her mother twitched then opened her mouth to reveal a row of sharpened teeth.

'Mother,' she wailed, hoping to reach the heart of whatever monster held the woman. 'Mother, please, don't do this.'

Her mother cocked her head to the side, a predator observing her prey. 'Come, Arlene,' she cooed, 'it shan't hurt much.'

Tears sprang to Arlene's eyes. How cruel, how cruel indeed to offer salvation when they'd been so close to death, only to bring them this.

'Mother, please,' she begged once more. 'Please don't—'

Her mother leapt for her, pinning her to the bed. She grinned down at her, mouth too wide, teeth too sharp and eyes wild and full of glee.

'It shan't hurt much, love, not much at all.'

Then she tore out Arlene's throat, and the world became the gush and flow of blood.

CHAPTER THIRTEEN
To Saucy Doubts & Fears

he morning sun found Joan in her father's shop, forge cold and unlit as she worked. She'd snuck back down here sometime in the small hours of the night after sleep refused to come.

Her father had gathered piles of scrap iron: broken pots and pans, pokers, horseshoes, anything that could be collected quickly. She pulled a dented pan out of the pile and focused. The metal rippled and sang as she fashioned it into a dagger with a smooth hilt. She took another moment to sharpen the blade before laying the flat edge across her two fingers to test the balance. The weight needed to be distributed perfectly to be wielded efficiently or thrown effectively. It teetered precariously before settling into a firm, straight line. Satisfied, Joan dropped it onto her growing pile of iron weapons and moved on to the next.

That's how James found her when he trudged down the stairs, bundled heavily against the early morning chill as he prepared to leave for the theatre.

'God's teeth, Joan,' James said. 'Have you slept at all?'

Joan shook her head and dropped another finished dagger onto the stack that nearly reached her knee. She considered it for a moment before taking it up again and passing it to her brother.

'Take this – it's iron.'

He grabbed it from her. 'The air feels dangerous, like it did back in the beginning of all this.'

'Well, now you're prepared,' Joan said, needlessly adjusting his cloak with anxious hands. 'Go straight to the theatre – you'll be safest there until I can join you.'

He swung open his bag and settled the iron dagger alongside his script pages for the day's performance. 'I know you have this task you've set for yourself, but you should try for some sleep.'

'And you should go before you're late again,' she said pointedly. He might be right but she was too, and only one of them needed to leave the house right now.

He rolled his eyes and squeezed her tightly in a quick hug before he jogged out the door.

The King's Men had a performance today, and their morning rehearsal began soon. *The Merchant of Venice* had no fights for her to oversee, but James had a large part as Portia, the sought-after heiress whose dowry sets off the plot of the play.

She kept watch long after he'd gone and tried to swallow around the lump in her throat. She desperately wanted to be walking alongside her brother as they made their way to the Globe, where they'd spend the next few hours rehearsing with their group of rowdy actors. But there was no time.

Everything was moving so quickly and they were still no closer to restoring the Pact than they'd been before. Tomorrow she'd begin her service directly under Titanea and closer to Cecil than she ever desired to be. The Orisha community in London had been warned of Cecil's dangerous knowledge, but if they wanted any hope of protecting themselves from Fae attacks, they needed iron. Joan had to craft their weapons today or not at all.

How could she pick time spent with the people who'd become her second family over the safety of every person within their community, within this country? She should be noble enough, heroic enough to make the choice easily, but as she stared off towards the Globe, that glorious wooden O, she felt her heart break.

Enough. If she hurried, she still might catch the end of rehearsal, and she'd at least be able to watch the show from the courtyard with the rest of the groundlings.

She squared her shoulders and grabbed another scrap of iron, cold determination letting her ignore the pieces of her shattered heart.

The sounds of a play well underway greeted Joan's ears as she approached the tiring-house door at the Globe. The small entry at the back of the white-walled building led straight to the halls and rooms behind the stage where the actors rested before and after shows and between scenes. She slipped through the door and into the cozy darkness inside. The voices from the stage echoed hollowly back here, filtered as they were by heavy curtains and the great wooden doors at centre stage.

'*The quality of mercy is not strained.*

It droppeth as the gentle rain from heaven
Upon the place beneath. It is twice blest:
It blesseth him that gives and him that takes.'

She could hear James giving his courtroom speech as Portia. It was one of his favourite parts because he not only got to play a woman pretending to be a man, but an heiress pretending to be a lawyer. It was one of the more complex roles given to the apprentices, and James acted it to perfection every time.

Joan stood at the bottom of the stairs, her chest tight. When would she be able to watch her brother perform from the yard, surrounded by the beautiful, chaotic energy of the groundlings?

When would she be able to watch him perform at all?

She shook herself. She couldn't lurk here in the dark forever. If James was giving his speech, it meant that not only were they nearly at the end of the play, but also the wooden doors facing the top of this staircase would be closed. She could ascend without accidentally revealing herself to the audience.

She'd wait in James's dressing area, maybe rest her eyes a bit, until the play was done. She headed up, stumbling only once in her exhaustion, then immediately cut off to her right.

'Awful late today, aren't you, Joan?'

Joan stilled halfway up to the tiring-house's first floor and turned to see Roz staring up at her. The older woman held an intricate gown in her arms, the blue one Joan had borrowed to meet the queen on Twelfth Night. It was for James to change into after the court scene, when Portia dropped her manly disguise.

Roz stepped closer and then frowned as she took Joan in, her expression worried. She glanced at the stage then back to Joan, her shoulders tense. Joan felt panic rising in her chest. What had Roz noticed? What would she do and say next?

Joan started back down the stairs, ready to beg Roz for her silence, but the older woman held up a hand.

'Go on,' Roz said firmly. 'I'll meet you in James's area as soon as I get him dressed for his next scene.'

Joan clamped her mouth shut and nodded before heading the rest of the way up to her brother's room. His next costume change was so quick, he wouldn't make it back up here until the end of the show. She'd be alone in the dressing area for a while. She slipped around the heavy curtain that gave James's space some privacy. She caught a glimpse of herself as she passed the mirror and flinched.

She looked completely worn down, with dark bruises under her eyes and rust stains along her sleeves.

She let out a deep, steadying breath and lifted herself onto one of the wooden boxes placed against the wall. At least the slice along her cheek had healed, leaving only a barely noticeable scar that would soon be gone too.

Bless her father's salves.

She leaned back, careful of her tender shoulder, and closed her eyes, letting the far-off, familiar sounds of a trial for a literal pound of flesh soothe her nerves.

She woke to Roz shaking her and gently calling her name. Joan blinked groggily and sat upright.

She looked up to thank Roz, who had stepped away and was threading a needle. She knotted the end of her thread, a deep green that matched the fabric of Joan's skirt exactly, then slipped a thimble out of the bag at her hip.

'Let's get this patched, shall we?' She smiled up at Joan then set to work on a tear in the skirt.

She hadn't noticed the rip but it must've happened while she'd been forging weapons. Gratitude welled up so thickly in her chest, she had to clear her throat to speak. 'Thank you, Roz.'

'We look out for each other here, don't we?' Roz pinched Joan's chin gently before getting back to sewing. 'And we both know that while you're good at many things, sewing is not one of them. Although that may change now that you'll be one of the queen's ladies.'

Joan laughed, the sound abrupt and watery. The people here within this theatre were her family too, not by blood but by bond. The knowledge that they were being torn away from her even sooner than she'd feared was breaking her heart.

She suddenly threw her arms around Roz, hugging the older woman tightly. She was crying and soaking Roz's dress but she couldn't make herself stop.

'Joan, I nearly stabbed you!' Roz patted her back with one hand and shushed her. 'Now, now. None of that.' She pulled away, smiling at Joan. 'We don't cry over good fortune.'

Joan choked out another laugh. 'Is it good fortune?' she asked honestly.

'Aye, Joan, because a woman has more power at court than she'd ever hope to have here.' She squeezed Joan's hand. 'Believe me on that.' She waited for Joan to nod before getting back to her sewing.

The woman was right. Joan might find a way to catch hold of all her dreams as a lady-in-waiting. But even if the position gave her some hope of becoming a goldsmith, it didn't make the parting any less painful.

She swiped away the tears wetting her cheeks and tried to collect herself as she watched Roz show off her perfect mending skills, for what was likely the last time.

CHAPTER FOURTEEN
Within This Wooden O

aster Shakespeare shrieked outright when Joan made her way downstairs after the performance. Burbage scowled heavily but bustled Nick, James and Rob off to the side while Shakespeare grabbed her face.

'Have you slept at all?' he said, frowning at her. 'You look terrible.'

Honestly, Joan thought she looked much better than she had when she'd stepped into the tiring-house.

Burbage came up on her other side, his expression sympathetic. 'Come on, we'd planned to give you a proper farewell fete at Yaughan's, but I think a quieter location would better suit.' He smiled and, with a gentle hand on her back, guided her out onto the stage. 'I already have the boys fetching what we need.'

Shakespeare followed, snatching up a wooden stool as he passed. He placed it against one of the tall wooden columns, then presented it to Joan with a flourish. He stepped back as Burbage carefully – unnecessarily – helped her sit.

'We'll need a table out here.' Burbage strode back towards the big wooden doors at the centre of the stage, throwing them open with a bang. 'Augustine, help me collect a table.' His voice echoed through the empty theatre as he disappeared back into the tiring-house.

Shakespeare shook his head and sighed. 'How are we supposed to send you off to court with any confidence when the day before you leave us you show up in this state?'

'You must,' Joan said before the icy chill of Titanea's boon could catch any thought of disobedience. She took a deep breath, hating to censor herself like this but hating that feeling of freezing to death more.

The power of the boon seemed to ice over her very heart and nearly shatter her bones before it released her. She felt the sharp pain of it threaten to return every time she even considered refusing Titanea's order.

But Shakespeare didn't know that. She'd told no one of the mistake she'd made before she'd realised who Lady Clifford and now Queen Anne truly were. An act of courtesy had damned her.

She glanced at the man who looked back at her with care and worry. Hadn't he been beside her when she'd feared she'd lost Ogun's blessing and the powers the Orisha bestowed along with it? He'd not judged her then. She prayed he wouldn't do so now.

'I owe Titanea two boons,' Joan said, shifting uncomfortably, 'because I thanked her before I knew who she was.' She took a breath as that creeping shame washed over her again. 'She used one to force me to come to court and I am compelled to obey.'

'Zounds, Joan. We've got to find some remedy for the way this trouble finds you.' Shakespeare wiped a hand over his face and snorted out a hollow laugh. 'At least you've gotten her to use one. I'm sure you can trick her into wasting the last. You're clever enough to outwit her.'

He winked at her, and Joan felt some of the weight on her heart lift. Master Shakespeare was one of the most brilliant minds she'd ever encountered. If he believed in her, she could well believe in herself too.

He crouched down in front of her. 'In any case, I have someone at court to look out for you. I've spoken to her, and she's vowed to assist you in any way she can. Her name is Aemilia Lanier. I trust her above all others so you may as well.'

'Thank you, Master Shakespeare.' She felt the smile bloom across her face. 'It's a good thing you're members of the king's household.'

His grin turned sly as he stood. 'Indeed, a privilege we intend to abuse most enthusiastically to make sure our best girl is safe in the palace.'

Just then, Burbage and Phillips appeared at the doors, carrying a sturdy wooden table between them. But while Burbage grunted under its weight, two white-knuckled hands gripping its underside, Phillips held it with one, his other carrying another stool. Shakespeare watched them with a raised eyebrow.

'Augustine,' Burbage grunted as he shifted his grip, 'since when did you get so strong, you old windbag?'

Phillips scowled, his bushy white brows winging together on his forehead. 'Watch yourself before I let go.'

But Master Burbage was right. In the three years that Joan had been working with the King's Men, Master Phillips had done his best to avoid exerting himself. They'd all attributed the extraordinary strength he'd displayed when Auberon had disrupted their performance of *A Midsummer Night's Dream* to the sudden rush of excitement. And the old man hadn't done anything since to dispel that notion.

Until now.

The two placed the table down with a deep thud. Burbage shook his hands vigorously as soon as it was out of his grip.

Joan felt something slide into place in her mind like a missing puzzle piece. She need only confirm it.

'Something tells me,' Shakespeare said, leaning towards Joan again, 'that Augustine could've carried that alone.'

Joan hummed quietly. 'Aye, I'd agree.' Joan beckoned the man over to them. 'But one question, Master Phillips.'

He strode over to them, and for the first time Joan noticed the youthful spring in his step. She held fast to that information too.

'Have you . . .' She paused, trying to choose the precise words that wouldn't let him wiggle out of answering.

Phillips rolled his eyes. 'Oh, out with it. I'll not riddle with you, Joan, so be plain and ask what you will.'

'Indeed,' she said as some of the tension within her released. 'Has your strength grown since the breaking of the Pact?'

Shakespeare snorted. 'Not starting easily, are we?'

'It has,' Phillips said, 'though it was slow until Titanea made her presence known on Twelfth Night.'

Interesting.

'Have you noticed any other changes?' Joan leaned forwards, taking the time to inspect Phillips for any visible differences.

He frowned then flexed his hands. 'Only this. I no longer feel the ravages of age upon me. We changelings grow old as our mortal counterparts would, with such aches and pains as age grants those who endure it. Barring an unnatural death, we leave this world only when we chose to return to the faerie realm.'

Now that she observed him closely, she could note everything he'd named. He seemed hale and spry and youthful; the glow she'd always seen about him shone more brightly than ever.

So, there was some difference within the Fae. Her struggle against the goblin yesterday hadn't been due to a lack of prowess but to a strengthening of her opponent. Relief flooded through her at the knowledge that she hadn't grown weaker. She could go to court comforted by the fact that she hadn't actually lost any of her skill.

The thought lifted her heart and just as quickly sent a chill down her spine. It left behind an entirely different problem. The Fae, with the Pact that protected the mortal realm well and truly gone, were regaining some of that which had made them so feared in the first place. If Master Phillips – a changeling and far, far less powerful than Titanea – had gained so much strength, what did that say about the red caps, the jacks-in-irons, the goblins?

What did it say of Titanea herself?

'Joan.' Armin appeared at the centre doors, arms wrapped around a basket of food nearly a third his size. 'Yaughan sends his best wishes by way of a feast.' His voice strained under the weight of his load.

Burbage hurried over to take it from him as Rob, Nick and James all filed in carrying more food, ale, cups and plates. They laid them out on the table as Roz appeared with several napkins, and even Sylvia and Mistress Woods came out to join them. Normally the door manager and bookkeeper never joined the company's festivities, but Joan figured her departure constituted a special occasion.

Her heart swelled with love for all these people, this second family of chaotic theatre makers who'd welcomed her into their fold with warmth and affection.

She'd miss them all desperately.

After some time, Shakespeare took up a lute. *'When that I was and a little tiny boy, with hey, ho, the wind and the rain ...'* He sang beautifully even as he played horridly, notes twanging clumsily from untrained fingers. *'A foolish thing was but a toy, for the rain it raineth every day.'*

Phillips snatched the instrument from his fumbling hands with a scowl. The old man quickly tuned its strings and took up the tune with infinitely more skill. They all knew the song, had danced to it at the end of every performance of *Twelfth Night*. They also knew it was Joan's favourite as was the play it closed: the story of shipwrecked twins and a countess in love with a boy who was really a girl in love with a duke who instead loved the countess and maybe the boy too. A merry, complicated plot the company had first performed before Queen Elizabeth on Joan's own birthday.

No other play sat more fondly in her heart.

'But when I came to man's estate' – Shakespeare winked at Joan and sang louder – *'With hey, ho, the wind and the rain, 'gainst knaves and thieves men shut their gate, for the rain it raineth every day.'*

'A dance, my dear,' Armin said.

He held out a hand to Joan. She grasped it and laughed when he pulled her up into a spin. He caught her round the waist, lifting their joined hands above their heads as they stepped around each other in a tight circle. Someone took up a steady stomping beat, their feet thudding against the wood stage and sending the sound echoing through the empty playhouse.

Armin twirled her away from him and leapt back. They crossed each other with a quick passing step that ended with a hop and a clap. He grabbed her hands, twisting her around herself and making her duck backwards under his arms. She laughed again, as the move always made her, and felt someone else grab hold of her. She straightened, letting another turn untangle her, and came face-to-face with Nick. She faltered.

He smiled down at her, and her heart seemed to skip a beat. 'Do you forget yourself now that I'm your partner?' He lifted their joined hands high, bringing their chests together as he slipped an arm around her waist.

She felt a fine tremor shiver through his palm and knew him to be as nervous as she. Her own answering smile slid across her face.

'Will you lead me?' She laced her fingers through his and watched the bob of his throat as he swallowed thickly. She felt power in the effect she had on him.

He turned them in a slow circle, his grip tightening as they moved. 'With pleasure, heart.'

She stumbled and he pulled her close. A sly smile slid over his face. Joan couldn't help herself – she threw her head back as a laugh burst from her, full and echoing. She heard Nick join her as they spun away from each other then back again. He grabbed her waist, lifting her with ease once, twice, then three times. He held her aloft on the third and spun her as she gripped his shoulders. She laughed harder. He set her on her feet and they tripped over each other. She snorted. He righted her. They turned again, touching wrists on one side and then the other, but she could barely keep time for giggling. They circled back-to-back, spun and clasped hands.

'Joan,' Nick said, her name like a prayer on his lips, his heart in his eyes. He spread their arms wide, drawing her in close.

She felt his breath on her face, his sandalwood-and-lilac scent surrounding her. The music sounded far off and faint. Did it still play? Did Shakespeare yet sing?

She felt she ought to say something, but the words stuck in her throat, her mind so filled with his eyes, his smile.

He leaned forwards and pressed his lips to hers in a sweet kiss. She ripped her hands away from his, throwing them around his neck and pulling him down to deepen it. He moaned, and the sound vibrated against her lips. His arms wrapped around her back, clutching her to him. They could get no closer without going further.

'Oy!' Shakespeare shouted. He forced them apart and set himself between them, glaring from one to the other. 'None of that in front of me. I'm yet chaperone to you both.'

Mrs Woods snorted. 'Where do you think they learned it, you wanton rogue?'

The whole company burst into raucous laughter as the man turned bright red.

'Do as I say, not as I do,' he muttered, fighting his own smile.

Just out of Shakespeare's sight, Joan reached for Nick and felt him clasp her hand in his own. Her heart ached with the thought of losing this place and the gathered family she loved as much as her own blood. She couldn't bear it, so she wouldn't allow it. She might leave them tomorrow, but it wouldn't be forever.

She swore it.

CHAPTER FIFTEEN
Interlude – Rawhead's Bloody Bones

ina Wood didn't know what possessed her to tell the horrid story to her baby brother tonight. Sure, Luke had ripped the head from her favourite doll, but the look of abject terror that had come over his face when she'd said Old Rawhead was coming to eat him for being naughty didn't fill her with the satisfaction she'd hoped for.

The matron had let them keep only one thing from their old lives when she'd taken them into her care two months ago. Rina had chosen the doll their mum had made her from scraps of her old clothes. It was imperfectly shaped but made with so much love Rina swore she could feel her mum's spirit when she held it close. But now it was ruined, head torn away and straw filling leaking out.

She had every right to be furious ... and yet ...

Rina could hear Luke's sniffling and feel his little body shaking beside her in their bed. Her heart sank as he whimpered then fell into more muffled sobs.

She sighed. Her brother was only five; he couldn't help but play recklessly. He didn't know any better. She rolled over, careful not to pull the covers off him in the chilly room, and gathered him up in her arms.

'I'm sorry, Luke,' she said, rubbing a hand along his back. 'Nothing's coming to get you. I was just angry about my doll.'

He nuzzled against her, tears soaking the front of her nightshirt. 'I'm sorry. I'll learn to sew so I can fix it.'

'We can fix it together.' She hugged him tighter, happy that they at least had each other even if their parents were gone.

The door to their room swung open suddenly, and the matron rushed in before slamming it shut behind her. She leaned back against it as she peered into the darkness of the room, her eyes wide and face white as her shift.

Rina sat up, keeping her hold on Luke. 'Mistress Gregg, what—'

Mistress Gregg shook her head back and forth as she lifted a trembling finger to her lips. Rina went silent, squeezing Luke and shushing him urgently.

SCREEEE.

Something scratched along the length of the door, and Rina saw the matron's whole body tense.

SCREEEE. SCREEEE. SCREEE.

The sound grew louder and louder. The matron shook violently, hands clamped over her mouth as tears sprang into her eyes.

SCREEEE. SCREEEE. SCREEE.

Rina ripped the blanket off her and Luke and dragged him out of the bed.

SCREEEE. SCREEEE. SCREEE.

She pulled him down beside her, crouching in the darkest corner she could find.

SCREEEE. SCREEEE. SCREEE.

The wooden door was starting to creak and groan under the loud scratches. Rina knew it wouldn't hold much longer. They'd need to be quick.

SCREEEEEEEEEE. SCREEEEEEEEE. SCREEEEEEEE.

She shifted her brother onto her back, felt his tiny arms lock around her neck as she raised herself into a crouch.

BOOM!

The door tore off its hinges and slammed into the hallway wall. The matron turned, a horrified moan escaping her as something dove forwards and dragged her to the ground. Rina leapt up, racing for the dooway as the matron screamed. The wet sounds of chewing and rending meat echoed in the darkness, but Rina just focused on running. As she sprinted along the hallway, she noticed every door was open, every room silent. Dark splatters of some liquid covered the walls and floor.

The matron always despaired that she'd never have quiet with so many children living under her roof. Rina didn't care to find out what horror had granted the woman's wish. She hurried down the stairs, her grip on Luke so tight she was sure she'd leave bruises.

It didn't matter, as long as she got them out.

She spotted the front door as something with too many legs thudded along the floor above and behind them. Moving fast.

The heavy locks that bolted them in safely every night now seemed to assure their death as the thing thumped along the stairs.

They didn't have time.

'Don't let go, Luke,' Rina hissed. She grabbed the matron's favourite quilt from her special embroidering chair and swung it over both their heads. Then she threw herself through the front window.

The glass shattered around them, jagged shards scratching her arms and legs, cutting her feet as she stumbled out onto the street. She flinched as one large piece stabbed into her bare sole. She limped forwards a few more steps before turning, just as something raised itself up in the broken window. Two piercing golden eyes, slitted like a cat's, peered out at her from a long, humanlike face so deep a green it could've been black. Six long limbs stuck out from either side of its body, each ending in a hand bearing long claws. It tilted its head to the side and revealed a mouth full of two rows of razor-sharp teeth.

Rina felt her heart drop. There was no escape now. Not with the thing so close. She prayed Luke would know enough to run while the beast devoured her. If he lived, she'd die happily.

The creature tensed, its long body preparing to leap.

'What's going on here?' someone shouted as the light of several lanterns and torches flowed out from the other houses along the street.

The creature hissed and skittered back into the darkness of the orphanage as someone pulled Rina towards them. She cried out as she put weight on her injured foot.

A woman crouched down in front of Rina, her face alarmed but gentle and blessedly ordinary. 'What happened, child?'

'Something's wrong,' the same voice from before called. 'Bring the light over here.'

Several men holding lanterns and torches and one brandishing what looked to be a sturdy cooking pan ran past Rina and the woman and into the silent building.

The woman ignored the commotion and focused on Rina, slowly pulled the blanket away. Rina heard Luke whimper as he was uncovered. She tightened her grip on him once more and felt him do the same. She was about to say something when one of the men returned, his face pale as the matron's had been.

'Kate, get the children inside,' he said firmly, only a slight tremble shaking his voice.

Kate frowned at him. 'What's happening?'

'Get the children inside. Now.'

Something in his tone made the woman, Kate's, eyes widen before she nodded and guided Rina and Luke away. Rina whimpered again as she put weight on her foot and the woman looked back at the man helplessly. His gaze softened and he strode forwards, lifting both Rina and Luke easily. Kate kept pace with him as he walked towards another house, several of its windows illuminated with warm light.

'Simon,' Kate whispered, 'what's going on?'

Rina felt Simon's grip on her tighten slightly, protectively, and felt a rush of relief flow through her.

He shuddered. 'Nothing of God, Kate. Nothing of God.'

As she looked to the orphanage they left behind, she spotted a pair of golden eyes gazing out of the upper window.

And Rina was sure she'd never felt so cold in her entire life.

CHAPTER SIXTEEN
Such Sweet Sorrow

he sun's bright morning light, filtered and bent by the window's glass, woke Joan from her barely restful sleep. She flopped onto her back, arm bumping James's where he lay bundled in the blanket beside her. They hadn't slept in the same bed since they were tiny, but knowing this was the last night she'd spend at home for a long time had made them sentimental.

He grunted as she hit him and flopped his arm across her face in retaliation. 'Did you sleep at all?'

'Hardly,' she said, shoving him away. 'You?'

He rolled over to face her and she did the same. 'How could I? I don't want you to go.'

James's eyes went shiny with tears. Joan felt her own threaten to spill as her throat tightened and her eyes burned.

I don't—

She stopped the thought before it could go any further, though she could already feel the fierce chill of the boon's magic biting at the edge of her awareness.

Titanea's command was absolute.

'I have to,' she said instead, and felt the cold fade away.

But it wouldn't be eternal.

James sighed and nodded.

He didn't know of the magic that tied Joan to the Fae queen; she'd told none but Master Shakespeare. Joan wouldn't trouble him with the fact that Titanea had political, social *and* supernatural power over her. She hated keeping secrets from her brother, but he had enough to worry about.

'I'll be all right.' She smiled at him, hoping she projected enough confidence to reassure him.

James cleared his throat and threw back the covers. 'Well, I'm glad Mistress Beckley is delivering all her creations directly to the palace. It means I can at least dress you for your first day at court. Let's pray you'll take some part of my lessons with you when you've got to pick your clothes alone.' He laughed, skipping out of the way as Joan lobbed a pillow at him. 'Now, we can't do blue. While it is indeed your colour, you wore it the last time we were at court. Let's see what else . . .' His voice faded as he dug deeper into Joan's closet.

Joan watched him, already feeling the ache of losing this ritual in her chest. She'd always known her brother wouldn't be choosing her clothing forever. They'd grow up, she'd marry and along with her running her own household she'd have to dress herself.

But she'd never expected the loss to come so soon.

She swiped at her eyes as James whooped loudly and dragged a cluster of brilliant yellow fabric out of her closet.

'This one,' he said triumphantly. 'Not many people can wear this shade of yellow with confidence, but it becomes you most spectacularly.'

He dragged his bundle over to the bed. 'And Baba Ben made it for you. We'll send you with as many pieces of your family as we can.'

The sob burst from Joan's throat, and she covered her face with her hands as the tears she'd been holding back finally fell. James made a distressed noise as he gathered her up into a hug. She felt him tremble and knew he was crying as well.

She squeezed him tighter.

She'd miss him so very, very much.

Just after breakfast, Joan found herself sitting sideways in one of their dining room chairs. Mrs Sands stood behind her, hands working quickly and expertly as they twisted and pinned her daughter's hair. Joan couldn't see what her mother was doing but what she could feel was the care and intention in her every movement.

'I'm sending you with some of Cassie's pomade,' Mrs Sands said. 'Make sure you use it frequently – the winter air is terribly dry and can make your hair look a fright.'

Joan nodded but her mother jerked her head back into place.

'Please don't move, love.'

James sat across from them, stuffing some things she couldn't see into her bags as he mumbled to himself. He wore a yellow jerkin and trousers that matched her gown. It suited his dark brown skin and black hair as perfectly as it did hers.

Her brother truly did have an excellent eye for these sorts of things.

Her mother slid one last pin into place, then turned Joan's head from side to side, inspecting her work.

'James,' she said, 'fetch my mirror from my room.'

James jumped up. 'Yes, ma'am.' He bolted up the stairs to their parents' room. He came back shortly, holding the large hand mirror. He spun it around to face Joan before he let her take it from him.

She gasped. Joan had never seen her hair look so beautiful. Several large twists wove through and around each other so expertly you couldn't tell where one ended and the next began. Smaller braids, each threaded with bright indigo ribbon, wound around the large twists. A few silver pins were placed throughout, their shiny round tops sparkling in the candlelit room.

Mrs Sands squeezed Joan's shoulders as she leaned down to meet her eye in the mirror's reflection. 'I'm sending you with your beauty well-armed, my love. You'll outshine all of those other ladies.'

Joan placed the mirror on the table and spun to bury her face in her mother's dress. She was soaking the front with her tears, but she doubted her mother cared.

'Careful not to ruin all my hard work,' Mrs Sands said, but Joan could hear the quaver in her voice.

She squeezed her tightly because today she still could, but tomorrow . . .

Joan pulled away, sniffling and swiping at her eyes. Her mother patted her shoulder gently even as she held back her own tears.

'Mistress Sands?' Nan said from somewhere near the stairs. 'Lord Salisbury has arrived with the carriage.'

They both turned to see Nan holding a deep navy gown, clearly expensive in both fabric and construction. She'd draped it across her arms gingerly as if it would attack her at any moment. She glanced at Joan before her gaze skittered off somewhere else.

Joan sighed. Even today, Nan let her shame hold her and kept her distance. Joan hoped the woman could forgive herself for what she'd done while under Auberon's control, even as she understood why she couldn't.

Certain things from that time would haunt Joan for the rest of her life, whether they'd truly been her fault or not.

Nan shifted the gown in her arms. 'It's been requested that the young mistress change into this.'

Joan immediately looked to James, watched the melancholy overtake his entire being as he realised they wouldn't even have this last day of their twin ritual.

She scowled.

The new gown might be lovely and expensive, but it hadn't been made with Baba Ben's love or chosen by James and his excellent sense of colour.

'Thank you, Nan, but I'll remain as I am. Have it packed with the rest of my things.' Joan smiled at Nan.

The woman barely glanced at her before she bustled up the stairs to put the dress into one of Joan's trunks. It was a tiny rebellion, an insignificant victory over Cecil and his demands, but it gave her a flush of pleasure anyway.

Joan turned to her brother. 'There's nothing else I'd rather be wearing. Besides, I distinctly recall you saying that such a deep blue wasn't my most flattering colour.'

James laughed, his grin brilliant as he applauded her. 'How wonderful to see you've learned something from me, sister dear.'

The carriage looked appropriately royal. Not lavish enough for the king or queen themselves but clearly a vehicle that belonged to their household.

It marked whoever rode in it as a member of court, above and separate from common men.

The door swung open, and Cecil stepped out into the sunshine, his black clothing immaculate even as annoyance twisted his tired face. He watched as Joan's belongings were loaded into the gilded monstrosity before his gaze shifted to her. He took in her cheery yellow dress, the opposite of the dark gown he'd ordered her to wear, and his scowl deepened.

Joan watched his face change and reached out to grip her father's hand tightly in defiance. He squeezed back, pulling her close so their shoulders pressed together.

'Hurry up,' Cecil sneered at the footmen. Having made his displeasure known, he slipped back into the carriage with nary a word to Joan or her family.

She had to admit, she preferred it that way.

The men loading her trunks quickened their pace, and Joan felt her heart race along with them. She could already feel distance opening between her and her family, even as she stood shoulder to shoulder with her father.

Tears pushed against her eyes again. She breathed deeply, doing her best to force them back. Crying within the warm safety of their home was one thing. Sobbing on the streets where Cecil could see and where neighbours and strangers alike had gathered to ogle her departure – that was another thing entirely.

Too soon, her last case was fastened to the back of the carriage. The driver swung himself up into his seat, taking the reins in hand and readying the horses. The footman stood stoically beside the door, ready to hand her up into the dim interior alongside Cecil.

Joan took another deep breath and felt it shudder through her body. She turned, wrapping her arms tightly around her father.

'Be careful, my love,' he whispered to her. 'You know how to find us should you need us.'

Joan nodded and said, 'I do.' The words barely made it out of her tight throat.

Her mother and brother joined them, wrapping her in a firm embrace. She closed her eyes, doing her best to memorise the warmth, the smells, the sounds of her family. She pulled away after what felt like both an eternity and the barest moment. Her father pressed a small box into her hands, covering them with both of his before he let her go.

The four of them separated. Joan stepped backwards towards the carriage as her family moved closer to their home. She tucked her father's gift safely into the small bag at her hip, running her fingers over the polished wood and clearing her throat as she tried to breathe through her tears.

From the doorway to the house, James watched her face for a moment, then his jaw clenched. He straightened his shoulders and swept into an elaborate and perfectly executed bow.

'May you be blessed, Lady Clifford,' he said loudly as he stood again.

Joan understood her cue. She curtsied back, inclining her head slightly at her brother. The focus on the movement allowed her the moment she needed to rein in her emotions. 'And you as well. Until we meet again.' She straightened, smiled at her family and turned to step into the carriage. She allowed herself to be guided up into the dark interior. She tried to ignore the breaking of her heart as the door clicked shut and the smell of old leather and polished wood surrounded her.

'Lady Clifford . . .' William Cecil sat within, dressed all in black from neck to wrist to ankle. 'Good morning.'

CHAPTER SEVENTEEN
The Spider's Tedious Snares

ave you grown used to your new title?' William said, his expression serious though his eyes seemed to sparkle with excitement. 'I hope you shall carry it as well as my sister might have.'

Rage filled her at the sight of the boy, and her palm itched to slap him across his smug face.

'Sit down, girl, you waste precious time.' Cecil glared from the opposite bench. His black clothing blended near perfectly with the inside of the carriage, giving him the appearance of a floating pale head in a dark abyss. A perfect match to his son.

No wonder she'd missed the boy at first.

Cecil banged twice on the roof of the carriage, and it lurched into motion. She arranged her skirts across the bench, careful not to touch William.

Bia hung discreetly at her wrist, catching the shifting light as the carriage bumped through the streets of London. She'd keep her focus there and let the sword's metal song bring her comfort.

They hit a particularly prodigious bump, the lurch of the carriage jostling her forwards so she had to catch herself against the seat or end up in Cecil's lap.

She'd rather die.

She shifted herself back, but William caught hold of her fingers and slid his hand over hers.

Her stomach sank.

She glanced up at Cecil, fearing the man's reaction when he noticed his son showing her such affection. But he'd fixed his gaze out the window and paid the two of them no mind. She attempted to slide away from William, but he crept his hand along the seat, matching her every move. She could finally do no more or risk catching his father's attention.

She felt sick.

She turned her attention to the passing city, letting her eye catch on any detail. Anything to avoid looking at either Cecil. A grocer opened for the day, his young apprentice struggling to arrange a stack of crates nearly as tall as he. A mother bustled one child along with a second strapped securely to her back. Another carriage rattled past in the opposite direction, its occupants obscured by draped curtains.

Before long, they reached Whitehall Palace. The carriage clattered towards the ornate front gates. She'd never used this entrance when she'd come along with the King's Men. The gate they used was smaller, plainer and on the opposite side of the Banqueting House. She couldn't help staring at the imposing metalwork, surely five times as tall as she. So much iron shaped and curled by hands without magic. Joan admired their craft even as a voice within her boasted that she could craft something far better.

They passed through the gate, and the carriage rumbled to a stop. She heard the footman dismounting, his shoes clattering on the ground as he hurried around the carriage. The door closest to Cecil swung open, and he stepped out onto the clean stones.

'Come along, William,' he said. 'Girl.' He spat the word like a curse.

Joan didn't care; she was just ready to be done with this thrice-damned ride. The footman reached out a hand, but William held her back. She glanced up, noticing that Cecil paid them no mind as he brushed dust from his clothes and scowled up at the palace entryway. She turned back to William and raised an eyebrow.

'Yes?'

He fished something out of his pocket and grinned at her. 'I have a gift.' He brought her hand up to his lips then slipped a gold ring on her index finger. 'It's a sign of my intent.'

Joan wanted to melt the band into a puddle on the floor of the carriage.

As if sensing her thoughts, he squeezed her hand between both of his. 'Wear it.'

'I don't want it,' she whispered back.

He leaned closer, his face intent. 'No? Then . . .' He gazed pointedly over her shoulder where she knew his father stood.

Fear and rage surged within her, each emotion feeding the other until she thought she'd choke on the bile rising in her throat. She squeezed his hand back, some of her anger cooling when he winced in pain. He wielded more power because of his father, but she'd always be stronger than him. He needed to remember that.

William snatched his hand away from hers, shaking it rapidly to stave off the ache of her grip. 'Wear it,' he hissed, then stepped out of the other side of the carriage.

Joan glared down at the gold ring, which was expensive and well-crafted from what she could see and sense. The vine detailing was a signature of the Tabbard family goldsmith shop, known for overcharging wealthy customers. Joan hoped the thing had cost William dearly. She planned to discard it as soon as opportunity allowed.

'Are you ready, miss?' The footman still waited for her, the expression on his light brown face carefully blank even as his gaze slipped quickly to the new accessory on her finger.

She let herself be helped down out of the carriage, and he held her hand delicately until she lighted on the ground.

'Thank you,' she said politely.

The man looked shocked and then smiled back as heat burned in his cheeks. He inclined his head and gestured towards where William and his father had already begun to ascend the short staircase. Joan picked up her skirts and strode after him. She refused to run, but she also wouldn't be left behind.

'Miss . . .' the footman said suddenly, making her turn back to him. His eyes cut to the Cecils before coming back to her. 'They expect power to get them anything. We must seem to obey, but don't give them all they ask.'

Joan felt a genuine smile spread across her face. 'Of course. Thank you . . .'

'Gregory.'

'Joan. Thank you, Gregory. I appreciate good advice.'

He gave a shallow bow that she returned before turning back towards the palace. She caught up to Cecil and his son, who stood watching her from the top of the stairs.

'A friend of yours?' William scowled at the footman.

Fear swept over Joan again, this time not for herself but for Gregory. The man had only shown her a bit of kindness; she couldn't allow him to be punished for that.

'No, my lord,' she said, forcing a soft detachment into her voice. 'Only saying thanks for a job well done. Is that not done here at court?'

Cecil squinted at her, then turned away. 'Enough, we waste time.'

He beckoned William over as the ornate doors were swung open before them. Together the three entered. Joan noticed guards in crimson uniforms held each door, their expressions serious. The man on the right was pale but suntanned while the man on the left had the same soft brown complexion as Joan. He offered Joan a discreet nod as she passed. She returned it, just the slightest inclination of her head.

His fellow ignored her as the two swung the great doors closed behind them.

The queen's chambers had changed in the two days since Joan was last been there. Fresh flowers filled nearly every corner of the space. Garlands hung from the ceiling, draped between pillars and crept down along the walls like vines. Vases perched on every surface that would allow it, each filled nearly to bursting. On every place those didn't touch lay baskets loaded with more flowers and clusters of herbs.

The trilling of birds echoed throughout the room, and Joan spotted several small, brightly coloured shapes flitting about. Fresh rushes covered the floors beneath plush rugs, their earthy smell blending with the heavy scent of flowers and herbs.

The sight was completely overwhelming, but the smell somehow pleasant, a harmonious blend of natural perfumes among a chaotic spray of plants.

Amid it all lounged Titanea, of course wearing Queen Anne's pale form and clothed in an impossibly purple gown. She lay upon a cluster of soft, bright pillows in all colours of the rainbow, her blonde hair piled delicately atop her head and threaded through with gold trinkets and fresh flowers. She smiled as Cecil showed Joan into the room.

They'd thankfully been forced to leave William behind, though the relief Joan felt at his absence was tempered by the feel of his ring on her finger.

'Ah, she's finally arrived. Welcome, dear Joan.' Titanea reached out her hands, and two of her pale ladies in clashing bright gowns immediately swooped in to take her arms. 'Or should I say, Lady Clifford?'

They lifted Titanea gently to her feet. Lady Goose Neck glared openly at the use of Joan's new title, her face just out of the queen's sight. A look passed between her and Foul-Breath.

Could I but slap those expressions from your faces . . .

Joan twitched as she felt an answering scowl beginning to overtake her. She wished she could tell these ladies that she loathed them both with an equal fervour but doubted that would be her most prudent move. Instead, she pursed her lips before forcing them quickly into a smile. She curtsied, bowing her head to better allow her to control her expressions.

'Your Majesty, I am grateful for your kind invitation to join this sisterhood.' Joan smiled sweetly as she straightened and saw Goose Neck's lips pitched downward in a fierce frown.

Yes, we're equals here, you long-throated sour grape.

But again Joan kept the words to herself. Now wasn't the time to reveal her innermost thoughts. Such looseness could see her punished. The simmer of Ogun's presence pulsed in her chest, beating in time with her heart and Bia's gentle hum but neither of them could help her against these snakes.

'Be gone, Salisbury,' the queen, said abruptly. 'We've no more need of you.'

Cecil flinched at her sudden dismissal. To his credit, his expression didn't change as he bowed deeply and left the room. He cut one last look at Joan, then the door swung closed in his face.

She wished it had hit him.

Titanea approached Joan, the ladies supporting her on either side in a way that clearly wasn't merely a show of power.

Now that Joan looked closely, Titanea's face looked weary. Pain or some other discomfort pinched the skin at the corners of her eyes and around her mouth.

It could've been a part of her illusion, the fine details to ensure no one questioned her playing as the newly healed queen of England. But something in the way she held herself, the whisper of barely contained rage that lent an edge of danger to the whole room, pointed to the truth.

Titanea had suffered severe harm because of her explosion.

Joan filed that information away and curtsied again as Titanea reached her. The queen's pale hand gripped Joan's chin, lifting her head until their gazes met. Blue eyes shifted to brown, the change visible to only Joan.

'It pleases us well to have you here' – a predator's grin spread across Titanea's lips, and her grip tightened – 'where we can observe your growth and your movements closely, dear Joan.' She leaned closer. 'And make sure you don't plot against us in the Tower.'

Joan ground her teeth together to halt any reaction to the queen's words even as a chill raced down her spine. Of course Goodfellow had revealed their first visit to Titanea. Joan prayed they'd held the secret of the second but knew that hope was a precarious thing.

Titanea let go abruptly, her eyes turning blue between one blink and the next. She flapped her hands at her ladies. 'Catherine, Penelope. We grow tired and desire now to rest. Rose, come.'

Goose Neck and Foul-Breath fluttered beneath Titanea's arms again and led her deeper into the comforts of the room. Rose appeared behind the queen, and Joan felt her heart stumble in her chest.

Rose was attired as a lady of the court, her grey gown dull in colour but clearly made of an expensive fabric and cut specifically to flatter her tall form. Four strings of pearls interspersed with black ribbon hung around her slim neck, but her beautiful hair had been forced into random twists and folds, showing a distinct lack of care. Her posture was erect and stiff, nothing of the relaxed ease that Joan was used to.

And now that she looked closely, Joan noticed the dark bruises beneath Rose's eyes and the slightest creases of perpetual frowning around her lips. Joan's heart lurched.

Clearly whatever Rose was experiencing here at court had diminished her. Joan hated that.

'Take Joan to her rooms and have her prepare for luncheon,' Titanea said before raising an eyebrow at Joan. 'In the dress we sent her this time.'

Joan flushed, her hands fisting in the skirts of her yellow gown. She didn't want to change into a new gown – the familiar fabric she wore felt as much a comfort to her as Bia at her wrist.

'Joan,' Titanea said her tone sharp, 'go change.'

Foul-Breath glanced at Goose Neck. 'She's refusing Her Highness's gift. How distasteful.'

'We shouldn't expect more of the creature,' Goose Neck said, glee behind the voicing of the insult. 'Does it have any manners?'

Joan felt her nails bite into her palms as she fought with every fibre of her being the desire to pummel these women. Their hatred wouldn't have changed in so short a time despite Titanea's chastisement at Twelfth

Night. Her 'sisters' in service to the queen clearly believed Joan to be so far beneath them they could refer to her as 'it' without consequence. They may feel so bold as to give voice to their disgusting spite, but Joan would not stand their treatment. Not when Titanea had made them all equals. She couldn't use her fists or sword to repay them, but she'd devise some way to . . .

'Silence, you clucking hens,' Titanea spat, glaring at each woman until they shrank under her gaze. She turned back to Joan with a smile. 'Go change, dear.'

Or they'd be handled by someone more powerful. Yes, while the true Queen Anne had allowed such behaviour, Titanea would never permit it unchallenged. Let the Fae queen punish them; Joan would not intervene.

She unclenched her fists and curtsied. Her hands shook as the fires of her rage dissipated, leaving her feeling wrung out and exhausted. She tucked them against the yellow fabric of her skirts and followed Rose out of the chambers. Another lady slipped past them as they walked out into the hallway. Pale and pretty, she looked hardly older than Joan or Rose, and she glowed with an inner light that marked her as Fae. She smiled plesantly at Joan as she closed the door in her face.

Rose immediately grabbed Joan's hand, threading their fingers together tightly and using the wide fabric of their skirts to obscure them. She gave Joan a sudden sideways look, her eyes showing alarm even though her smile stayed pleasant and gentle. Her gaze darted around the candlelit hall then settled back on Joan.

Ah.

They were being watched – and of course they were, this was the royal court.

'I knew this couldn't be the gown she sent for you,' Rose said quietly. 'I've seen no one here dare wear such a shade of yellow. It wouldn't flatter any of them half as well as it does you.'

Joan sighed. 'The queen is so kind in her generosity and I very much look forwards to wearing her gift' – she racked her brain for a proper excuse – 'when it is not in danger of bearing the marks of rough travel.'

Or I'll shove it to the back of my closet where it'll never see the light of day.

Her tongue may have to be schooled to brandish lies and petty half-truths, but at least her thoughts were still her own.

'You look beautiful,' Rose said, her warm breath whispering against the skin of Joan's ear. 'The dress she sent wouldn't have done you such justice.'

Joan felt her face grow even hotter as her heart raced. 'You flatter me.'

'I wish you hadn't come, but I'm glad you're here. Quite selfishly, in fact.'

Joan pulled Rose closer as they made their way through winding hallways. She tried to note distinguishing features to help her find her way alone. The attempt was valiant, but her mind refused to retain any more information. She gave up after they passed what seemed to be the hundredth cluster of candles jutting from the wall.

She'd learn her way soon enough.

Besides, being close to Rose was far too distracting and unfortunately, the changes in the other girl were obvious. Joan squeezed her hand, smiling when she glanced her way. Rose's severe expression lightened for a moment as she caressed Joan's fingers.

A new resolve rushed through Joan.

Whatever weighed upon Rose, stealing her vibrance, would not prevail so long as Joan was here.

'Here we are,' Rose finally said, stopping before a heavy wooden door. 'These are the rooms of the former Lady Clifford.' Her eyes went sad. 'May she rest in peace.'

Joan felt her stomach turn. 'They've given me a dead girl's title, why not her rooms as well?' She turned to Rose. 'Do you know what happened to her? The real Lady Clifford?'

'Only the queen knows.' Rose shifted uncomfortably. 'I admit, I fear the answer.'

Joan did too, but even still she'd ask Titanea herself. The Fae queen's response might be the thing to steel Joan's resolve. She doubted the young girl could've committed any sin heavy enough to excuse her disposal.

Light to your spirit, Lady Clifford. I'm sorry I've been given all that was yours but I will care for it as my own.

She sent the prayer up quickly as Rose swung the door to her new lodgings open, revealing a set of rooms as large as the top floor of Joan's entire house.

She tried not to feel impressed but failed miserably. The spacious main area was hung with beautiful tapestries showing pastoral scenes of shepherdesses with their flocks, foxes outrunning hounds and hunters, and one extremely detailed depiction of a unicorn bowing its head to a pale blonde maiden who bore a striking resemblance to the former Lady Clifford. Joan didn't let her gaze linger on that one for too long. A large bed sat against one wall. Heavy emerald velvet looped around the four tall, polished wood posts and cascaded down to pool on the floor. A fire blazed merrily in the large hearth across from the bed, a fluffy animal skin rug laid in front of it.

The rest of the room was just as lavish as the bed: high-backed chairs and heavy wooden tables polished to a near reflective shine, puffy pillows and thick blankets on every surface. Someone had unpacked Joan's things. Her brush, comb and jewellery box sat atop the dressing table near the wardrobe, which was filled with unfamiliar dresses and cloaks, and the deep blue gown she'd been ordered – twice – to wear. Her own clothing had been stuffed hastily to one side, overtaken by Mistress Beckley's creations.

The woman worked lightning fast, Joan couldn't deny that.

'They've at least aired them out before you arrived,' Rose said as she stood awkwardly near one of the chairs.

Joan moved towards her, but a knock on the door stopped her in her tracks. 'Enter,' Joan called.

A young woman with pale brown skin – a servant, judging from her clothing and the silent, unobtrusive way she moved – eased open the door. 'My lady.' She gave a quick dip of a curtsy then shifted her gaze to Rose. 'Mistress Rose, Her Highness has asked you return to her chambers.'

'Thank you, Grace,' Rose said. Her shoulders slumped but she managed a smile at Joan. 'I'll see you for luncheon in your new gown.' She nodded to the servant and slipped out into the hall.

Grace made to follow after.

'Wait,' Joan called. 'Grace, was it?'

The girl froze and stepped back into the doorway, her gaze cast to the ground. 'Yes. Grace Foster, my lady.'

'Might I trouble you, Grace,' Joan said, putting as much genuine warmth into her voice as she could, 'to help me get changed?'

Joan knew outside the palace, some invisible bond connected people of her complexion. She remembered the kindness the footman had shown her and the brief acknowledgment she'd received from the guard. She hoped the girl would agree and find Joan genial enough to trust. Servants witnessed far more in the households where they worked than most realised. Joan needed every ally she could find in this place.

Grace nodded after a long moment and slipped into the room. She scurried over to the wardrobe. 'Which one, my lady?'

'The dark blue one, please.' Joan reached into her bag to retrieve her father's gift as Grace gathered the gown and laid it across the large bed.

Joan smiled as she ran her fingers over the smooth wood of the box again, then opened it. Well-oiled hinges swung silently to reveal a cushion of black velvet. On that pillow lay a bracelet made of delicate gold loops, with three charms dangling from it: a mermaid, an open fan and a key. A note had been tucked into the interior of the box's lid. Joan opened it to see her father's neat handwriting.

Wear this and think of us.

With all our love,

Father, Mother & James

Joan immediately tucked it and the box back into her bag, then set it on her dressing table. She turned the bracelet over in her hands, feeling the effort and craftsmanship her father had put into it. That loving care had found its way into the metal and stood out beyond the song it whispered to her. It was a sharp contrast to the ring that clung to her finger, though that had as much to do with its giver as its crafter.

The bracelet had no clasp, but her father knew she had no need for one. She opened one of the gold links with a touch, looped the whole thing around the opposite wrist from where she wore Bia, then closed it again. The gold slid together easily and smoothed over as if it had never been separated.

She touched the bracelet at her wrist, fingers plucking at the tiny key charm, and wished desperately she could put things back as they were.

CHAPTER EIGHTEEN
Cheek by Jowl

oan followed along behind Titanea and her ladies as they made their way to the Great Hall to greet King James. Foul-Breath and Goose Neck flanked the queen closely, not touching her this time, but ready to support her should her exhaustion overtake her. The unnamed Fae woman trailed behind them, her gaze fixed on her queen. Beside her, Rose moved with her tall frame bowed as if she were trying to make herself invisible.

Joan was even more convinced that this fragile constitution wasn't for show. Not even Titanea could disguise the distaste on her face whenever someone had to help her stand or sit or walk. If the Fae were gaining strength as Master Phillips had proven back at the theatre, then Joan didn't understand how Titanea was still so weak.

She'd have to ask Rose at the next opportunity. Hopefully that night.

'What, not excited to meet the king, girl?' Lady Snort – the least openly confrontational of the lot so far – said. None of the ladies had yet used Joan's name or title, though they'd avoided directly insulting her within Titanea's hearing. Snort – whose face bore its signature pinched scowl – walked at the rear of their group alongside Joan.

I'd look eternally sour too, if I had the personality of wet parchment.

Joan rolled her eyes. 'I merely breathe, nothing more.' The doors of the hall came into view, and Joan couldn't resist one parting shot as they swung open before them. 'The last time I stood before the king, he granted me a title. How could such a thing not breed excitement?' She hid her smile behind her hand as Snort's sputters were drowned out by the trumpet fanfare announcing their arrival.

The queen and her train entered to the sounds of music and quiet conversation. The room had already filled with courtiers and lesser royals, some standing and some seated at the long wooden tables that had been arranged throughout.

Joan realised she'd never seen this space; her work with the King's Men was confined to the Banqueting House. This room was far sturdier, having been built as part of the original palace instead of hastily erected long after. Not a single window lined the walls, allowing no chill wind nor any sunlight. Indeed, darkness loomed although Joan knew it to be the middle of the afternoon. Instead, tall torches sat like a line of sentinels, their light steady in the draftless room save for the occasional flicker.

King James sat on a raised dais at the far end, sprawled comfortably on his throne with one leg thrown over the arm and the other stretched out before him.

He looked as if he wanted to be anywhere but here.

Joan couldn't blame him.

Philip stood just behind the king's right shoulder, excitement over-taking his face as he spotted the queen and her train. Behind them both and nearly in complete shadow stood Cecil, his glare murderous enough to have struck Joan dead if it had held such power. She smiled at him just because she could and watched him turn an unbecoming shade of purple.

On the king's other side stood Lord Fentoun in his crimson uniform. He noticed her gaze and winked. Joan grinned back, this time genuinely.

The queen's group approached the royal dais, whispers and stares following in Joan's wake as they passed. At the base she curtsied along with the rest, a unified move that surprised her in its unpracticed ease, before Titanea made her way up onto the dais. Her much smaller and slightly less embellished throne sat to the right of the king's. Joan wondered if Titanea hated it and the power imbalance it indicated. If she did, her face revealed nothing of her distaste. The ladies fanned out beside and behind her, with Foul-Breath and Goose Neck standing closest.

The king's gaze slid over Titanea as she caressed his hand. He raised an eyebrow. 'You have me abandon my hunting expedition for naught but boredom.'

'Not so, lord,' Titanea laughed, and it sounded completely genuine. 'We have many pleasures in mind.' She tangled their fingers together and they both glanced up at Philip.

The smile the younger man returned was lewd enough to make Joan avert her gaze.

'Stop thinking of what's proper when you can have both of us.'

Rose's words sprang to Joan's mind unbidden, and she found her eyes trained on the girl who'd said them.

'Shall we take in some entertainments here first?' Philip said smoothly as he let his hand brush against the king's shoulder.

The king groaned. 'Not more dancing . . .'

Philip looked lost for a moment before Cecil stepped forwards, his gaze locked on Joan.

'Your Majesty,' he said, bending into a deep bow, 'I've heard word the queen's newest lady-in-waiting is an accomplished sword fighter.'

Joan paled. What was the man playing at?

'A swords . . . woman, you say?' King James straightened, his lips quirking in a smile. 'How delightfully unusual.'

Cecil bared his teeth at her. 'Indeed, my liege. Shall we have her demonstrate her skill? Perhaps against one of your grooms?'

'A duel between a lady and a gentleman? Why, that is quite the entertainment indeed! Finally, some intelligence from you, Salisbury.'

Cecil's expression pinched for the briefest moment before he bowed once again.

The king turned to squint at Titanea and her ladies. 'Which one is she again? The brown one?' He pointed at Rose then shook his head. 'No, not that one. Ah, yes, the dark brown one. Step forwards, girl.'

Joan felt her heart plummet to her feet even as she came from behind the queen's throne.

'She's a scrawny one, but I'll trust your word, Salisbury. Get the girl some trousers.' He leaned towards Joan, a wide grin on his face and excitement in his eyes. 'No matter how good you are, you can't best a man wearing that gown.'

I've bested two men at once while wearing a gown.

But she clenched her teeth around the thought and instead curtsied, saying, 'I thank you for your generous offer, Your Majesty.'

He shooed her off the dais, and someone gently touched Joan's arm. Joan turned to see Grace, the young maid from earlier, standing at her elbow.

'This way, my lady,' she said softly, and led the way to a side room where she closed the door behind them. She held out a pair of black wool trousers to Joan. 'Shall I help you dress in these, lady?'

'Yes, please, Grace.' Joan shook herself, then tugged at the ties at the side of her skirts and underpinnings.

Her mind spun. If she dared wear a pair of trousers out into the streets of London, she'd be instantly arrested. Yet, here in the palace, the very people who made those laws and in whose name they were carried out were offering her men's clothes to better prepare her for a duel. Surely this was some great jest, and she would be made a fool of as soon as she reentered the Great Hall.

Grace held the trousers by the waist and leaned over to let Joan step into them. The wool was expensive and soft, but the feel of the fabric rubbing against her legs was still odd and uncomfortable. She pulled them up, lacing them tightly around her hips.

'It's safest to let them feel they've humbled you,' Grace said suddenly.

Joan's head shot up from where she'd been fumbling with closing her trousers. 'What?'

'I'm sorry, my lady.' The girl paled and lowered her gaze. 'I didn't mean to speak out of turn. I had thought—'

Joan reached out to touch her arm. 'No, you didn't. It's fine.' She waited for the girl to lift her eyes again, then smiled gently. 'It's fine, truly. Thank you for your wise words, Grace,' Joan said sincerely. 'Any others you can offer?'

A bright smile spread across Grace's face as her entire body seemed to relax. 'Indeed, lady. Let them have their wins against you and you won't make yourself a target here.'

'I'm already a target,' Joan snorted. 'As I'm sure you can see.'

Grace pursed her lips as she shook her head. 'This is but a game. They're capable of far more deadly things if they consider you a threat. Mind yourself.'

'I'll do my best to hold your advice.' Joan nodded and finished knotting the ties on her trousers. She held out her arms with a flourish. 'How do I look? Honestly?'

'Utterly uncomfortable.'

Joan laughed and heard Grace join her. 'Yes, well, these offer much less freedom than skirts.' She shifted her hips and pulled the fabric away from her rear. The constant press of wool against her nethers was unpleasant to say the least.

She would've been better fighting in her original clothing, although the heavy navy gown Mistress Beckley had designed lacked the ease of movement Baba managed to integrate into his works.

She pulled imaginary imperfections off the trousers as she struggled to get control of her emotions. She missed Baba Ben ardently, and prayed he was still well. They planned to visit him once Joan got settled at court, but this sudden exhibition showed that day might prove far off indeed. Waiting for such a thing before they continued their discovery of the Pact's requirements would be foolish.

At the first chance, Joan would get word to her family and sneak away from the palace. Then, with James's help, they'd work to contact the ancestor who'd forged the first Pact and all this would be done.

'Are you ready, my lady?' Grace stood near the door, Joan's heavy overgown and skirts bundled in her arms.

Joan shook herself and nodded. She'd kept on her bodice and chemise but tucked and tied the latter so it wouldn't hang to her knees like usual. The ties on her cream stockings were hidden by the lower hems of the trousers, and her shoes were blessedly her own still.

She was – in a way – properly attired for this duel, so there was no more need to linger.

They both left the tiny side dressing room, Grace disappearing into the crowd with practiced ease. Joan had assumed she'd be greeted with raucous laughter and taunts, but her entrance didn't even disrupt the usual court chatter. Someone had cleared a large circle of space in front of the royal dais, allowing the king and queen a perfect view of the event to come.

'Who'll challenge this slip of a girl?' the king said, his voice echoing through the room. 'Come forth, any of you.' He waved his hand in the general direction of the men who stood behind him.

Joan glanced up and happened to catch Rose's eye. The tall girl couldn't seem to decide whether she was horrified or amused, her face shifting awkwardly between the two emotions as she tugged at her fingers. Joan offered her a confident smile and Rose hesitantly returned it, her hands slowing in their panicked fluttering.

'I will, my liege,' a familiar voice proclaimed.

Hushed whispers shot across the room as Lord Fentoun stepped forwards.

CHAPTER NINETEEN

Put to the Arbitrament of Swords

ing James laughed broadly. 'A duel against the captain of my guard? Give us a good show, Thomas.'

Lord Fentoun bowed his head and shot a grin at Joan. He removed his formal crimson doublet as he descended from the dais, leaving himself clad in only a shirt and his black trousers. Joan idly noticed that they matched hers, before she let the panic of fighting the captain of the king's guard overtake her.

This was real. This duel was happening.

Another guard in a crimson uniform handed her a sword – a plain, unbalanced thing so abused she knew its presentation had been meant as an insult. She wished she could at least wield Bia, felt the sword pulsing jealously at her wrist, but there'd be no way to explain how she'd produced a hidden sword or why she kept one in the first place. Joan touched her fingertips to the ragged blade, discreetly shifting the metal until it laid evenly along the edge and countered the weight of the guard nicely.

Not that anyone was watching her. All eyes were on Lord Fentoun as he drew his own blade with a flourish, flicking it through the air with a quick whistle that drew a few cheers from the crowd. He cut a dashing figure, though she doubted having a young girl as his opponent would boost anyone's already glowing opinion of the guard.

Ogun's presence cooled in her chest, making her notice for the first time how hotly it had burned from the moment she'd stepped into the queen's chamber. The Orisha thankfully hadn't tried to possess her again, but he felt the danger in Titanea's presence.

Joan still wasn't sure whether the great spirit responded to the Fae queen's current threat or what he remembered from the past. The possibility of it being the latter was enough to still her hand.

She prayed she'd not regret it.

'Shall we begin, Lady Clifford?' Lord Fentoun bowed to her, pulling her from her racing thoughts as he slid into an easy stance, sword at the ready.

Joan cleared her throat. She doubted she'd ever get used to being called by the dead girl's title, but it was a shield she wouldn't refuse. 'Of course, Lord Fentoun.' She grounded herself, sliding her feet far apart and bending her knees before raising her blade to be ready to block his first attack.

Here at least was something familiar among the stares and whispers. Strangeness surrounded her on all sides but in a fight there was comfort.

Lord Fentoun grinned again and lunged towards her. The move was lazy and easy to read. Joan sidestepped him, knocking his blade away with a tap. He raised an eyebrow but collected himself quickly and attacked again. He sliced at her belly and she blocked. She caught the flat of his sword on hers and flung it over their heads and away. The speed of her parry threw him off-balance and he stumbled a few steps past her.

She scowled. He was toying with her; not a single one of his attacks had been serious. Anger blazed in the pit of her stomach.

Fine, if they wanted to make a spectacle of her, she'd give them a show.

She rushed forwards just as Fentoun turned to face her. She swung a wide cut at his shoulder that she knew he'd block. Their blades connected with a clang and she softened her wrist, riding the force of his parry to slice at his other shoulder. His arm shot across his body to block her again. Metal rang against metal as she planted her feet to lock him in place. Her free hand grabbed hold of his elbow and she shoved with all her might.

Fentoun yelped as he was propelled backwards, unprepared for her strength. He twisted his body, slamming one hand against the ground to stop himself from falling flat. He righted himself with a toss of his blonde hair and narrowed his eyes at Joan. She grinned at the fire she saw there.

Good, now he would take her seriously.

The whispers of the crowd grew louder as Fentoun bowed his head to the king, never taking his eyes off Joan.

'Your Majesty, shall the *child*' – he emphasised 'child,' the word holding some warning Joan chose to ignore – 'and I fight until one of us holds the other's sword?'

King James laughed again. 'She's putting you through your paces, Thomas. But, yes, the duel shall end with the victor holding both blades.' He leaned back, his grin turning sharp. 'Though a bit of blood wouldn't displease me.'

'I serve at your pleasure, my liege,' Fentoun said, and brought his sword up in a quick salute. 'Until I have your sword.'

Joan did the same then threw herself backwards as he rushed her. Their blades tangled together. He twisted their arms around, binding her over so quickly the sword slipped from her shocked fingers and flew through the air. Their eyes met, satisfaction and relief battling in his gaze.

I'm not done yet, Lord Fentoun.

Joan clenched her jaw and dove for her blade. She snatched it from the air, tucking herself into a forwards roll and propelling herself back to her feet. She spun and parried his next two blows with ease.

He was fast when he wasn't holding back, each move coming without hesitation.

But she was faster.

The wonderful familiarity of throwing herself into a fight rushed through her as she ducked under his third swing, coming up behind him. She pressed her back against his and matched his pivot, sticking close as he turned. She spun in to face him. Their swords clashed with an echoing clang.

He grabbed her wrist and jerked her towards him. His face loomed close between the locked tension of their shaking blades.

She raised an eyebrow at him. 'Not the easy win you expected, my lord?'

'For God's sake, child, lose,' he hissed through clenched teeth, 'if you ever hope to find peace in this place.' His voice was barely a whisper so none but she could hear his words. 'Don't give them more reason to want you dead.'

Her joy cooled so suddenly, it was as if she'd been doused in icy water.

He was absolutely right. Winning against the captain of the king's guard would bring her nothing but more misery.

Over Fentoun's shoulder she caught Cecil's eye, his lips curled up in a smile at her struggle.

That fiery anger within her blazed forth again, but not fuelled by the presence of Ogun. No, this was purely her. She was already a target and source of wonderment in this pit of vipers. Win or lose, she'd find no peace here.

Bia, having hummed sullenly at her wrist the entire fight, pulsed along with her anger. The staccato beat further heated her blood. She cast one last glance at Cecil and his detested grin.

He hoped to humble her, but she'd not allow it.

Enough of this petty sport.

She'd cleave the satisfaction from his face with her win and damn the rest.

Joan relaxed her body, easing her press against Fentoun's sword. He shoved his blade hard against hers, and she let the attack move her slightly as he stepped into her space. Confidently, he twisted her arm to force her to the ground. She leaned backwards and he followed, pitching his weight too far forwards.

There.

She planted her back foot and jerked him towards her, wrenching her wrist free from his hold as she pushed their connected swords in the opposite direction. He yelped as his body turned sideways, off-balance. She smacked her palm against the flat of his blade just above the hilt. It popped out of his clenched fist as he fell. He went sprawling across the floor with a loud grunt, his sword clattering to the ground behind him.

She tucked her foot beneath it and kicked it into the air. She grabbed hold of it with her free hand, noting the superior balance and craftsmanship as she spun both swords in quick arcs that whistled through the air.

'I have your sword, Lord Fentoun,' she said, unable and unwilling to suppress the pride in her voice.

She turned to the royal dais and saluted the king, barely glimpsing Philip behind him, his face serious. She glanced at Cecil, prepared to revel in his soured expression.

But his smile held as his gaze swept over the room behind her.

Then the whispers began.

She heard Lord Fentoun gather himself from the ground and come stand beside her. She passed him his sword, not daring to look at his face.

'Your new companion fights well, my queen,' he said loudly enough to echo through the space.

The king leaned forwards. 'Her skill must be incredible to have bested you, Thomas. Or am I in need of a new captain of my personal guard?'

Lord Fentoun stiffened beside her as a smattering of laughter sounded around the hall. Joan wanted to curl up and disappear. She hadn't considered who else her win might endanger.

She should have listened.

'She is one to keep an eye on indeed,' Cecil said smoothly.

And that was the way of it. She'd saved her pride and fallen into Cecil's trap.

If only she'd listened.

King James gave her a long, considering look before he sat back with a casual wave. 'Well fought, girl. Now someone get her out of these trousers before the other ladies decide to make this the new fashion.'

The entire room burst into overly loud laughter, and the king called for some musicians to play. Lord Fentoun looped Joan's arm through his as the sounds of a viol and drum began. The crowd closed in around them, no longer keeping the circle clear now that the duel had been won. Fentoun guided her deftly through the sudden crush of people, avoiding everyone as the laughter and whispers followed in their wake.

They approached the door to that same side room where she had changed before, and he slipped her hand from his arm.

'I won't ask where you learned to fight with such skill or how you bear such great strength,' he said quietly, not looking at her. 'But take care.

There was already a target on you because you are different and because of your sudden elevation. You've given them more reason to hate you now.'

Joan nodded. 'Of course. Thank you for your wise words, my lord' – she felt her cheeks flush with shame – 'even if I lacked the mind to heed them.'

'You're welcome, my lady. Though, that said' – he finally turned his gaze to her, his eyes shining with soft pride – 'it was thrilling to fight such a skilled opponent, child though she may be.'

Joan barked out a surprised laugh. 'Thank you, my lord.'

Lord Fentoun grinned back at her and dipped his head in a quick bow before he disappeared back into the crowd. Joan slipped into the dressing room to find Grace already waiting with her original clothes. Grace gave a soft smile and took the sword from Joan's hands.

Good riddance to poor craftsmanship.

'My lady,' Grace said, 'I fear—'

'I know.' Joan flushed as she recalled how quickly the other girl's excellent advice had flown from her mind in the heat of a fight.

Next time, she would listen.

Joan returned to the Great Hall filled with shame. She'd played right into Cecil's devices by not losing her fight with Lord Fentoun. The man had outwitted her easily, and she'd pay for her overconfidence.

The whispers that followed her earlier had doubled, paired now with outright looks of suspicion. She did her best to ignore them as she ascended the stairs up to the royal dais, and Ogun's presence swelled within her once again.

Goose Neck sneered at her and leaned over to Foul-Breath as she approached. 'What a brute that child is . . .'

'Indeed,' Foul-Breath said. 'Practically an animal.'

Joan clenched her fists to keep from reacting to their insults, the Orisha's heat in her chest fuelling her anger with ease. She tried to school her expression, to remain pleasantly blank despite the rage she felt and by the way the two women giggled, she knew she'd failed.

'Cease your incessant caterwauling, you vile wretches,' Titanea shouted, drawing all eyes to her immediately.

Goose Neck gasped, her hand clutching her chest as true pain crossed her face. 'My lady . . .' She rushed to Titanea, kneeling at her side. 'My lady, I know you find this *girl*' – she spat the word as she glared at Joan – 'and her presence novel but you need not defend her.' She waited for some reaction from the queen and continued when she received none. 'First you sit her beside you as an honoured guest, then you elevate her and welcome her into your household.' Her voice raised with passion as she clutched the queen's arm. 'Now you berate us when we treat her as she deserves? For what reason, my queen? Why do you flout us so at her—'

Goose Neck's head whipped to the side as Titanea slapped her. Gasps rippled through the crowd in the silence after, and Foul-Breath paled where she stood behind her fellow.

'You dare question your queen? Impudent, treasonous wretches,' Titanea hissed the words at the two women.

Goose Neck went white as paper as Foul-Breath rushed up to clutch the woman's shaking shoulders. 'No, my queen, we mean you no harm and have served you faithfully for three years. You know the deep love we bear you.'

'Enough!' The glare Titanea levelled at them made both women seem to shrivel up. 'How we loathe your presence now. Out of our sight and do not return to us until we have summoned you.'

Goose Neck jerked back as if she'd been slapped again before she turned wild eyes to Joan. 'Look what you've caused, you beastly girl!' She surged forwards, clawing for Joan's face like a cornered cat.

Joan leaned to the side, knocking the woman's hands away with a sharp hit to her wrists. Goose Neck's momentum sent her tumbling down the stairs shrieking. She hit the floor hard and sprawled gracelessly across the fresh rushes. Laughter exploded in her wake.

'Remove them,' Titanea said dryly, gesturing to Goose Neck on the ground and Foul-Breath who remained on the dais.

Lord Fentoun grabbed Foul-Breath's arm and dragged her pleading and sputtering down the stairs. Joan stepped aside to let them pass. The foul-breathed woman reached for her. Joan swatted her hand away. Two guards were already collecting Goose Neck from the floor.

'Your Highness, please,' the woman screeched, her long neck straining as she struggled against the men who held her. 'We have served you faithfully!'

Fentoun gave Foul-Breath over to the care of another guard and returned to the dais as the two women were marched out of the Great Hall, Goose Neck's wailed pleas echoing until the doors closed in her face.

The whispers were loud in the sudden silence. Joan noticed they seemed full of talk of the two disgraced women, her own duel seemingly forgotten in the face of a far juicier scandal. She moved to take her place again behind Titanea's throne.

The queen beckoned her over, patting Joan's hand gently when she obliged. 'It would've been more prudent to lose that duel.'

'Yes, it would have,' Joan said, her smile dropping from her face.

Titanea gave her that wolf's grin again. 'But what a glorious win it was, dear Joan. You fight like a demon; she would've been proud.'

Joan started, wondering what 'she' Titanea referred to, her brain racing to find some connection.

Speak not of her.

Ogun hissed the words inside her head, the venom in them throwing Joan off-kilter. Bia pulsed aggressively at her wrist.

The queen urged her closer with a crooked finger. 'These mortals behave poorly in the presence of a greatness beyond their own, especially when it presents in a form they do not expect. They are unworthy of us, remember that.' She touched Joan's cheek, her face warm and kind. 'They shall pay for taunting you, we swear it.'

Joan felt a chill rush through her at the words. She almost pitied what Titanea planned for Goose Neck and Foul-Breath but they'd come to the proper reward for their hatred. She couldn't stop such justice, nor did she want to.

She'd save her pity for those who deserved it.

'You are too kind, Your Highness,' Joan said with a curtsy.

Titanea smiled her wolf's grin again. 'Well said. Well learned.'

Joan inclined her head and stepped back to her place. The memory of the agony the boon caused taught better than any words could. She shivered at the thought of the pain.

Her mind latched on to Titanea's words, on Ogun's reaction and Bia's that followed close after. This 'she' they mentioned, was this the ancestor they needed to contact? The one who'd forged the first Pact?

She felt some confirmation within herself, not from Ogun but some instinct of her own that knew it to be true.

So, the spirit they needed to contact was a woman. She'd get this information to Baba somehow, and though the clue was small, it gave them a target, and that's what they needed more than anything.

'Joan,' Philip said as he leaned towards her, 'have you met my wife, Susan?'

She blinked, startled from her racing thoughts and raised an eyebrow. Of all people, she hadn't expected Philip to be married. He grinned at her look and reached out his hand. The one that clasped it in return was just as pale but glowed with an inner light. Joan's eyes went wide.

'We've seen each other,' the same Fae woman who'd been part of Titanea's train since this morning said, 'but we haven't had the pleasure of being introduced.' She inclined her head to Joan.

Philip smiled slyly. 'I suppose you'll stand closer to the queen now that Catherine and Penelope have been booted. If you'll believe it of my lovely wife,' he whispered to Joan behind his raised hand, 'she's also Lord Salisbury's niece.'

Oh.

Joan looked to Susan in surprise.

'You won't hold my true nature against me, will you Joan?' She smiled as she said it, the glint in her eyes showing she knew Joan would glean her true meaning.

Philip laughed. 'Of course, she won't! She knows our family is as much the will of fate as our faces. We've been blessed in one way but cursed in another.'

Joan considered telling the man his wife wasn't his wife at all. That she'd been replaced by a being from another world, but the genuine joy that crossed his face when he looked at the woman stilled her tongue.

There'd be time for it later. She'd leave him to his peace for now.

CHAPTER TWENTY
In the Coiled Night

hat was foolish,' Rose said as she barged into Joan's room that night.

Joan held the door open as the other girl shoved past her, biting down on the scathing reply at the tip of her tongue. Rose was right, she had been foolish. So instead of arguing, Joan wrapped Rose up in a tight hug, a far better use of the time they finally had together.

'I thought you'd never get away from her.' She squeezed tightly and felt Rose's arms slip around her shoulders.

Rose snorted. 'She wouldn't let me go, so I had to wait until she fell asleep.'

Joan pulled away, clasping Rose's hand in both of hers. Rose's fingers were cold and trembling.

Rose took a deep, shuddering breath. 'I wish with everything in me that you hadn't come to this wretched place.' She pulled back and stared at Joan. 'But I'm glad you're here with me.'

'Rose—'

She kissed Joan suddenly, the quickest press of lips, before she leaned away. 'You should've lost today.'

'So I've been scolded many a time over.' Joan shook herself to clear her racing thoughts and the urge to lean up for another kiss. 'I miscalculated. Grace and Lord Fentoun both advised me against winning and even Titanea chastised me.'

Rose frowned. 'Did she?'

'Is that strange?'

'It is . . . worth noting. She likes you, genuinely, but I don't know if it's a gift or curse.'

Joan agreed and hated that only time would reveal which. She squeezed Rose's hands, hoping to distract her mind before it wandered close to disaster.

'That man you fought,' Rose said, 'Thomas Erskine. He's the groom of the stool and captain of the king's guard. You're lucky it was he and not another.'

Joan remembered the whispers after her win bandying about her name as well as his. 'He's been extremely kind to me, and I fear I've sullied his reputation.' Her face went hot with shame. 'I find myself out of my element with the battles here.'

Rose tangled their fingers together. 'As am I, but we've each other now. Perhaps our wits together shall prove weapon enough.' Rose squeezed her hands, then let go to sweep deeper into the room. 'I couldn't properly see the opulence of this place before I had to rush back to the queen's side. Do you like it?'

Joan shrugged. 'It's beautiful, but I miss my room at home.' She hugged herself as that familiar loneliness swept over her. She'd barely changed anything in the room, only laying out the blanket her grandmother had made before she'd died – a cheery emerald and grey that matched the burgundy-and-grey one she'd made for James – and her smaller personal items and cosmetics.

It was hard to feel at home here when she couldn't stop wondering what had happened to the real Lady Clifford. Stepping into a ghost's life was unsettling, to say the least.

She prayed the girl hadn't suffered.

'What is this?' Rose stood at the room's dark wooden dressing table that doubled as Joan's desk. She held up a dark coloured jar, frowning at its contents.

Joan smiled and moved to gently take it from the other girl. 'It's a cream for your hair. It smells lovely.' She twisted off the top and held out to Rose. 'See?'

Rose hummed and grabbed Joan's wrist, tugging her close as she leaned forwards to sniff. Joan's heart thudded in her chest.

'I recognise this scent.' Rose looked up, her face suddenly very close to Joan's. 'I had thought it was your perfume.'

Joan shook her head. 'No . . . it's . . .' Her gaze dropped to Rose's lips, near enough that all she'd have to do is lean the barest bit . . .

'Can I ask you a favour, Joan?'

Joan swallowed, her voice stuck in her suddenly dry throat. She cleared it and tried to speak again. 'Yes? Anything.'

'Could you do my hair?'

She felt the tense moment between them break at Rose's innocent question. 'Ah, yes, of course.' She dropped down on her heels and stepped back.

'Yours is always so beautiful.' Rose's fingertips brushed along Joan's cheek before gently caressing her hair. 'I haven't the knowledge to create such art.'

Joan's heart raced as whatever had been pulled taut between them tensed again, making the air feel thick with the potential for . . . something. She caught Rose's wrist. 'You needn't flatter me so to get your way.'

She reached around the other girl to grab her hair tools, their bodies pressing close when Rose didn't move. It took Joan two tries to pick up her comb but eventually she gathered everything she needed.

'Can you grab that basin,' she said softly, afraid that speaking any louder than a whisper would break this moment, 'and bring it over?'

Rose nodded, letting Joan slide back around her before following her over to the bed. Joan spread her tools out on the blanket and sat down. She gestured to the floor in front of her. Rose carefully placed the half-full basin of water beside Joan, then dropped down to sit between her feet, letting her back slide along Joan's shins on her way to the floor.

A shiver raced up Joan's spine, but she set to work anyway. Whoever had been dressing Rose's hair had been haphazard in their efforts at best. Her beautiful curls had been brushed and pulled into a dry snarl of knots. Joan felt her heart break at the obvious mistreatment.

She dipped her hands into the basin and started working water through the parched strands. By the time she'd gotten Rose's hair properly wet, she'd drenched the front of her skirt. But the curls had already started to revive a bit. She made four sections then reached for her hair cream next, gently and generously massaging it in before combing the tangles out.

'I can't believe you bested Lord Fentoun,' Rose said as Joan worked, her voice soft and dreamy. 'Well, I can believe your skill, but I did not expect such audacity.'

Joan smiled though she knew Rose couldn't see her. 'Neither did

Lord Fentoun.'

She parted Rose's hair into smaller portions and set to twisting them. Rose hummed softly as she worked, her body relaxing against Joan's legs. She was twisting through the third large section when she felt Rose's thumb rubbing along her ankle.

Her hands slipped, dropping the cluster of hair she'd been holding. It unraveled immediately. Water sloshed over the edge of the basin, soaking the side of her skirt.

'Rose—' She cleared her throat. The touch scorched even through her wool stockings. 'Rose, I can't concentrate when you do that.'

Rose pressed her face against Joan's leg. 'Good,' she whispered and ran her hand up her calf. 'Good.' She tilted her head back, dark eyes locking with Joan's. 'I'd like to give you something. Is that all right?'

Something in her gaze pinned Joan in place. A promise she couldn't name.

Rose turned so she kneeled at Joan's feet. 'You can say no. I swear, it won't make me think of you any differently however you answer.'

What was the question? Joan could barely think, especially when Rose's touch seemed to burn all the way through the fabric of her clothes. The girl's hands pressed against her knees as she stood. She loomed over Joan and traced her way along her face to her chin.

She leaned close, her breath hot against Joan's ear. 'May I give you this gift?'

Oh.

Joan wanted, but was she ready? She leaned back, watching Rose's face and saw nothing but patience and affection in the other girl's gaze. She closed her eyes and asked herself again.

I want this. Am I ready?

She breathed, suddenly so very sure of her answer, and pressed her lips against Rose's palm. Rose's other hand slid along Joan's throat, brushing against the pendant that hung round her neck. They both froze as it jangled against its chain.

'Is this from your player, Nick?' Rose said softly.

Joan reached for the pendant, gripping the cool metal. 'He intends to court me. Formally.'

'You know I don't begrudge you his affections.' Rose laid her hand over Joan's. 'Don't feel you have to make a choice.'

Joan didn't think her face could grow any hotter. She knew she was red from her cheeks to the tips of her ears but she didn't pull away.

Stop thinking of what's proper when you could have both of us.

She knew how Rose felt on the matter, but what of Nick? Would he agree that she need not make a choice, or would the thought of being part of such an arrangement break his heart?

She had to speak with him before she moved further with either of them. She could do so tomorrow, when the King's Men would appear here for another court performance. The thought filled her with a different kind of fear, but she refused to let that keep her from being honest with someone she cared for.

She took another deep breath, clasping Rose's hand with hers. 'Let me finish your hair, Rose,' she said into the dimness of the room and prayed her resolve would overrule her passion.

She'd withdraw until everything was clear and equal between the three of them. But after . . .

She cleared her throat and set back to her task.

CHAPTER TWENTY-ONE
Unpolished & Unvarnished

oan slipped through the doors leading into the Banqueting Hall's side room where the King's Men always prepared for a royal performance. She'd watched for the last hour from her room across the courtyard as the players fumbled through the fights that she'd taught them. She knew from the clumsy passes that they were rehearsing for *Troilus and Cressida*, the first play they'd trusted her with nearly three years ago. Of course, they'd performed it since then, but never without her present to review and keep them in sync.

They were lucky the day was still early yet.

She pulled back the hood of her black wool cloak, and James spotted her immediately.

'Joan!' he shouted and ran to wrap her up in a tight hug.

She squeezed him back, then let go with reluctance. She held on to his arm, though, just because she could. Nick was approaching them when Master Shakespeare stepped directly into her view. He appeared so suddenly, she couldn't help but jump.

The tall man grabbed her arms, looking her over carefully. 'Are you well, Joan? I heard about your duel.' He sighed, his face disappointed. 'Did you not think to lose swiftly?'

'You had a duel?' James blurted with absolutely no discretion. 'You *won* a duel with someone at the royal court?'

Master Burbage jogged over, a wide grin on his face. 'Our Joan's been fighting at court? That's my girl.'

'Who'd you duel, Joan?' Nick said as he joined them too. 'That doesn't seem wise.'

Joan sighed, dropping her face into her hands. 'It was immensely unwise, but I didn't have a choice. I duelled the captain of the guard on His Majesty's order. Lord Salisbury suggested it, and yes, I won.' She bit her lip, bracing for their reactions.

The gathered men groaned, knowing the consequences her own pride had blinded her to.

'Lass, you do know how to find trouble,' Burbage said, shaking his head.

She huffed out a breath. He wasn't wrong but . . . 'This isn't what I've come here for. I happened to be watching you all practice the fights in the courtyard. They look terrible.'

Nick, Burbage, and Shakespeare all had the grace to look ashamed.

'Who's been drilling them since I couldn't?'

Shakespeare cleared his throat and tugged at his beard. 'Ah, well, we haven't . . . there isn't . . .' He sniffed and rolled his shoulders. 'We haven't actually replaced you yet.'

Joan had a moment to be touched by their reluctance to put someone else in her position before she rolled her eyes. It likely had as much to do with laziness as with tender feelings. But neither mattered when they had quality and a reputation to uphold.

'Gather the players and bring me a sword,' she said striding towards the performance space with a grinning James close on her heels. 'I'm fixing this immediately.' She paused for a moment and turned back to Nick. 'Thank you for remembering what I've taught. It's made the pleasure of seeing you even greater.'

He smiled brightly at her. 'I wouldn't dare forget.'

'Could we – ' She cleared her suddenly dry throat as her heart thudded nervously in her chest. 'Could we speak later? Privately?'

He blinked owlishly but nodded. His eyes shifted to her hand. He frowned, and she knew he'd spotted William Cecil's ring. 'Who—'

'Joan!' James shouted once more, running back to grab her hand. 'Come if you want to run these fights.'

She smiled at Nick and let herself be led away like a coward. She'd tell Nick the truth of it later when she'd had time to consider the smoothest answer.

She and James had walked only a few steps before he squeezed her hand tightly.

'I miss you,' he said.

Tears sprang to her eyes, and she blinked them back. 'I miss you too. Terribly.'

'It's quite obvious you do.' James tugged her close so he could wrap his arm around her shoulders. 'And what are you wearing? Did you get dressed in the dark?'

Joan burst out laughing and hugged her brother tightly as she realised she somehow missed his sharp tongue most of all.

Hours later, Joan hurried along the hallways looking for the golden sconce she'd marked to help her find her way to the queen's chambers. So far she'd had no luck.

Perhaps she'd get Rose or Grace to draw her a map of the labyrinthine ways through Whitehall Palace. Anything was better than this senseless wandering.

She had hoped to return sooner but the players had been so sloppy in their execution, it had been all she could do to keep someone from losing an eye in a stage battle. Their practice had run long, and she'd found no time to talk to Nick.

That part was worst of all because she feared they wouldn't have another opportunity soon.

Ah!

She finally spotted the thrice-damned sconce marked with the subtle arrow pattern up ahead. It pointed to the hallway she needed that branched off to the right just beyond it. She picked up her pace, glancing behind her as she rounded the corner, and just barely avoided slamming into someone. They grabbed hold of her arm as she stepped around them, and Joan found herself face-to-face with Cecil.

'It's far from proper,' he sneered, 'for one of Her Majesty's ladies to consort with players.'

Joan scowled back. 'I'm on my way to Her Majesty's chambers.'

'You think I'm not aware of everything that happens within this palace, girl?' He dragged her along with him as he strode towards the queen's rooms. He glared at her over his shoulder. 'Lying to me is pointless.'

They approached the ornate wooden door that marked Her Majesty's parlour, and Cecil half shoved Joan inside.

Titanea looked up from where she lounged among a cascade of pillows and raised one blonde eyebrow. 'Have you forgotten yourself and your manners, Lord Salisbury?'

'My apologies, your grace,' Cecil said, bowing deeply, 'but I found Lady Clifford lurking in the hall and thought to return her to your side.'

The queen pushed herself up onto her elbows. 'And enter here without announcing yourself or awaiting permission? How presumptuous.' She beckoned Joan over with the wave of one thin, pale hand. 'A moment of privacy with dear Joan, ladies.' She looked up at Cecil through her lashes, the look somehow both bored and enraged. 'Salisbury, you're dismissed.'

Cecil's face went red, but he pinched his mouth closed and, with another deep bow, left the room. Titanea's ladies followed after him with equal displeasure. Snort sniffed in that way of hers that inspired Joan's nickname for her as she moved to another part of the room, making sure to slam her shoulder into Joan's as they passed each other. Joan clenched her jaw and tried to breathe through the rage.

She wouldn't give the woman the satisfaction of a response. Instead she just imagined shoving her through a window and into one of the rose bushes planted beneath. It made bearing the insult much easier.

Rose and Susan were the last to leave Titanea's side. Rose didn't look at Joan when she passed but their hands brushed together discreetly. Her hair was still in the careful arrangement of twists and braids Joan had done for her last night.

Joan's face burned at the memory, and she found herself battling a very different kind of heat.

She glanced up to see Titanea smiling at her gently as she patted one of the pillows beside her. Joan crossed over to her and sat delicately. She laid her hands in her lap, letting Bia rest against the back of her wrist.

The hidden sword's hum was always louder near Titanea. By now, Joan found its thrum soothing, along with Ogun's pulsing heat in her chest. In the presence of such uncertainty, the feel of both were welcome constants.

'How are the players?' Titanea said suddenly. 'That is where you were, is it not?'

Joan stiffened. 'I don't—'

'Joan, you sweet, sweet girl' – she turned, her gaze locking directly on Joan's – 'don't lie.'

'I'm—'

Titanea surged forwards, grabbing Joan's chin in one hand. 'You will not lie to me again.' She pressed one sharp nail into Joan's skin as her blue eyes flashed brown. 'You will not lie in my presence again. Ever.'

Joan knew Titanea had invoked a boon even before the icy force washed over her. She cried out as the piercing pain hit her. The feeling overwhelmed her. It was as if every part of her body froze at once and her bones shattered into fragments.

'You know the pain will stop when you agree,' Titanea whispered gently. 'Will you lie before me again?'

Joan shook her head though she could barely move as her body trembled with pain and cold. 'No . . .' She forced the words out of a tight throat. She could barely breathe. 'No, I won't lie before you again.'

The chill disappeared immediately but the ache of it lingered, leaving her shaking violently. Joan could feel Bia's frantic pulsing at her wrist and wished more than anything she could draw the sword now.

Titanea pinched her chin again. 'What dark thought brings such fire to your eyes, Joan?'

'I'm imagining running you through,' Joan said, half startled by the words falling from her lips.

The queen burst into laughter and released her. 'You're welcome to try. Although you should consider the consequences of murdering the queen.' Her grin turned sharp. 'If not for yourself then for your family or your dear players. We might like to see that playwright hang for his audacious slander.'

The shiver that ran through Joan then was pure fear.

Titanea leaned back, raising her voice so the whole room could hear. 'But you need not worry, we love you still. Now go change. We're to hear a play, and we want you wearing something lovely instead of functional. You are dismissed.'

Joan didn't wait for any other instruction. She surged to her feet and bolted from the room.

Titanea had used the last of the boons Joan owed her. Relief flooded through her even as fear clenched her heart. That magic no longer loomed over her but oh, at what a cost. For where the first had been nearly squandered, the second had been used to perfection. With a single command, Titanea had made Joan a danger to all she loved.

What secrets could Joan keep if she couldn't lie? She might be forced to confess that they even now plotted with Baba Ben to restore the Pact and sought to send Titanea back to the Fae realm.

What havoc would she wreak then? Joan doubted any affection the Fae queen held for her would be dashed in the face of that truth. And Joan felt ill prepared for those consequences.

 lfie hated having the furthest stall in the meat market. After ten years of working in this spot in Smithfield – first with his parents and now by himself – he'd grown to expect a certain amount of theft. He still didn't like it, but at least it was no longer a shocking occurrence.

At least until these few days past.

What had once been a cut or two of meat disappearing a couple times a week – 'alms for the poor,' his father had called it, rest his soul – now he'd lose the stock of an entire table while his back was turned. Alfie didn't mind beggars taking a few shanks; folks needed to eat and if they were quick enough to not be caught, he wasn't one to raise an alarm and hunt them down. But this was too much. Hell, he'd be in the poorhouse along with them if this kept up. And with the crowds of buyers thinning with every day, Alfie found himself barely taking enough coin home even when he did sell all his wares.

He doubted Thurlow or Brun with their stalls at the centre of the long market had to deal with any such issues. And speak of the man, Alfie spotted Thurlow's sturdy form walking down the pathway towards him, his dark apron pulled taut over his large belly, his white-streaked black hair braided over one shoulder.

The man was more than three times Alfie's age, had taught him just as much about the market as his own father had. And one lesson had been to never leave your stall alone at midday.

Alfie wiped his hands off on his work cloth and hurried around the front to meet the old man. 'Something wrong, sir? What brings you all the way down here?'

'Alfie,' Thurlow said, his deep brown face ashen as his eyes darted between Alfie and the way from which he'd come. 'Alfie, my boy, go home early today. I'll watch your stall myself and bring you your pay come close.'

Alfie raised an eyebrow. 'Thank you kindly, sir, but I couldn't ask you—'

'No trouble. You should go.' Thurlow reached over and put a hand on Alfie's shoulder, the older man trembling hard enough to vibrate Alfie's whole slim body.

'Sir, what's—'

'Well, doesn't this all look fresh,' a smooth voice said.

Thurlow went suddenly still, his eyes locking with Alfie's. There was a pleading in them, something he'd never seen from the usually gruff old man. He would've asked more, but he had a customer. Alfie patted Thurlow's hand gently and turned to the woman looking over his collection of meats.

The woman was older than Alfie, but still quite young. She had a plain but pleasant face, her pale skin only slightly pinked by the sun. Her brown hair was tucked under a tan cap, and she held a basket on one arm. She smiled at Alfie, and he felt a chill race down his spine. He glanced at Thurlow, whose brow was covered in sweat.

What was happening?

'Are you all right, young man?' the woman asked, her voice far more soothing than her smile.

Alfie shook himself. 'Yes, ma'am, sorry, ma'am. How can I help?' He tried to move towards the woman but Thurlow's hand clamped down on his shoulder, squeezing like a vice.

'The boy was just heading off on an errand for me, ma'am,' the old man said as he stared pointedly at Alfie. 'I'll be the one helping you.'

Alfie started to speak but Thurlow's grip dug in hard enough to hurt. He clamped his mouth shut. Thurlow let go and slipped around to the back of the stall.

He leaned in close as he passed Alfie, his voice an urgent whisper. 'Run. For God's sake, Alfie, run while you can.'

'All this whispering' – the woman was suddenly in front of them, her eyes cutting from one to the other – 'will make me think you're talking about me.' She smiled again, and something about the curve and spread of her mouth felt wrong.

She tilted her head to the side, a move that reminded Alfie of his family cat when she scented a mouse. Between one blink and the next, her eyes shifted from brown to red. Something dribbled from beneath her cap and down along one side of her face and then the other, a deep crimson liquid that looked and moved like blood. Impossibly long fingers gripped her basket.

Fear greater than anything he'd ever experienced overtook Alfie in that moment. Why hadn't he listened? Why hadn't he run?

'Which of you shall I devour first? Young and supple?' The woman's smile spread to nearly split her face in half, her teeth sharpened to dangerous points. 'Or old and seasoned?'

'Oh my, this is inconvenient.'

Alfie dared to look away and saw two other women standing on the path just beyond his stall. Both had skin as brown as his own, though one was clearly wealthy – maybe a merchant's wife from the way she was dressed – while the one cowering a bit behind her, holding a basket of wrapped meats, must be her servant.

'Nan, dear' –the wealthy woman removed her cloak and passed it to her maid – 'you and these gentlemen find somewhere safe while I handle this.' She reached out and seemed to pull a shiny silver cane from thin air, never taking her eyes off the monster standing before his stall.

The maid jerked her head in a half nod then scampered towards Alfie and Thurlow. 'Come, come,' she hissed, 'the mistress has it handled.'

Alfie started to protest, but then Thurlow grabbed him by the shirt collar and dragged him after the small woman.

'Shall I eat them after I've finished you?' the monster cooed.

The wealthy woman laughed. 'It's funny that you think you'll have that chance.' She twirled her cane as if it were the most natural thing in the world. 'But you'll trouble these people no more.'

The monster dove for the woman, and Alfie lost sight of them as Thurlow dragged him down behind a table.

'Wait, we have to help her.' He tried to move but the old man's grip stayed firm. 'That woman, your mistress, she'll be killed. We have to help her!'

The maid shook her head rapidly, her eyes trained on the ground. 'No. No, Mistress Sands knows how to handle these creatures.' She looked up, locking eyes with Alfie. 'She'll be fine.' There was no doubt in her gaze though her hands still shook.

Her confidence was palpable but still . . . he had to be sure. He slowly eased up, lifting his head above the table just enough to get a clear view.

The wealthy woman ducked under the wild swing of a supernaturally long arm and struck out with her cane, cracking it across the monster's jaw. The thing shrieked as a smoking wound opened where the weapon had touched, then again as the woman hit it across the temple then the back of the neck.

Alfie dropped back to safety, his heart racing with fear and more than a little admiration, half in love with this avenging angel who'd stepped in to save them.

'But since we have time here together,' the maid hiding along with him blurted, 'how much are your lamb shanks today?'

Thurlow stared at her for a long moment before he burst into hysterical laughter. He nudged Alfie with an elbow. 'Well, tell her, my boy. Might as well make a sale.'

Alfie blinked rapidly, then, with a quick shake of his head to rattle his mind into its correct place, ran down his prices.

hen Joan arrived back at her room, Grace was carefully spreading a crimson dress on the bed. She had planned to change out of her serviceable black gown, as Titanea demanded, but she hadn't expected to be given something so striking. The fabric itself stood out in the dimness of London in winter, the brocade's colour bright and woven all through with cavorting peacocks in cream and a red so dark it was nearly purple. Matching slashed sleeves were striped in crimson and cream and gathered periodically along their length so they bubbled out multiple times until they cinched at her wrists.

The beauty of it had sent a burst of anger through her, for how could she complain about being put in something so lovely? And she absolutely wanted to complain. Instead, she asked Grace to help wind a crimson ribbon through her hair and set her pearl-and-silver hairpins in strategic places.

Her pleasure and distaste warred, one never fully overtaking the other, until Grace presented her with Titanea's final gift: a large, three-layered ruff. The curls of hard white fabric were incredibly uncomfortable. Even Grace grimaced as she pinned it securely around Joan's neck.

Ruffs were a luxury Joan had never desired to wear, and being forced into one had only proven her dislike well-founded. The stiff, curling white fabric circled her throat like a collar, and she could barely turn her head in any direction, but it made her posture impeccable.

Not a worthy trade-off – but Joan had to hold tightly to the positive aspects of her current situation lest her frustration appear plainly upon her face. As she found herself filing into the hall at the back of the queen's train alongside Snort, Titanea's calculation was unmistakable.

The crimson colour marked her as a member of the queen's household. It showed the power of Joan's position as a lady, but just as equally announced that she belonged to Titanea. A fact made much more true now that the queen had taken away Joan's ability to lie to her.

The only other person dressed in the same colour – besides the royal guard – was Rose, though her dress was less extravagant than Joan's. So went the Fae queen's affections, though Joan felt as much a captive as her friend.

Their group finally settled in their seats on the queen's dais, the false Susan and Snort claiming the chairs on either side of Titanea as soon as they had the queen comfortable in her own.

Joan let them – she had no desire to be seated beside the queen in this spectacle of a gown.

'Pardon me, Your Highness. If I might ask a favour?'

Joan glanced up at the familiar voice. William Cecil – dressed in expensive black velvet tailored to fit him perfectly – bowed before the queen, though his gaze was locked on Joan.

This couldn't be good.

'Might I request the company of Lady Clifford for the viewing of today's performance?' His voice held a balance of coy nonchalance and pleading that could only be perfected through years of practice in such volatile interactions.

Joan scowled at his feigned innocence and wished she could curse the boy outright. He was brazen, but he'd also obviously learned some subterfuge from his father the spymaster. If she hadn't known of his threats firsthand, she might've been charmed by him too.

As it was, she just wanted to punch him in the nose. She glanced at Titanea, knowing her answer but hoping against it nonetheless.

The queen smiled indulgently. 'Of course, young Lord Cranborne. Joan.' She waved Joan over towards William. 'Enjoy each other's company. Just not too much.' She laughed brightly.

Not-Susan and Snort joined in, a clutch of twittering birds. Only Rose remained silent, the frown on her face severe as she watched William.

Joan forced a smile, curtsying then stepping down to take William's extended arm. He patted her hand and grinned at her. She managed one quick glance back at Rose as the boy led her away.

Hopefully, this wouldn't be as troublesome as she feared.

'Father, it's as you said.' William presented Joan with a flourish as they reached his seats. 'Her Highness gave her permission. We may watch her for any untowards behaviour.'

Robert Cecil glared as if his gaze could incinerate her on the spot, then shifted to a soft smile as his son turned to face him.

She curtsied. 'Lord Salisbury.'

'Lady Clifford,' he said, then gestured to the girl sitting beside him. 'You must remember my daughter, Frances, from whom you filched your place as one of the queen's ladies.'

Frances nodded to her from her seat on her father's other side. Her worried gaze shifted from Joan to the immense ruff around her neck, then to William and back again.

Joan nearly scowled but then the absurdity of the moment hit her. Here she was, a lady-in-waiting to the queen of the Fae who wore the face of the dead mortal queen, dressed head-to-toe in crimson that marked her new station, on the arm of a boy who courted her by threat who was also the son of a man who wanted her dead, and collared by a ruff that completely blocked her from seeing her own feet. She might've laughed at her predicament but couldn't be sure a scream wouldn't burst forth instead.

'I'm ready for this play to begin.' King James's voice echoed through the hall. He sat on a separate platform closer to the stage, with Philip and Lord Fentoun flanking him on either side. Philip sent a single worried glance Joan's way before he turned his attention back to the king.

Cecil pointed to the empty space on the bench beside him. 'Sit, Lady Clifford.'

William watched her slide in between himself and his father.

Joan dared one glance at Rose. The other girl had one eyebrow raised and both lips pressed tightly together. She glared at William but sat too far away to do anything but that.

'Do try to enjoy the play,' William whispered as he patted her hand discreetly. His eyes settled on the gold ring she still wore and he smiled.

The musicians striking their first chord saved her from saying anything more.

They were nearing the end of the play, a frenzy of skirmishes that would end with Greece destroying Troy and leave a heartbroken and defeated

Troilus in the ruins of his home. Joan was sure she'd scored nail marks along the fabric of her skirts, such were her nerves watching each of the small running battles.

But her fellows had done blessedly well so far, their few stumbles small enough for only Joan to notice.

She took a deep breath and tried to relax herself as Nick ran onstage for the next scene.

Joan leapt to her feet, her heart in her throat. She couldn't watch this scene from here. She could scarcely breathe for all the anxiety she held between the botched fights onstage and the Cecil men flanking her.

'Pardon,' she said and slipped away before anyone could stop her. She positioned herself in the aisle between the raised stands and the edge of the queen's dais, tucked against the back wall. Here she could see the stage clearly while out of view of most of the audience whose benches sat above her.

Here she need not keep her worry invisible.

'O traitor Diomed! Turn thy false face, thou traitor,' Nick shouted, holding his sword aloft. 'And pay the life thou owest me for my horse!'

He wore a silver chest plate, dented but polished to a high shine, and his long black hair hung down his back in a loose braid. He looked incredibly dashing, but he always did as Troilus. It was the other reason Joan had committed the lines of this play to memory so easily.

A blonde man with pale skin ran in from the opposite entrance, also in shining armour and brandishing a sword. 'Ha! Art thou there?'

Diomedes, Troilus's Greek rival for Cressida's love. This was Samuel's part.

Joan's heart clenched at the memory of the boy who'd been murdered so ruthlessly by Auberon. The sight of him bloody and pale, the feel of him clenching her hand as the light left his eyes, that limp stillness when he'd died haunted her nearly every day. Perhaps if she'd been more clever, had recognised Auberon's ploy sooner, she could have saved her friend.

Or perhaps it would've made no difference at all.

Oliver Poole, the man the King's Men had hired to take over all of Samuel's parts, played well enough.

But Joan felt he was a pale comparison to the boy they'd lost. Oliver may have shared Samuel's height and blonde hair but something in his delivery lacked the cocksure bravado her friend had exuded so easily.

Not that she or any of them had said as much to Oliver, though they'd all felt it.

'I'll fight with him alone. Stand, Diomed.' Another hired man, this one with sleek black hair and golden tanned skin, appeared through the upstage entrance armed and armoured.

Jack Mills was their usual Ajax, had played the part in every performance since the play's first hearing. His well-practiced energy helped balance whatever Oliver lacked.

Joan had made a point of reviewing the fights with Oliver that morning, particularly this one that would have him facing off against Nick alongside Jack in a complicated travelling pass of swords that would move them across and off the stage. Even Samuel had messed this up on occasion, and all three players had earned scars from a missed step or some other hesitation.

But Oliver didn't have the benefit of nearly three years of practice.

'Why are you hiding here?'

Joan jumped as William Cecil whispered the words into her ear. Why was he so close?

He touched her arm with his other hand and leaned nearer still. 'Are you all right? I wouldn't think the swordplay could frighten you.'

Nick spun his sword with a flourish. *'Come, both you cogging Greeks.'* He pointed his weapon at Jack then Oliver. *'Have at you both!'*

Joan shushed the boy as her attention locked onto the stage. She felt every muscle in her body tense as Nick, Oliver and Jack rushed towards one another.

It will all be fine.

They'd practiced this twice this morning under her watchful eye. There was no need to fear.

Nick blocked Oliver's swing, swords ringing against each other. He stepped in and grabbed Oliver's wrist, spinning around his body and forcing the other man's blade up to knock against Jack's wild swing. Nick shoved Oliver against Jack, then hopped back out of reach as the two men collected themselves.

That was the first pass done with no mistakes. Joan released a breath and flexed the aching fingers she'd held fisted at her belly. They only had one more set of moves to do to carry them offstage, but this sequence was the most complex.

A hand gently slid along her face and she hissed, turning and coming nose to nose with William. Before she could react, he gripped the back of her neck and smashed their lips together.

Joan squawked in alarm as she pulled away.

'Don't,' he said firmly. 'If you do something I dislike, I'll tell my father immediately.'

Fear engulfed her again, though she glared at the boy with all the venom she could muster. He tucked her arm around his with a smile, patting her hand.

Damn this boy.

She turned her gaze back to the performers and locked eyes with Nick. The bare devastation on his face told her everything.

He'd seen William's kiss, her seeming acceptance, their linked arms now and assumed the worst.

Shite. Shite!

Nick looked lost for a moment before he dove back into his stage fight. He and Oliver charged towards each other, Nick swiping at Oliver in a cut that barely cleared the man's head as he ducked. Oliver drove his pommel up towards Nick's chin. Nick caught it with his free hand, then used all his weight to spin Oliver around behind him and shove him away with his foot. Nick dropped down as Jack's wide cut sailed over him, then rolled to the side. Jack's blade slammed into the floor right where he'd been. Nick sprang to his feet.

Joan's heart raced in her chest. They were doing what she'd taught but going entirely too fast, and Nick was a beat ahead.

But of course he was. He was distracted and distraught and both made this fight all the more dangerous.

Oliver attacked Nick's back and as he blocked, their swords connected barely a moment into the swing. Nick used his quillon to toss Oliver's sword into the air. Oliver let the momentum carry his weapon up and then braced for another shove that never came. Nick spun a move too soon.

No.

Joan's heart dropped. Time seemed to slow.

No.

Nick was supposed to push Oliver away, taking himself safely out of reach for Jack's stab to his gut. But they were too close, in true striking distance with Jack's blade, which was driving straight towards Nick.

No!

The blades were dull, but both men moved with enough force to run Nick through and make the damage worse for the sword's blunt edge.

'Stop!' Joan ripped herself away from William, reaching for the stage. The panic of her racing heart seemed to rush through her, and all her focus shifted to that moving blade. Her whole body went burning hot.

Don't.

Her fingertips felt like they were on fire. A picture appeared in her mind, as clearly as if she were watching it happen. The tip of Jack's blade turned liquid and harmlessly curled around Nick's waist before solidifying again.

Joan gasped, shivering as the intense heat she'd felt left her body all at once. The world around her slowly came into focus. She saw Nick, his arms held over his head as Jack's blade pressed into his belly. Both men stared at each other with wide eyes.

No!

Shame and despair flooded through Joan, though she wasn't sure what she'd hoped would happen from this far away. Despite all her power, she'd just allowed someone she loved to be harmed.

Suddenly, Nick brought his blade down in a tight arc that knocked Jack's off to the side. The sword swung away with no resistance, revealing the wide curve at its tip.

Just as Joan had imagined it.

Relief flooded her so quickly her knees buckled and she collapsed to the floor.

'*Come, both you cogging Greeks,*' he repeated his earlier line. '*Have at you both!*' Nick rolled along Jack's body then bolted offstage with the other two men following close behind.

The silent crowd burst into raucous cheers. All Joan could do was blink from where she'd dropped.

She'd done it. She'd saved Nick.

But how?

William crouched down in front of her and patted her head. 'Such a passionate reaction. It looks real but it's all pretend. No one really gets hurt. I thought you of all people would know that.' He pulled her to her feet. 'Now I'll return to our seats and you'll soon follow so we can watch the end of the play together.'

'Yes, yes, of course,' Joan said distractedly. She flexed her hand. 'Of course.'

William stood and with one last expectant look, walked back to where his father sat. Joan ignored the boy and his command, watching the next scene of the play from her place on the floor.

Her fingers still buzzed from the heat that had flowed through them. Heat from her controlling metal without touching it. Something she'd been sure she couldn't accomplish after her thrashing in Baba's workshop.

But she'd done it here, and if she'd managed it in the midst of breath-stealing panic, maybe, with training, she could use this power whenever she had the need.

Quietly, she curled her hand into a tight fist and laid it in her lap.

CHAPTER TWENTY-FOUR

Ever Running Before the Clock

nce the play had thankfully concluded – and Joan could finally calm her racing heart – all the actors cleared the stage save for Shakespeare, Armin, and Burbage.

'Lords and ladies,' Shakespeare said, his voice echoing through the large room, 'we humbly thank you for the attention you've paid our story and now offer you this gift.'

Burbage stepped forwards holding his hands aloft. 'A song from our dear Robert Armin, performed extempore.'

Armin's head whipped to Burbage as applause and excited chatter rushed through the crowd. Joan snorted into her fist as she tried to hold in her laughter. Armin hated making up songs on the spot, even though he was extremely skilled at it.

'Indeed,' the man said through clenched teeth. He turned to the musicians behind them and waved a hand. 'A madrigal, then. Mid-tempo, I think. One, two, three, four.' He snapped out the rhythm with his fingers, the music sweeping in after his count. They played through a couple bars before he began singing. *'Oh, love, where hast thou flown ere now—'*

Shakespeare and Burbage joined in immediately, encouraging the crowd to sing along as well. *'Oh, love, where hast thou flown ere now—'*

'When foul fair ladies break their vow?'

'When foul fair ladies break their vow?'

The audience laughed heartily and shout-sang along with Shakespeare and Burbage. Joan smiled at their enthusiasm, the noise bouncing around her where she still sat tucked between the stalls and the dais.

Someone touched her shoulder, and she looked up to see a woman standing over her.

She was about a head taller than Joan with a full figure embraced by a well-made gown of black and cream with gold detailing. Her skin was pale but held a hint of warmth, similar to Master Shakespeare's. Her spiralling curls of black hair were pinned atop her head and fixed with a band of brass and white ornaments.

'Come with me,' she said. Something behind Joan caught her eye and she jerked her head towards the door. 'Hurry.'

Joan turned to see William striding towards her, a scowl on his face.

Joan scrambled to her feet and followed after the woman who'd come to retrieve her, not caring where they were going in that moment. Her heart raced and she was sure her face showed some of her shock and fear. She'd like to think she wasn't running away from the boy, but her pace was far from leisurely. That look in William's eye promised dire consequences. She hated the panic his threat inspired.

'Did you choose to sit with Lord Cranborne,' the woman said as they slipped around behind the singing crowd and out into the hallway, 'or did Her Highness send you to be ogled by him?'

Joan snorted. 'Her Highness sent me at his request.' She clamped her mouth shut suddenly, realising what she'd confessed to a stranger.

'Mary's tit, that's worse,' the woman said before glancing around to ensure they were alone. She noticed some hesitation in Joan's expression because her pink lips tilted up in a smile. 'I'm Aemilia Lanier. Will has told me much about you, Joan.'

Joan's eyes widened. 'You're Master Shakespeare's friend at court?' The woman nodded, and Joan curtsied quickly. 'A pleasure to meet you, Lady Lanier.'

'It's Mistress Lanier, actually, but you may call me Aemilia.' Her brown eyes twinkled, and she winked at Joan before leading them along a winding path of wood-panelled walls and endless sconces.

Joan looked around, the halls around them suddenly becoming quite familiar. 'Where are we going?'

'I was asked to get you a bit more time with your company.' Aemilia looked around before slipping them both through a side door that opened into the preparation area for the King's Men. 'Use it wisely.'

James appeared from nowhere, and Joan stumbled back as he flung himself into her arms. He grunted as the ruff she wore forced his upper body backwards at a sharp angle.

'This thing is hideous. Why would you ever wear it?' He pulled away and dragged her over to his curtained dressing area.

'Titanea made me. Listen, James, I have to tell you—'

He pushed her down onto his stool then pulled at the ruff. 'Where are the pins for this?'

'On the left side,' Joan said automatically, shoulders relaxing as he pulled the monstrosity from around her neck. 'But I have to tell you—'

'Less talking more unlacing. We don't have much time to trade.'

Joan frowned. 'Trade?'

She took a good look at her brother, who still wore his Cressida gown. But instead of the wig of flowing black curls, he wore one that had a sweep of dark brown twists and braids pinned up and twined with a crimson ribbon.

Styled exactly like her hair.

'What's going on?' she blurted.

James huffed out a breath but kept unlacing the back of his green dress. 'Do you want to ask questions or do you want some time with Nick?'

'What?'

He rolled his eyes. 'Questions, then. We're trading clothes so while you talk to Nick, I can walk about with Aemilia pretending to be you. Now are you done?'

She pointed at the wig. 'Who . . . ?'

'Ah, Roz did it during the play. Quite the match, isn't it?' He flapped his hands at her. 'Now move, you're wasting the time you could be spending with Nick.'

Joan shook herself and snapped into action. James was right, she was wasting the precious time her friends had given her.

When James put on the crimson dress with the ruff and the wig, he did look like her match. They were twins, after all. Besides, she doubted anyone here knew her well enough to pick out the subtle differences in their faces.

'Can you get here tonight,' Joan said as he adjusted his hair in the mirror, 'around the strike of one by the Abbey clock?'

James nodded, tugging at the sleeves of his – her – dress. Westminster Abbey sat closest to Whitehall, its hourly bells easy to hear from within the palace.

Joan clasped his hand. 'You and mother must retrieve me from here, then we'll go to Baba. Time is of the essence and we have to try to contact that ancestor tonight.'

'It shall be done,' James said. 'Now good luck.' He slipped through the curtain to find Aemilia, turning around and winking at Joan just before he disappeared.

Joan rolled her eyes and checked herself in James's mirror needlessly. The green Cressida dress was beautiful, she knew that, but the thought of seeing Nick had her tugging and brushing at the fabric's imaginary imperfections.

'Joan.'

She spun. Nick stood just inside the alcove, the heavy curtain swinging back into place behind him. He'd removed his armour and now stood in only a shirt and his trousers. His thick black hair hung around his shoulders in soft waves that Joan suddenly longed to run her fingers through. He strode over to her in two long steps, caught her face gently between his hands, and kissed her deeply.

Joan moaned and clutched at his arms as his soft lips pressed against hers. Every thought left her mind but his lilac-and-sandalwood scent and the play of his muscles beneath his shirt. He tilted his head, deepening their kiss. Heat rushed through her as she felt his tongue slip into her mouth.

Yes . . .

He pulled away suddenly. 'You saved me,' he said, breaths coming quick and harsh. 'When Jack nearly ran me through, you bent the sword.'

'I did,' she said, trying to focus on what was being said and not the movement of his lips or the flex of his arms. 'You ... you need to remember your timing.'

His eyes went wide. 'Ah, I'm sorry, I ...' He stepped away from her, hands dropping to his sides as his face went carefully blank. 'If my suit has become an inconvenience for you—'

'No,' she blurted.

An inconvenience? Never.

His gaze landed on the gold ring before he cleared his throat and looked away. 'I do love you, Joan—'

He loved her? Her heart soared at the words. She'd known his feelings deep enough to want to court her, but hearing him name it so directly was different. She couldn't have kept the smile from her face even if she'd tried.

'—but if you'd rather someone befitting your current station, I will withdraw.'

The memory of Nick's face, the briefest moment of devastation laid bare as he'd seen William Cecil kiss her.

He thought she wanted William Cecil?

No. Never.

'I've despised nothing more than the kiss I received from that boy today,' she said firmly. She tore the gold ring from her finger and dropped it to the floor.

Nick's eyes widened. '"Despised"? But ... you didn't ...'

'Nick,' she said firmly as she placed her hands on his chest, 'I love you, but please stop talking.' She grasped his shirt and hauled him down for another kiss.

He responded quickly, his body leaning in close. She knew the moment her words registered in his mind because his arms wrapped around her back and crushed her tightly against him.

He groaned and she slipped her arms up around his neck. His hand against her back held their bodies together so she could feel every hard angle of him. She speared her fingers through his soft hair as his touch threatened to overwhelm her.

He nuzzled her chin and released a low hum that seemed to vibrate through her whole body. 'I'd like to . . . May I?' His hand rested against her skirt and she knew exactly what he was asking.

She shifted so she could gaze into his eyes, darker and more beautiful than she'd ever seen them.

May I give you this gift?

The memory of Rose's words, whispered in the dark of night, made her pull back. 'Nick, wait.'

'Yes,' he said, pressing kisses along her neck.

Joan leaned into him for a moment longer, the feel of his lips making her dizzy. He moaned against her skin, and she thought her knees might buckle. She gently pushed against his shoulders. She couldn't think when he did that, and she needed her wits about her now. He leaned back, his half-lidded gaze nearly making her dive back into kissing him again.

But no. Love was involved, and she needed to be honest. Whatever the consequences, she owed all their hearts that.

'I love you, Nicholas Tooley,' she blurted, fear clenching her chest as she watched him. 'But I also love another.'

He jerked back as if she'd stuck him.

'It will never be William Cecil,' she hissed. 'Nor any man but you.'

Realisation bloomed over his face. 'It's that girl, Rose, isn't it?'

She nodded. Her words seemed to be caught in her throat.

'I see,' he said quietly.

She threw her arms around his waist, burying her face in his shirt. 'Please, Nick, please don't doubt my feelings for you.' She willed the tears not to fall.

'There was a time I fancied myself in love with Master Shakespeare,' he said suddenly. He rubbed his hands along her back. 'He is, of course, far too old for me.'

Joan looked up at him, face stricken.

'This is not to doubt your feelings for Rose.' He ran his fingers along her cheek. 'But rather to say that in seeing how he and Mistress Shakespeare are together, I believe there is room for more than one person in the human heart.'

Stop thinking of what's proper when you could have both of us.

Joan leaned into his touch, the relief that rushed through her making her dizzy.

'Love us both or neither,' he said, pulling away to smile at her. 'It won't change my feelings for you, Joan Sands.'

She gazed into his eyes, darker and more beautiful than she'd ever seen them. It made her bold. She slid her hand up along the back of his neck, felt him shiver at her touch. 'Swear it.'

'With all my heart.'

And she drew him in for a deep kiss.

CHAPTER TWENTY-FIVE
To Trust the Air

he bell at Westminster Abbey rang one as Joan slipped through the door of the storage room where the players usually changed. She'd donned her black cloak and retraced her steps from earlier. Most of the palace lay asleep at this late hour, still she'd stuck to the shadows along her route as a precaution. Fortunately, she'd not encountered a single soul.

James and the company had bought her nearly an hour with Nick. When she and James had finally switched back, he'd told her how he'd spent the time avoiding William Cecil and Titanea both. Joan felt sorry for his struggle but she wouldn't have given up a moment with Nick to save her brother from it.

Even now excitement still thrummed through her and made it easy for her to stay awake this late.

She eased the door shut behind her, waiting until it clicked closed before she dared pull the shutters on the lantern she held. A few moments later, a shimmering doorway opened in the middle of the room. She stepped through without a word and came out into the cell in the Tower of London, her mother and brother already preparing for their ceremony.

Baba Ben looked up at her from where he sat on the floor with his legs crossed. When he recognised her, he turned back to his task. His fingers flew across a handkerchief pulled taut on a small wooden embroidery hoop, working a needle and thread. A lump of silvery metal lay near him.

Her mother crouched close by, James huddled beside her as he poured oils into a basin of water at her direction. She glanced up at Joan, twisting her hand to close the doorway behind her.

'We'll begin as soon as Ben is ready,' she said, the slightest hint of tension in her voice.

Baba scowled but stayed focused on his design, an intricate pattern of sunflowers bursting across the white fabric.

Watching him push and pull the thread expertly almost felt normal. But this stark cell loomed far more menacingly than the warmth of his shop's workroom. Its darkness seemed to devour Joan's very life force, leaving her weak. The weight of despair was overwhelming. She couldn't imagine how her godfather felt having been trapped here for months.

The act of creation soothed him. They were similar in that, had connected over it multiple times throughout the years. But not even this task could banish the weariness that drooped his eyes and slumped his shoulders.

He doesn't deserve this.

Joan swore she'd return him to his home and his art. Before they resealed the Pact and removed Titanea from the crown, Joan would use her new place at court to ensure his release.

Even as she thought it, an icy wind battered the high windows, rattling the glass before slipping through to whip around the room. The stone walls and wooden floor held the chill covetously and robbed the cell of any warmth.

Baba flexed his fingers for a moment before setting back to his task. 'Are you keeping safe at court?'

'Yes,' Joan lied. She cleared her throat and shifted to a half-truth. 'It's far more boring than I'd imagined.'

Her godfather hummed. 'Fascinating. I wouldn't call a duel with the captain of the king's guard "boring," but perhaps such things are more novel for youths.'

'How did you find out about that?' Joan said, her whole face going hot.

He raised an eyebrow. 'Your mother told me.'

'Mother knows?' Joan flinched, glancing over her shoulder as her mother shot her a reproachful look.

Oh yes, her mother absolutely knew.

He looked directly into her eyes. 'Every battle isn't meant to be won.' Something in his expression shifted, and he suddenly seemed far away. 'Sometimes the only way to win is by losing.'

'I'm sorry,' she said, wrapping her arms around herself. She always managed to disappoint her godfather, no matter how hard she tried. She'd make it up to him once they renewed the Pact and freed him of this place. She'd prove she could be a proper goddaughter.

He sighed then grabbed the metal beside him – a slab of iron, she reasoned – pulling a piece off as if it were wet clay and not solid metal. He touched it to his wrist. It slid around his arm easily as he fashioned it into a bracelet. He held the remaining nugget of iron against the handkerchief.

Tiny threadlike tendrils burst from the slab's edges and wove themselves through the fabric.

Satisfied, he released the tension on the hoop and removed the handkerchief. As he held it up, the sunflowers sparkled in the light, infused as they were with bits of iron.

'Carry this with you,' he said. He laid the cloth over his palm. 'Should you need a weapon . . .' The iron fragments sprang up at his touch, gathering into a sharp point at the centre of the handkerchief before flowing back into the design.

Joan reached for it, a smile crossing her lips. 'Thank you, Baba.' She felt the metal singing through it as soon as it touched her fingers. 'I'll keep it close, but . . .' She laid the cloth in her lap then tugged at the sword that hung round her wrist. Bia unwrapped itself, straightening and growing as it sprang into her hand. 'I'm always armed.'

Bia hummed as it always did but much more loudly. The sound seemed to vibrate Joan's very bones. She tightened her grip and tried to breathe through the sensation.

'Where did you get this blade?'

Joan looked up at Baba, whose face had gone grey. His wide eyes stared first at the sword then at her, his breath suddenly coming in quick puffs.

'I . . .' She bit her lip, trying to focus through Bia's humming, which kept growing louder and louder. 'It came to me at the theatre, I'm not sure how.'

Was she shouting? It felt like she was, but she could barely hear anything else over the sword's noise. Her godfather reached out for the blade and Joan felt panic rush through her as his fingers closed around the hilt.

No! It's not meant for his hand!

She shook her head, the words ringing in her ears in a repeating shriek that seemed to rattle her skull. She breathed deeply and let him take the sword from her shaking hands.

He stared at it, fingers brushing over the dogs engraved along the hilt and guard. His eyes narrowed in concentration as he tried to make Bia change.

Take it back. Take it back!

It screamed in Joan's head.

'Baba,' she said, her voice hoarse in her own ears, 'may I have it back?' She reached for the sword, fingers outstretched and trembling. 'Please.'

He looked up in alarm. Whatever he saw in her face had him shoving the hilt back into her grip and clasping her hands around it. Immediately the wailing stopped and Bia's hum became more bearable.

Her breath rushed out of her in a huff as she doubled over, clutching the sword to her chest.

'Ben, what's happening?' her mother half shouted as she hurried over. 'No, James, keep working.'

Joan felt her godfather wrap his arms around her and leaned into him as she tried to calm her breathing.

He rubbed her back in soothing circles as he spoke to her mother. 'What was it Ogun said when he came down? That we have all we need.' He squeezed her, his grip almost too tight. 'We do, right here.'

'Bia is the key,' Joan said as realisation washed over her. She pulled back, looking between her mother and her godfather. 'We need this blade to forge a new Pact.'

Baba smiled at her, his eyes sad. 'Yes, and only you can wield it.'

Joan gasped, her heart beating hard in her chest even as she knew his words to be true. She'd felt like she was dying when Baba had held the sword for a mere moment. Bia had chosen her, but for what?

Shouting and the sound of boots rushing up the stairs echoed outside the room. Goodfellow appeared suddenly in the room, breathing heavily, their eyes wide and wild.

'You have to go,' they whispered harshly, 'someone's coming—'

Baba tensed beside her. 'Bess, take the children and leave.'

Someone slammed into the cell door before the metallic scraping of a key in the lock sent them all scrambling. Joan's mother leapt to her feet, drawing the shape of her doorway in the air. James tipped his basin of water onto the floor, filling the cell with the scent of fragrant oils. Baba pulled Joan up alongside him, and she shrank Bia again. She wrapped it around her wrist where it clanged lightly against the gold bracelet and charms her father had given her.

The door creaked on its hinges as it began to swing open before Goodfellow stopped it with the heel of their foot. They flapped their hands frantically, urging them all to hurry.

'This sword is the key,' Baba repeated as he hugged Joan tightly. 'Do not let it out of your sight.'

Joan pulled out of his arms. 'Yes, but we need you to figure out the rest. Come on.' She tugged him towards her mother's doorway. 'Please. What good is having the sword if you don't tell me how to use it?'

The voices outside grew louder even as they were muffled by the heavy wooden door.

'Keep that handkerchief with you,' Baba whispered, 'in case you get challenged again.' He slipped his hands from hers and pushed her away.

She reached for him, panic rising in her. 'No, Baba, please. I need you to help me. We can't do this without you.'

'You have everything you need,' he said softly. 'Go. You can't be found here and I can't be found gone.'

James grabbed her arm, tugging her away even as she scrambled to grab Baba again.

Damn Titanea and her commands. Joan needed to get her godfather out of here. They could deal with the consequences once they were all safe.

The door rattled with a heavy thud as someone rammed their shoulder against it. Baba's gaze locked with Goodfellow's as the two communicated some secret over her head.

Baba smiled down at her. 'Make me proud, Joan.'

Goodfellow rushed her, snagging her around the waist with one arm and grabbing James with the other. The three of them slammed into her mother, then collapsed through the magical doorway in a heap. Joan scrambled to her feet, determined to drag Baba to safety if she had to. However stubborn he might be, she was worse.

The door to Baba's cell screamed on its hinges as a man shoved it open.

'That's him,' the man growled as two others stepped into the cell behind them.

No!

She stumbled forwards, Bia leaping into her grasp. Goodfellow grabbed her shoulder to wrench her away, but Joan twisted out of their grip. She dove back towards the cell as the magical doorway blinked out of existence. Joan went sprawling across the floor in its absence, left with nothing but air and silence in the darkness of the storage room in the palace.

She met Goodfellow's gaze, rage stealing her words. They clenched their jaw and disappeared.

Shock overcame Joan for a moment before she spun on her mother, who crouched on the floor, her hand still outstretched.

'I—' She blinked at Joan and her face crumpled in horrified despair.

James stood slowly, rubbing the arm he'd fallen on. 'Goodfellow will protect Baba.' The words came haltingly, as if he barely believed them himself. 'It will be all right.' He nodded distractedly and turned to pick up the broken pieces of the basin behind him.

The anger flooded out of Joan all at once, replaced with an anguish so deep she trembled with it.

CHAPTER TWENTY-SIX
Courtly & Fashionable Performance

oan jerked awake, pulled from her restless sleep by some unknown thing. She pressed a hand against her racing heart and tried to tell herself there was no fight imminent. Bright sunlight peeked in through her curtained windows. The last she remembered, after leaving behind her mother and brother and dragging herself back to her rooms, was lying awake in the darkness too afraid to sleep because what if Baba was . . .

No. She wouldn't give that thought life.

The blazing sun meant she'd slept, even if it felt like she hadn't.

Knock. Knock. Knock.

She turned to the door and felt her nerves settle. That impatient rapping must've woken her. She huffed out a breath and pressed her palms against eyes that felt dry and swollen.

'One moment,' she called as she dragged herself out from under the covers. She pulled her robe from the hook near her bed and wrapped it around herself as she rushed to the door.

Joan swung it open, and Grace dipped into a curtsy immediately. She held a silver tray balanced on one hand, a sealed letter and a sprig of holly propped at the centre of it.

Her eyes darted up and down the hall before her smile shifted into a grimace. 'A message for you, my lady.'

Joan frowned. She knew immediately from the crisp, nearly white paper and gold-flecked seal that it was from a wealthy sender. That didn't bode well. She stepped aside and waved Grace in before closing the door.

'Do you know who it's from?' Joan said. She plucked the letter and the holly from the tray and sat at her dressing table to read it.

Grace shook her head. 'It was given to someone else, but as soon as I heard it was for you I offered to deliver it myself.' She relaxed a little, leaning against Joan's bed as she flipped the tray in her grip. 'I wondered if you'd prefer a friendly ear to help plan your response.'

Joan smiled gratefully at the girl then turned her attention back to the letter. The *C* pressed into the gilded wax narrowed her list of suspects, though Joan wasn't sure which of the two Cecil men she dreaded hearing from more.

'Damnation,' she said as she cracked the seal.

Lady Clifford,

It would please me greatly if you would agree to be my guest at the Old Palace Yard in Westminster for this afternoon's occasion. I have already acquired Her Highness's approval and eagerly await your acceptance.

Yours truly,

William Cecil
Lord Cranborne

Joan cursed and threw the letter onto her table. The memory of William's actions at yesterday's performance turned her stomach. She'd already removed his ring, transforming it into another bearing her father's signature designs and passing it along to Grace to keep or sell as she saw fit.

Joan had no idea what occasion William spoke of in the letter, but he'd already informed Titanea of his intentions so Joan knew denial wasn't an option. She'd have to spend more time with William and his miserable father. A sudden chill overtook her as she remembered the cold look on William's face when she'd refused to return to his side.

Was this his moment to follow through with his threats? Was she being forced into a trap?

'What does it say?' Grace came closer, her face full of concern.

Joan shook her head and gestured towards the letter as if it were a poisonous snake waiting to strike.

'I can't read.' Grace glanced down at it, then handed it to Joan. 'You'll have to tell me what it says.'

Joan sat up, her face burning red immediately. 'Ah, I'm sorry! I didn't realise.' She fumbled with the letter. 'I could teach you, if you'd like.'

'I'm not ashamed of it,' Grace said gently. She laid a hand on Joan's shoulder and squeezed. 'I know what I need, and it serves me well. I know that holly means that whoever sent this to you is hoping for something.'

Joan sighed and dropped her face into her hands. 'Not hoping but demanding. William Cecil has invited me to be his guest today, and the queen has approved it.'

'An unwanted but unavoidable suit.' Grace nodded and strode over to Joan's wardrobe. She flung the doors open. 'We'll need the appropriate armour for such a battle.' She grinned at Joan. 'I may not read, but this I know quite well.'

Some time and several bouts of panic later, another knock sounded at Joan's door.

'Just a moment,' Joan called.

Grace finished securing the laces at the back of her deep-blue-and-gold dress and moved to tie the sleeves. Joan took over one of the sleeves, while Grace hurriedly handled the other, closing all four loops in the time it took Joan to do two. Grace smiled then crossed to open the door.

'Joan.'

She spun at the sound of her name to see Rose standing in the hall.

'Why are we meeting with Robert Cecil today?' she said as she strode into the room.

Grace locked eyes with Joan quickly and smiled again before she slipped out, closing the door behind her.

Joan dropped the last sleeve string and turned to Rose. 'His son William has requested my company.' She gestured towards the letter that sat open on her dressing table before plucking up the sprig of holly. 'Are you coming with me?'

'I am.' Rose quickly tied Joan's sleeve then let her fingers slide down the length of her arm. 'Her Highness is sending me as your chaperone.'

Joan shivered at the touch before the words truly hit her. 'He wants to marry me. Will she force it on me?' Her stomach heaved, and she tasted bile at the back of her throat.

'She can't,' Rose said, grabbing both of Joan's shoulders. 'She can command it, but you don't have to listen.'

Relief rushed through Joan so quickly her knees buckled. Rose caught her under the elbows, pulling her close to keep her upright.

A mirthless laugh burst from her. 'She could have.' Another laugh. 'I owed her two boons but she's used them both.' She couldn't stop now, the sound tumbling from her. 'She could have commanded me to do anything, but she's used them both.' Her belly hitched. She couldn't breathe.

The memory of that icy pain made her bones ache and her muscles clench. Yes, she was trapped here at court. Yes, she could no longer lie before the Fae queen. But what more could she have been forced into doing? What hells could Titanea have wrought on Joan's life for her own entertainment?

Another disaster had been so close, avoided so narrowly.

She took a gasping breath. Her head felt light, the room suddenly growing dimmer. She heard Rose calling her name but she couldn't—

Then gentle hands slid over her face and soft lips pressed against her own. Joan blinked then melted into the kiss, her racing heart settling into a steady, hard thump.

'It's all right,' Rose whispered, stroking her hair. 'She's used them up. You're safe.' She pressed their foreheads together. 'We can tell William Cecil to go to hell if you'd like.'

Joan sighed, feeling her breathing calm to match Rose's. 'I want to but he's sworn to tell his father if I refuse him. I don't know if the man would rejoice or try to have me beheaded. Likely both.'

'I'm with you, and together we can thwart whatever that boy has planned.'

Joan laced their fingers together and smiled. She'd make it through today with Rose by her side.

But some creeping fear still slipped its fingers around her heart. The anxiety of last night's desperate flight from the Tower lingered while this day felt off-kilter on its own, as if danger lurked just beyond her vision. She dreaded finding out what misfortune awaited.

he carriage navigated through a roiling crowd of people as it arrived at the Old Palace Yard at Westminster. When she alighted, Joan noticed several wooden platforms had been assembled and set throughout the large courtyard. The gallows stood tall, the central stage around which the multitude of spectators gathered, and framed by the gaping front of the ruined House of Lords. Joan reached out, and Rose's hand slipped into hers.

She felt the same about public executions as she did about bearbaiting. The brutality of watching a life expire for sport always set her on edge. She looped her arm through Rose's and felt the other girl press in close.

Today would prove challenging indeed.

'Ah, Lady Clifford.' William Cecil approached them, his lips pressed into a thin line. He wore all black, the only exception being his white stockings and the glimpses of his shirt peeking through his slashed sleeves. 'I'm glad you've come. This way. We have the most excellent vantage point.'

He held out his arm, glaring when Joan didn't move. She reluctantly slipped away from Rose to join the boy. Rose squeezed her fingers as they parted, then fell into step behind William and Joan. The three ascended the steps to a high platform. Several velvet chairs had been placed under a canvas shelter shielding both from the sun and the day's chill wind.

'They're executing the rest of the traitors of the Gunpowder Plot,' William said as he guided her towards where his father stood. 'It's terribly exciting.'

Joan frowned. Yes, they'd arrested men plotting to kill the king, the ones who'd originally planted those barrels of gunpowder, but Titanea had been the one to see the plan to a sort of success. Of course, none would believe it, especially if Joan did the telling.

William glanced at her, eyes sparkling. 'Father seemed glad to have you come today. I believe we are well on our way to him accepting you as my wife.'

Joan doubted it completely but kept silent.

Robert Cecil stood at the edge of the platform, hands clasped behind his back. He glanced over when they approached, his expression unreadable as he laid eyes on Joan. She looked away, anxiety rising in her chest. Challenging Cecil today felt particularly dangerous. He was in complete control here, and he'd no doubt exercise his powers against her should she give him the slightest reason.

'Take your seats, William,' Cecil said, his voice gentle as he spoke to his son. 'We'll begin soon.'

William grinned, then dragged Joan over to the chairs. A trio of them sat ahead of the others.

He handed Joan into one in the centre then glanced up at Rose. 'Ah, your lady can sit behind us.'

Joan forced a smile to her lips, making brief eye contact with Rose as the girl moved to settle into the chair behind her.

William sat on her right, and Joan glanced warily at the empty one on her left.

'Will your sister be joining us today?' she asked.

William laughed. 'No, Frances hates these sorts of things. She says it's too monstrous.'

Cecil turned then, as if sensing her panic. He strolled over to them in his usual slow way, eyes locked on Joan.

She lifted her chin. She refused to fidget under his glare, however fast her heart raced.

He slid into the seat beside her, his unnerving stare constant. 'Have you witnessed many executions, Lady Clifford?'

'I have not, my lord.' She kept her words curt but unfailingly polite.

She and her family avoided public executions, and even though Joan herself had killed – had beheaded Auberon with her own hands. Watching the life leave someone's eyes changed your relationship with death.

Cecil leaned back as if he'd heard her thoughts. 'Well, you are used to violence in other venues. I will warn that the castration and evisceration tend to become quite noisy. Such is the fate for traitors to the crown.' He smiled then, and Joan had never hated an expression more. 'The burning of witches tends to be a quieter affair. Perhaps you'll attend such an occasion one day.'

Zounds.

Cecil knew her secrets and should he reveal them, Joan doubted anything could save her from the fire.

A guard stepped into place beside Cecil, the sharp blade of his halberd glinting in the light. Joan swallowed and laid her sweating hands in her lap. Murmurs and shouts rumbled through the crowd as the clacking of wooden wheels echoed on the courtyard's stones. Boos and cheers rose in equal measure rising to a cacophony.

The prisoners had arrived.

Something on the cart rolling in caught her eye, an odd shift of the light. She looked past Cecil and there, with the other traitors headed to their death, lay one glowing figure. His swollen and raw face gave no clue as to his identity. Joan faintly remembered a man who stood with Herne in the undercroft that November morning. This had to be him, but how had he allowed himself to be caught?

This man was one of the Fae. Did they know that only iron could kill him?

'One last thing before we get underway, Lady Clifford,' Cecil said suddenly.

She turned but didn't speak as Cecil leaned closer.

'The storage rooms of the Banqueting House are no place for a young girl to be at night.' A smile spread across his lips, cocky and knowing. 'Nor is the Tower of London.'

Joan's heart jerked, then beat double-time.

No. How did he . . . ?

William looked up at her. 'Are you well? Is this too much for you?'

Joan blinked. When had she even stood? She couldn't think. The air seemed too close, too thick. How did you breathe again?

'Nonsense,' Cecil said. 'I'm sure she's fine. Do not depart yet.' Cecil grabbed her wrist and jerked her back down into her seat. 'The excitement is just beginning.'

He smiled at her again, and she pressed her trembling hands into the fabric of her skirts to hide her fear.

CHAPTER TWENTY-EIGHT

Interlude – The Execution of 'Guy Fawkes'

he incredible noise of the crowd nearly drowned out the three men weeping and praying in the cart alongside him. Guy Fawkes likely would've cried out to his God in concert with his fellow prisoners, but Guy Fawkes had died long ago, devoured by the being who now wore his shape.

Not-Guy Fawkes's head lolled to one side, where he let his gaze take in the mortals gathered for this execution. Their delicious bloodlust tasted sweet on his tongue. He gorged himself on it, greedily drinking both that and the fear of his fellows. The immense torture they'd subjected him to had broken this body so expertly he'd been a breath from death – had he been mortal. But as a being of nightmares and darkness, their lashes and burning and rending of bones fed him like mother's milk. Between the pain of their rough handling and the despair flowing through the very walls of the Tower of London, he found himself so delightfully full he could barely move.

It had been too long since he'd fed so well. While the rest of the Wild Hunt roamed freely, he'd been trapped wearing this mortal's shape. But he'd soon be free.

The cart jerked to a stop, and guards dragged a screaming Thomas Wintour up to the scaffold. Not-Guy rolled his head to watch as the man thrashed and sobbed. The executioner slipped the rope around Thomas's neck, and Not-Guy knew the moment he lost hope. He drank up that devastation with a groan of overfull pleasure.

Thomas hung from the noose for a long while, body jerking this way and that as he suffocated, eyes bulging and pale face red with the strain. They cut him down just as his twitching slowed, refusing him the grace of an easy death. The crowd cheered as they then dragged him away, gasping and moaning, and fixed him to a wooden table.

When the knife took his genitals, the monstrous screams filled Not-Guy's ears like the sweetest music. The agony and fear joined with the excitement and pleasure and slid down his gullet as honeyed as the best dessert. He sighed where he lay in the cart, bringing his shackled hands to rub his distended belly.

Thomas died not long after they split him open to draw out his innards. Not-Guy nearly wept at the loss of such delightful pain. Would that Thomas had lived through to being cut to pieces. The air went still with that life extinguished, though both Not-Guy and the crowd bubbled with anticipation. There were three left to be punished, two to be tormented ahead of him.

Ambrose Rookwood's sobbing prayers grew to hysterical shrieks as they dragged him forth next. Next to Not-Guy, Robert Keyes left off his pleas heavenwards and merely wept. Not-Guy chuckled in his true voice, the sound hoarse and rattling like old dry bones in a jostled coffin.

Robert looked up, his pale face splotchy and wet with tears and snot. 'You laugh at the hour of our death?'

'I laugh for my freedom,' Not-Guy whispered. He longed to release this mortal shape, to prowl the night with his kin. Yes, he'd eat his fill of the horrors here and rejoice in the feast, but he belonged with the Hunt.

And soon to the Hunt would he return.

Cheers rose again, then throat-tearing cries as the executioners set their knives to Ambrose's flesh.

'Relish your last moments, Robert,' Not-Guy said, grinning as Ambrose's anguish washed over him. 'The torment sounds agonising.' His gaze drifted over to his fellow prisoner, the smile cracking his dry lips so he tasted blood. He licked it away.

Robert went white as his shirt. 'God have mercy, they've driven you mad.' His shackles clanked as he frantically crossed himself, not hiding his Catholic faith in these final moments.

Not-Guy bared his teeth and, for a second, let them reveal their sharp points as his eyes shifted to their natural fathomless black. He felt Robert's terror wash over him in a delightful rush. He groaned and closed his eyes.

Then he felt Ambrose die.

He lifted his head, locking his inky gaze with Robert's. 'Don't die right when they rip your guts out. I'm not yet full.'

'What are you?' Robert whispered, scrambling away from him in the cart. 'Monster.' The sudden weight change shifted the whole cart to one side. 'Demon. A demon from hell!' Then they plucked Robert from the cart and dragged him to the gallows.

Not-Guy closed his eyes. A feast of this magnitude happened so rarely, he wanted to truly enjoy these last moments of mortal agony.

When Robert died in a rush of panic as the knife split open his belly, Not-Guy opened his eyes. This was it.

They'd drag him to the gallows to be hung and castrated and eviscerated, then cut into pieces to mount on their great bridge. There Herne and the Wild Hunt would find him. They'd gather his pieces and welcome him home, where he'd make himself whole and true again.

The executioners pulled him from the cart and dragged him up the wooden stairs. One held his swaying body while the other tightened the noose around his neck.

He enjoyed this torment, but most of all he anticipated the freedom to come. He felt the rough rope pressing into his skin. Yes, that joy lay close at hand.

But now? Now he'd give them a show.

The noose went taut, pulling just enough to lift his heels off the boards. Not-Guy grinned again and flung himself towards the crowd.

His body flew over the side of the high platform, then jerked to a sudden stop as the rope reached its end. The crowd gasped, some screaming as the bones in his neck snapped with a loud crack. His head hung at an odd angle and he swung back and forth like a forgotten toy.

They thought him dead, but he knew himself to be finally alive again. Let them cut and carve. He'd be home come nightfall.

But, just to enjoy his last tastes of disgust and fear, he let the smile linger on his face.

A fine finish to the best feast of his life.

CHAPTER TWENTY-NINE
Thy Sands Have All Run Out

oan turned her face away as the Fae prisoner launched himself from the gallows. Suffering through the brutality of the rest had already been awful – she needn't see this final act.

Cecil proved his point. The traitors had been executed and Joan could follow them into the grave whenever the man chose. She felt numb with fear, too exhausted to even be reckless.

She wanted to go home.

She felt William's eyes on her.

'Apologies, Lord Salisbury, Lord Cranborne,' she said, pushing to her feet and swallowing against the lump in her throat, 'but I'm afraid today's excitement was too much for me. If you'll pardon my abrupt departure.'

William leaned back in his seat and gave her a considering look. 'Are you sure? There is more yet to see.'

'No,' she blurted. 'No, it's fine. I've seen enough of your father's great victory.' She dipped into a brief curtsy and felt Rose come up and take her arm on her other side. 'Congratulations to you, Lord Salisbury.'

William glanced down at her hand and a scowl overtook his face. 'You took off my ring.'

'What ring?' Cecil said, his expression going cold as he stood.

William met her eyes as a slight smile came to his lips. 'Why, the ring she begged of me, father.'

Joan felt as if she'd been doused in icy water.

'I see.' Cecil laid a hand on his son's shoulder, then beckoned Joan. 'If you desire to go, I will escort you.' He didn't bother looking at Rose. 'Your girl can follow behind.'

Joan stepped away from Rose and looped her arm through Cecil's, pretending the move took no thought or effort when all she wanted was to run in the opposite direction. 'Of course, Lord Salisbury.'

He snatched at Joan's hand, shoving it into the crook of his elbow. 'I'll return shortly, William.' He said the words gently even as he squeezed Joan's fingers like he hoped to break them.

He wasn't strong enough for that, but it had never been clearer that he could do far worse. They descended the stairs, and the halberd-wielding guard fell into step behind Rose. Rose met Joan's eyes for a moment, her jaw clenched. She flexed her fingers, and Joan shook her head in a quick, discreet jerk.

Yes, they could fight their way past Cecil and his single guard, but the political and social ramifications of such actions would be massive.

Their coach sat not far ahead, its doors already open with the footman, Gregory, waiting to help them inside. They need only endure a short walk, though it already seemed to stretch into eternity.

'I'll see you dead before I let you have my son,' Cecil sneered.

Joan huffed out a mirthless laugh. 'Worry not. I want nothing to do with him.'

'Don't lie to me, girl.' He stopped suddenly, turning to glare at her with every bit of spite he held in his heart. He shifted his grip, digging his fingers into the flesh of her arm as he shook her hard. 'You're nothing to me. Best remember that.'

Joan scowled back, exhaustion making her bold. 'How could I forget, my lord? I feel nothing but loathing for your son.' She glanced over her shoulder to find William peering at them from the edge of the platform, satisfaction all over his face. She sent him a dark look and cursed him in her head. 'I despise him and would never lie about that.'

Shock stole the man's voice as he dropped her arm and immediately looked back at his son. Joan locked eyes with Rose and then continued towards the coach with purposeful steps.

She'd scored the tiniest victory against that vile man, but if she lingered in his company, she knew his next viper strike would be that much harsher.

'One last thing before you go, girl,' Cecil called after them. 'There was a prisoner in the Tower who was known to you, one Benjamin Wick, yes? I recognised his name when I saw it on that list of yours.'

Joan's heart jerked to a stop then beat double-time.

No.

'He was found dead this morning. Murdered in his cell sometime in the night.' Glee slid across his worn face, shifting it into something gruesome. 'I hope you weren't close.'

Murdered?

She couldn't breathe. She felt as if she was falling but couldn't make her body move to stop it.

Murdered?

Everything around her seemed to disappear. Her world narrowed to this man, who spoke devastation casually, as if it were the weather.

'It is far easier to kill a single prisoner in the Tower of London than any of His Majesty's favoured players,' he sneered. 'Do not underestimate my power. I could destroy everything if it is my will. Nothing you love is safe from my wrath.' Then he was gone, walking away and back up to the wooden platform.

Someone grabbed her arm. She looked up. Rose? Her mouth moved, but Joan couldn't hear her past the rushing sound in her ears. Then she was in the darkness of the carriage. She saw Gregory slam the door closed, and they were rumbling along quickly. She jerked back and forth as they rattled away from Westminster. Rose held her hand but the world wouldn't come into focus.

Her face was wet. Was she crying? She touched her cheek and felt the tears there.

'Baba . . . my godfather . . .' Her throat constricted around the words. 'My godfather is dead.'

She'd feared this but had held on to the hope that he'd lived, until Cecil had so callously confirmed it.

Her godfather was gone, leaving Joan alone to restore the Pact as the only child of Ogun left. She who was only just remembering to thank the Orisha properly, but even now still remained lax in her practices.

She who could no longer lie before Titanea.

Rose touched her face gently. 'It could be a lie. We both know Lord Salisbury would say such a thing only to hurt you.'

'We went to see Baba last night and Cecil knows.' Joan shook her head, feeling a sob break in her chest. 'He knows everything and he sent someone to murder Baba to teach me a lesson.'

Every harm, every threat Cecil brought to her loved ones had been to spite Joan. And now she'd doomed them all as sure as if she'd murdered her godfather by her own hand.

The pure pleasure on Cecil's face had confirmed the truth of his words. No lie could've brought him such joy. Besides, she's seen the men herself last night just as her mother had closed the doorway. If only she'd been faster. If only she'd dragged Baba along, he'd still be . . .

She curled in on herself, as if hoping the pain wouldn't rip her apart if she made herself smaller. Her brilliant and kind godfather was gone. She'd thought she knew this pain, had felt it when Samuel was murdered, but that was nothing compared to this. Rose pulled her close, shushing her softly and rubbing her back.

'I want to go home,' Joan said. She swiped at the tears streaming down her cheeks. 'I need to see my family. I need to tell them to leave the city.'

Rose grabbed her wrist, curling their hands together. 'You can't. We have to return to the palace. Cecil is watching you closely. If you go home, he may target them next.'

Joan clenched her jaw. Rose was right. Joan was sure if she sought out her family tonight, he'd see them arrested or worse.

But her godfather was dead, and their hope gone along with him.

CHAPTER THIRTY
Of Thwarted Bargins

he early dawn light burned against Joan's tired eyes as she scribbled frantically across several pieces of parchment. The candle on her dressing table had long since gone out, and though the sun's glow was yet weak, Joan refused to stop. She still wore her navy gown, the fabric wrinkled and creased, and the dust of yesterday's travels stained the hem. She'd taken down her hair if only as a task to distract her anxious hands. She tugged one of the loosened twists now and struggled to focus.

Knock. Knock. Knock.

She jerked upright and stared at the door.

Knock. Knock. Knock.

She shuffled her papers into a sloppy stack, trying not to smudge the wet ink. A rush of absolute fear overtook her. She'd laid out point by point how she'd help everyone she loved escape the city. If any one of these pages fell into the wrong hands, that work would be for naught. She glanced at the fireplace, ready to cast the whole lot into the flames.

Calm down. It could be Grace.

Joan breathed deeply and shoved the papers to the side of her dressing table. She placed her brush on top of them as further disguise before approaching the door. A servant, his pale face looking grey in the dim morning light, balanced a platter of food in both his hands.

'Your breakfast, my lady,' he said blandly, only the slightest irritation entering his voice as he shifted the weight of the tray.

Joan threw open her door and stepped aside to allow him in. 'Yes, thank you.' She watched him place the food on the low table in front of the fire, checking to see if his eyes strayed to other parts of the room. 'Grace said she would bring my meal. Is she not in this morning?'

'She wasn't available, my lady.' He adjusted the position of the tray, then he straightened and returned to the hall.

Joan followed him to the doorway and frowned as he disappeared around a corner. The man hadn't looked her in the eye the entire time he'd been in her presence. Perhaps some extreme sense of formality caused him to behave so – but it was still strange.

She couldn't think on it further. The sun continued to creep up higher. She was losing time.

Sighing, she dropped into one of the chairs by the fireplace, sinking deep in its soft cushions. Her shoulders and back felt the strain of her night's work, and she groaned at the insistent ache. She'd close her eyes for a moment and then she'd eat.

She only needed a moment.

Bam!

Joan leapt to her feet, eyes darting to the door as a full-size Bia materialised in her hand. Grace stood there. Her wild look took in Joan and then locked on the silver breakfast tray. She bolted for it, snatching up a goblet from one side and tossing it into the fire.

'Grace, what—'

The flames roared, blazing a sickly green as the liquid splashed over them. Joan jumped back as the heat rolled over her.

'Poisoned,' Grace gasped. She laid a hand against her chest and doubled over in exhaustion. 'I was—' She took a gulping breath. 'I was afraid I'd be too late.'

Joan looked between the simmering green fire and Grace. 'Who sent it?'

'I heard rumours' – she stopped again, coughing a bit – 'that the Countess of Suffolk intended to move against you.'

The Countess of Suffolk? It took Joan a long moment to recall who she knew with that title.

Lady Goose Neck. Of course, that long-throated terror would be the next to try killing her.

Joan took her own calming breath as she helped Grace into a chair. She knelt in front of her, grasping the girl's hands. 'Thank you, Grace. You saved my life.'

'You're very welcome.' Grace smiled at her, then collapsed back into the chair. 'Lord, I've not run like that since I was a child. It's much harder now.'

They both laughed at that even as Joan's mind turned over this newest threat.

'Oh, there's something else! The King's Men are performing here today, a new play at His Majesty's request.' She patted Joan's hand. 'That's good news, at least.'

No. They can't be here.

Joan forced the smile to remain on her face as her every plan shattered around her. They were supposed to be at the Globe on the other side of the river. She'd get word to them and they could escape into the countryside with hardly any notice.

But instead they'd be here, in the palace and within Cecil's reach.

She slipped away from Grace and went to the desk, grabbing her stack of papers, the plans she'd spent the whole night arranging and rearranging to protect those she loved most.

Without a word, she cast them all into the fire. The flames blazed again, devouring every sheet.

Grace sat up as the flames blazed again. 'What was that?'

'Nothing,' Joan said as the earthy smell of burning paper filled the room. 'Nothing at all.'

She'd been too afraid to risk seeing the players before their performance and even more afraid to send Grace with a message of warning. Not that it mattered. The King's Men didn't have the luxury of refusing a royal summons. They would've been here even if she could have given them fair warning.

Joan sat on the floor before the fire, knees hugged to her chest as Grace bustled around the room. The dancing flames cast a flickering orange glow over everything. Joan stared into their depths, wishing some safe plan to magically leap into her brain. She heard the faint clanging of swords and knew the King's Men were practicing in the courtyard opposite her window. The drawn curtains protected her from the sight of them but not the sounds. She hugged herself tighter.

She saw Grace approach again from the corner of her eye.

'Are you all right?' Grace said. She hesitated a moment then touched Joan's shoulder.

No, I'm afraid everyone I love is in danger and there's nothing I can do to prevent it.

Joan forced a smile to her lips. 'I'm tired,' she said simply, the words not a lie.

'Of course. You've already survived an attempted poisoning.' She squeezed Joan's shoulder. 'That alone's a day's worth of emotions, but the queen has requested your presence.' She went to Joan's closet then glanced back with a smile. 'Let's make sure you're wearing your best when Lady Suffolk sees she failed spectacularly.'

Joan dropped her face to her knees. Lady Goose Neck would be so disappointed if she knew how little Joan worried about her attempted murder. With Cecil and his son both against her, a bit of poisoning meant nothing at all.

Another wave of exhaustion slammed into her. She screwed her eyes shut and breathed deeply.

'Shall you wear the emerald gown?' Grace presented the skirt in question. 'Green is very becoming on you, and if there were ever a time to flaunt your beauty, it's today.'

Advantage is a better soldier than rashness.

The words leapt to Joan's mind unprompted, a single line from one of Master Shakespeare's plays. She squeezed herself tightly, taking another deep breath.

She had two enemies to watch for today, one of whom thought she was dead or at least near to it. Cecil couldn't move against the players in front of the whole court, and Lady Goose-Neck couldn't move against Joan in front of Titanea.

It wasn't enough of an advantage, but maybe she could give herself even more . . .

'Actually,' she said, lifting her head from her knees, 'I'd like to wear the yellow one.'

Grace smiled and pulled out the gown Joan had worn when she'd first arrived at the palace. 'This is excellently made! Is this also Mistress Beckley's work?'

'No, my godfather made it.' The words seemed to tear at her very heart as she said them. Yes, this gown was her own, the last tie to her life before this and the mentor she'd lost so tragically. It was both a reminder and a talisman, memorial and defiance.

She'd wear nothing else but this.

'The handkerchief too?' Grace held it up, the iron threads hidden in the sunflowers sparkling in the firelight. 'It matches so well.'

Joan closed her eyes. Her head still felt heavy, grief and exhaustion battling to drag her into a deep sleep, but she fought the feeling viciously. Baba was gone, taken from her when she'd been unprepared, but the rest of her loved ones were still very much alive.

And as long as she still breathed, as long as she carried Ogun within her, there was hope of restoring the Pact. Even trapped as she was under Cecil's careful watch, that man couldn't stop them all. She needed to behave as such.

She'd dress for battle in this armour. Though light, it suited her purpose well.

hakespeare would've thought that over a decade of seeing his plays performed before the crown would prepare him for this night, but his hands shook as hard, his stomach felt as full of lead, and his nerves plagued him as aggressively as they had that very first time.

'Breathe, man,' Burbage said as he slapped him on the back. 'Unless you've another player to serve as your replacement after you drop dead.'

Shakespeare snorted and scowled at the shorter man. 'You think you're helping, but you're not.'

'Come now.' Burbage clasped his hand around the back of Shakespeare's neck and tugged him down to stare directly into his eyes. ''Tis masterfully written and well prepared.' He raised an eyebrow. 'Do you doubt your fellows after all these years?'

'Of course not. Especially not you, Richard.'

Burbage grinned and pressed a loud, smacking kiss to Shakespeare's forehead. 'That's right! Nothing but raucous applause.'

'Nothing but.' He nodded, holding his smile until Burbage was well out of sight.

His friend was right, and it should've been enough to settle his mind. And yet . . .

He rubbed his hand against his chest, a dull pressure pulsing through him with every rapid beat of his heart.

Something still felt amiss. But was it fear for the play or some other looming misfortune? Not for the first time he wished he'd been more intuitive like his mother or his daughter Judith. They'd have easily made sense of whatever this feeling was.

'Master Shakespeare, do you have a moment?'

He turned to see James approaching and realised this was the first time today he'd heard from the boy outside of rehearsal. Shakespeare sighed. Such was the playing of a new piece. And without Joan to add her craft and masterful eye to the fights, setting the staging had taken double the time.

But did he even have a moment for the boy now?

'Ah, I'll . . .' James looked him over and saw something that made him purse his lips and shake his head. 'I'll speak of it after our performance.' He already wore his costume for the lady he'd be playing this time but held his wig. His hands flexed on the hairpiece, squeezing it tightly before letting it go with a sudden full-body jerk. He cleared his throat. 'Have an excellent show.' Then he scurried off.

Mary's milky teat.

James – dependable, remarkable James – was never nervous before a show. Hell, they'd once had a bolt of lightning strike the stage in the middle of *All's Well That Ends Well* and the boy had paused only long enough in his speech to allow the booming echo of thunder to disperse.

But something had clearly unsettled him now.

However unnerved Shakespeare had felt until then, seeing James in such a state left his palms sweating. He felt a headache forming behind his eyes and rubbed his temples in an attempt to quell it.

'They've all been seated – Will, are you ready?' Phillips said as he stepped away from the heavy velvet curtains that separated them from the stage. He glowed faintly, though few could see it.

Shakespeare himself hadn't been able to until he'd reclaimed his birthright and connected with Oshun again, inspired by Joan and her determination against Auberon. What more had he missed in his years of stubborn, childish refusal?

But he need not get distracted, their start was nigh.

'Aye, I am,' he said, sounding far more confident than he felt. He turned to the rest of the players milling about and preparing to go onstage. 'Company, to a show well-played.'

'To a show well-played' echoed throughout the back room, all voices raised as one.

It bolstered him a bit as he slipped from the safety of his fellows and out through the centre curtain. The king sat on the highest dais, surrounded by his grooms. He leaned over to whisper to the striking young man beside him, then gently stroked his hair. Not far off sat the queen – Titanea as Shakespeare knew her to truly be – with her ladies close by. He spotted Joan in a bright yellow gown, her face set and determined. His gaze shifted over the rest of the crowd and he noticed the pale, long-necked woman who kept glancing at Joan as if she were a ghost.

There was a story there that he'd get later. If not from Joan herself then from Aemilia.

But enough of that.

'Your majesties,' he said loudly, voice carrying to every corner of the wide room. 'Lords and ladies, what we present to you today is the first performance of a new play – a Scottish play.'

He paused as murmurs swept through the crowd then held up his hands to quiet them. He grinned as they went silent. Yes, this was when he felt most powerful, with the great multitude at his command. Nerves forgotten, he continued on.

'Today you'll hear a tale of bloody war and victorious knights, of kings and kingdoms, of prophecies and witches and bitter betrayal.' He knew he had them in his hands then, all eyes on him and every ear straining to catch the smallest sound falling from his lips. He grinned, spreading his arms wide as red smoke rolled through the curtains to curl around his feet. 'For we bring you *The Tragedy of Macbeth*.'

Artificial thunder boomed as he spun to exit, and the three witches slithered onstage cackling and howling.

'When shall we three meet again? / In thunder, lightning or in rain?'

Once he'd disappeared from sight, Shakespeare let out a sigh of relief. That dull ache lingered in his chest, but the thrill of the work overrode it. If he felt this come the end of their two hours' traffic, he'd investigate it, perhaps bring it up to Augustine and Richard. But for now, he'd play.

'We shall not spend a large expense of time / Before we reckon with your several loves . . .'

Oliver stood centre stage delivering Malcolm's final speech. The boy spoke well, but Shakespeare still found himself wishing for Samuel's charisma and draw, for the boy they'd lost. He realised now he'd written the speech with Samuel's voice in mind, his cadence and delivery. Even now he heard the dead boy speaking the words in his head.

Shakespeare let the curtain slip closed as he cleared his throat quietly, tears burning against his eyes. He forced them away along with the memory of Samuel's broken and bloody body.

One dead boy haunting his memories was more than enough. Adding another to mourn was torture.

'Come on, you fool,' Burbage hissed, grabbing his arm to drag him onstage.

Shakespeare let out a startled noise as he noticed the applause and the musicians playing their final song. He gave Burbage a grateful smile before they both swept into their closing dance.

He risked a glance at the king, who looked pleased as he lounged across his chair. Shakespeare noticed one of the queen's ladies approaching to whisper to the king before he was forced to look away or miss his next steps. Eventually they finished, the trumpet ending with a final complicated flourish. The audience burst into another round of loud applause, and Shakespeare finally let himself relax.

His newest play had been enjoyed by all, and this first royal performance would certainly bring attention to every subsequent showing of it at the Globe.

His mind at ease, his gaze swept the crowd, noticing for the first time an abundance of glowing figures.

He frowned.

Had there always been this many Fae at court?

He bowed again alongside the company, his mind racing. A sudden rush of movement caught his eye as he straightened and caught sight of Lord Salisbury shoving his way towards the queen. Something in the set of the man's face sent a chill down Shakespeare's spine. He looked feral.

Shakespeare followed the man's gaze, his heart thudding in his chest as he realised where he looked and at whom.

Shite!

Cecil wasn't moving towards the queen. He was heading straight for Joan.

he king held up a hand, silencing the room immediately. He leaned forwards in his chair but didn't stand. 'My queen has something to say.' He gestured to the queen, who smiled back at him.

'A request has been made that we wish to answer.' Something in her mien shifted, and Joan glimpsed the true face of the queen of the Fae. 'Today we announce and grant full blessings to the betrothal of William Cecil, Viscount Cranborne, and Joan Sands, Baroness of Clifford. May your union be happy and fruitful.'

What?

Several voices shouted at once, but Joan could barely hear them over the rushing of blood in her ears. She found herself looking at Nick before she could stop herself. The tall boy had gone pale, his face stricken. She turned to Rose, who watched the queen with an equally horrified expression.

'I object to this betrothal!' Lord Salisbury stood from his seat, his face a mask of barely controlled rage.

Oh no . . .

King James scowled but turned his gaze to the short man. 'On what grounds do you deny your queen?'

Oh no . . . no, no, no.

'That girl will never marry my son,' Salisbury sneered, jabbing a finger at Joan, 'because she's a witch.'

No.

Joan's eyes widened as every person in the room turned to gape at her. William and his father's plans collided to see her dead.

The king raised an eyebrow as a slow smile spread across his face. 'A witch, you say?'

And, damn them, it might prove the most effective of all. Shakespeare's new tragedy played directly into the king's superstitions, driving him down a dangerous path as his excitement drew the whole court along with him.

She wouldn't be surprised if they tried to burn her on that same stage.

Her heart raced as King James's gaze slid over to her. Philip looked aghast, and Joan caught Lord Fentoun's eye over the king's other shoulder. The man's face scrunched up in disgust and he looked away.

William Cecil tried to grab his father's arm. 'Father! What are you doing?' Cecil shook him off.

'I'll not have you married off only to be cuckolded by Satan himself,' Cecil said before turning to sneer at Joan. 'She should be burned for her crimes against God, not rewarded.'

Titanea laughed, the sound stark against the hushed whispers. 'This is absurd.'

'She is a witch,' Goose Neck shouted as she shoved her way through the crowd, Foul-Breath beside her. She looked ragged, her face pale and her eyes engulfed by dark circles. 'I've seen her use dark magic. We've all seen her do it!' She waved her hand at Snort and Not-Susan, who still stood beside Titanea, Snort now glowing as surely as Not-Susan did.

The disgraced lady-in-waiting had seen an opportunity to finish Joan where the morning's poison had not and she'd surely spew any foul lie to achieve her ends.

Rage burst in Joan's chest. 'Lies! I've done no dark magic!' She stood, glaring at Goose Neck, who flinched under her gaze.

'We did indeed,' Foul-Breath said from her friend's side, sombre faced as she crossed herself, 'but dared not speak of it in fear of our lives.'

Cecil smiled. 'Two witnesses presenting testimony along with my own should serve as proof enough, Your Majesty.'

William had dropped back into his seat and stared silently beside his father, his eyes wide with shock. Joan wanted to scream at him. This was where his threats had led. Had he not realised what the consequences would be?

'Not when that proof comes from a murderer,' Joan shouted. 'The Countess of Suffolk should speak of how she tried to poison me this morning.'

Titanea's cold gaze shifted to the woman. 'Poison,' she hissed. 'You sent poison to our dear Joan?'

Goose Neck paled but clamped her mouth shut.

Encouraged by Titanea's response, Joan turned to the queen. 'I am no witch. Please, Your Highness.'

If Titanea held any affection for her, she'd save her now. She'd know Joan spoke the truth, for her second boon wouldn't allow a lie in her presence.

'Words are not proof,' Titanea scoffed, 'especially not from the mouths of poisoners.' She turned to Joan. 'Are you a witch, Joan? Answer me true.'

Joan shook her head, relief rushing through her. 'No, Your Highness, I am not a witch.'

'These are hefty charges, girl.' The king stroked his beard, eyes narrowed in gleeful contemplation. 'Do you practice magic?'

Titanea snorted loudly, the sound unladylike and full of derision. 'This is ridiculous. She's already answered—'

'Quiet, Anne!' King James thundered, slamming his fist against the arm of his throne. The men around him leaned away, intimidated by his rage. 'You do not rule here – I do. The girl must answer to me.' He scowled at the queen then at Joan. 'Speak, girl. Do you practice magic? Answer your king!'

Titanea's eyes widened, then narrowed as fury overtook her face.

Joan might've been afraid of that look but the answer to the king's question pressed against her gritted teeth. Thanks to Titanea's boon, Joan could do nothing but say 'Yes.'

'Arrest her quickly,' Cecil said, his severe voice at odds with the glee spreading over his face, 'before she casts some new wickedness on us all.'

This is how I die.

Fear surged through her.

'Your Highness,' she called out to Titanea. 'Your Highness, please!'

She'd faced her death before, but this – this could not be escaped by fighting. Neither her sword nor Ogun could save her from the wrath of the mortal king.

I'll be burned alive.

She heard James scream her name, turned to see him flinging himself towards her as Phillips held him back.

Good, he didn't need to get drawn into this too.

'Your Highness, please, if you love me at all—'

'Why do you call out to the queen?' Cecil shouted. 'Have you swayed her by magic?'

'No,' Joan said, letting the easier answer burst forth as she racked her brain for the right way to speak the other.

Lord Fentoun moved towards her, every bit of his usual friendly demeanour gone. Not that she expected any less. She knew how this court felt about magic, about witches. Philip was suddenly in his way, somehow managing to step in front of Fentoun and block wherever he moved.

She had one ally here at least.

Another guard attacked Joan first. She ducked under his swing and grabbed his wrist, twisting his sword out of his grasp as she shoved him away. She used that blade to parry the next man who ran up behind her and let the momentum send his sword flying across the room.

Joan dared a glance at Titanea, who watched all with an unmovable expression. The true response to Cecil's question burned in her throat but she couldn't devise a response that wouldn't expose the Fae queen. Joan knocked a third yeoman flat and squared off with the fourth.

The first hints of the boon's icy-cold magic surged through her bones and she faltered. The guard charged her, and she threw her body to the side a moment too late, cried out as his blade sliced along her arm. She grabbed the wound and felt blood rush hotly over her fingers.

Bia pulsed at her wrist.

Enough.

This was Titanea making her stance known. She valued Joan only so long as she didn't disrupt her own plans. If only she'd realised it before now.

If only she'd had faith . . .

'I call to her because she is Titanea, queen of the Fae, and she's protected me before.' Joan let the truth fall from her lips as guards surrounded her. 'Queen Anne died in the rubble of the House of Lords, and the Fae impostor who sits upon her throne might have spared my life.'

Gasps and shouts echoed through the hall at Joan's words. The chill released her now that she'd fulfilled its demands. She glared at Titanea, daring her to react or deny, knowing she was caught by her own trap.

King James stood, his face stricken as he looked to his queen. 'Is this true? Is what she says true?'

'We had hoped to enjoy ourselves a bit longer' – Titanea rose slowly from her seat, that wolf's smile spreading across her lips – 'but we find our secrets all revealed.' Light seemed to ripple over her form before the shape of Queen Anne sloughed off her, pale skin giving way to a deep brown complexion like a snake shedding its skin. Titanea rolled her neck and spread her arms, relishing the feel of being in her true form once again. 'It is as the girl says.'

She surged forwards, shifting from the dais to stand in front of Goose Neck in the span of a blink. The woman gasped as Titanea's fingers wrapped around her throat and then pulled back, dragging a clump of flesh and gore with her. A river of crimson flowed over Goose Neck's hands and bubbled out through her lips. Foul-Breath shrieked beside her, the hysterical sound echoing through the hall. Titanea was suddenly behind her and her hand burst through Foul-Breath's chest, the woman's still-beating heart clutched in her fist. Foul-Breath's eyes went wide as the scream died on her lips and blood flowed down the front of her gown.

'We abhor liars,' Titanea said. She pulled her hand free, staring directly at Cecil as she took a bite out of the woman's heart. She spat the piece at the man, her mouth painted crimson. She laughed as he turned pale and swayed on his feet before she tossed the rest of the heart into the crowd.

A phantom wind sent the candles flickering and the tapestries thrashing against their hangings. A horse neighed, the sound twisted as if the creature were only a breath away from death. A wild howling like a hundred screams and death rattles, like nightmares creeping from the darkest corners of a moonless night came soon after, first whisper-quiet then growing louder and closer with each passing minute.

Titanea's smile turned feral as she looked to the king. 'You don't deserve the land you rule. We look forwards to taking it back from you.'

On the dais, Not-Susan and the false Snort shed their glamours, their mortal guises disappearing in an instant. Each grew by a head and a half, their thin forms the sickly bluish brown of a drowned body and dripping with water. Not-Susan smiled, and dark liquid bubbled from the edges of her lips.

Screams sounded from throughout the hall as all around them the Fae revealed themselves. Joan's eyes widened. When had so many at court been replaced? More than half of those gathered glowed and shifted as magic flowed over them.

This was Titanea's work, and Joan had been too preoccupied with Cecil to take notice.

The Fae queen turned to Joan as the shadows in the room seemed to grow and lengthen, slithering up along the walls and stretching over the floors. 'Your life is ours, child. Remember that.'

A horse made of pure darkness and its cloaked rider appeared in the air above the crowd. Both descended, moving as if on solid ground. They landed before Titanea, who tipped her head back as the rider – Herne the Hunter, leader of the Wild Hunt – dismounted to approach her queen. The Hunt's shrieking grew to a cacophony, then went suddenly quiet. Titanea reached up to caress Herne's cheek somewhere in the shadows of her hood.

'You've been so patient,' she said, as Herne leaned into her touch like a cat. 'For nearly two thousand years we've waited.'

Ogun flared, a blazing inferno in her chest as Bia vibrated hard enough to ring.

Titanea smiled out over the crowd as all manner of creature seemed to be birthed from the darkness, joining their fellows among the court. 'Now feast.'

Then all hell broke loose.

 oan didn't think. She leapt down the stairs to the queen's dais and ran towards the stage, towards the company.

'Get your swords,' she shouted to the King's Men. 'Arm yourselves!'

James caught her eye then bolted back through the curtain in a dead sprint, Nick and Rob following right behind him. The stage blades were dull and plain steel, but they'd serve until she could reach them.

The screams of mortal fear and Fae glee thundered through the hall. Two jacks-in-iron grabbed at whoever was nearest, their tall bodies towering over the courtiers desperately trying to escape them. One grabbed hold of a woman and tore her head from her shoulders with ease. It used her hair to attach it to the thick chains circling its body, her mouth open in a silent, eternal scream that matched the other trophies the creature wore.

Joan hiked up her skirts, ducking under the flying body of a yeoman tossed by a blue-skinned goblin. She threw herself to the side as the guard's bloody arm flew back towards her, a trail of gore following in its wake.

'No,' Titanea whispered in Joan's ear, suddenly very close. 'No, you stay with us, Iron Blade.' Her elbow locked around Joan's throat. 'We can watch them fall together, and relish in their suffering.'

Joan tried to twist away, and Titanea squeezed until she could barely breathe. Pain lanced through her and spots danced at the corners of her vision as Joan clawed at the arm that held her fast. She forced iron down over her palm.

'We had hoped to keep our conquest subtle.' She batted Joan's hand away idly, avoiding her metal swipe. 'But this is far more fun.' She pressed harder and Joan felt her throat close.

Her head buzzed as the world around her started to fade to darkness. Her limbs seemed to rebel against her mind's commands, each move a struggle.

Something slammed into them and they pitched suddenly sideways, Titanea losing her grip. Arms wrapped around Joan as she gasped and choked, desperately sucking in air. She rubbed her throat as her vision settled and gazed right into the face of Goodfellow.

'What—' Joan coughed and tried again. 'What are you doing?'

They smiled thinly. 'The little I can to protect you. I've brought your parents. Your mother is a hell of a fighter.' They jerked their chin towards something behind her.

Joan turned to see her mother hopping from bench to bench, swiping at Titanea with the metal canes she wielded in each hand. The Fae queen grunted and jerked as each hit connected. Joan smiled. She'd coated her mother's weapons in iron herself.

But still, as excellent as her mother was, she shouldn't have been able to occupy Titanea so thoroughly. The way the Fae queen's slow moves nearly matched pace with Joan's mother's sent a sudden chill down Joan's spine.

'She's not at full strength yet, is she?' She turned to Goodfellow, afraid of their answer. 'Titanea.'

Their face turned grim. 'No, nowhere near. You can't win here, so you need to run.'

Joan closed her eyes as the sounds of fighting and death surrounded them. Courtiers stumbled over their fellows, both alive and dead, as they sought to escape the Fae who hunted them. Joan didn't see any of the King's Men among the fallen but that didn't mean they all still lived.

But running now was as good as handing Titanea and her Fae the city of London. What would it mean if they lost this place?

Fight.

No, she wouldn't let any of her people fall here.

'No, we can't run,' Joan said resolutely. 'Go find the king, and we can—'

'This is the last help I can give you, Iron Blade.' Goodfellow said, their gaze darting around to take in the carnage. They looked back at Joan, their eyes bright with tears as they pulled her into a tight hug. 'Please, protect my Rose.' Then they disappeared into the air.

Joan stumbled forwards as they faded, heart breaking even as she understood. 'I will, I promise.' She whispered the words into the emptiness, not knowing if they heard but needing to speak it nonetheless.

Fight.

I will, she thought.

Ogun's presence blazed again, and Joan felt her resolve strengthen. The Orisha was with her, within her, giving her strength and guiding her hand.

She was made for this fight and she would not lose.

She touched a hand to her wrist, and Bia leapt forth into her waiting grip. Sending iron flowing down the blade, she sliced through a fast-moving goblin. It shrieked and split in two, falling out of her way. Another moved to replace it, then curled out of her way as she raised her sword. It jumped past her and landed on a screaming courtier, his clothes shredded and his face already bloody with deep scratches.

Joan flung out her hand, sending an iron spike through its heart as it tried to tear out the poor man's throat. The goblin collapsed. The man coughed and scrambled away, sobbing out a string of prayers.

All around her the Fae terrorised the royal court, toppling benches and tearing down tapestries. She couldn't see where Titanea and her mother's fighting had drawn them now and she still hadn't glimpsed her father, but she had to trust that her family could take care of themselves.

Some movement nearby caught her eye, and Joan threw herself backwards as claws lightly scraped along her neck. Her hand flew to her throat, feeling the sting of shallow wounds and the wetness of blood. The creature skittered towards her on six spiderlike legs, each ending in human hands.

A sharp-toothed smile spread across its face and it swiped at her again. Joan whipped Baba's handkerchief from her bodice, forging its iron threads together to make a shield. She knocked the creature's claws away, and it hissed as it touched the metal. Joan blocked its next blow, slicing its hand off with a quick swing of her sword. It hissed again, and she slammed the handkerchief into its face. The smell of burning flesh filled the air.

It fell backwards shrieking and moaning, its face smoking and raw where she'd touched it. Joan stepped on its writhing body and then vaulted over the last few benches to land onstage.

'Joan! Give me those gloves like before,' Burbage shouted, running towards her with his fists outstretched. 'But with spikes, to really hurt.'

She couldn't help the laugh that burst out of her. She tapped Bia's blade against her wrist, wrapping it around her forearm as she softened the handkerchief and tucked it back into her gown. Her hands free, she clasped them over Burbage's. Iron slid across his knuckles then spiked up between her fingers in four sharp blades. He pulled away, and his fist shot past her head. Something screeched behind her, the noise cut short by a wet crack. She spun to see the face of a red cap collapsed around Burbage's fist, its long arms going limp at its sides.

'Now I'm ready – thanks, lass.' He grinned and stepped around her, kicking the red cap's body away. He flexed his fingers then dove into the fight with a bright yell.

Joan turned again, and James shoved a bundle of swords into her grip. She wrapped her arms around them before they could tumble to the floor. She counted seven total in her fumbling.

'Do your thing,' he flapped his hand at her then blew a jack-in-irons off its feet with a gust of wind from his palm. 'Go, go, go.'

Only she and Burbage were armed well enough to do damage to the Fae, and if she didn't hurry, the other players would soon be overpowered. Joan nodded and set to work as screams and shrieks and groans and growls quickened her hands. She sent iron flowing over the first sword. It caught the light as the metal covered the blade and the edge sharpened finely enough to cleave with ease. She tossed the finished sword to James who immediately threw it to Rob. She quickly prepared another, which James passed to Nick. The one after went to Shakespeare.

'Stop giving away every sword I make for you, you fool,' she shouted at James over the squelching noise of battle.

He glared at her. 'Less yelling, more arming.'

She screamed in frustration and grabbed up the remaining four blades. She'd never tried manipulating more than a single sword at once, wasn't sure she even could, but now wasn't the time for doubt. She breathed deeply, shutting out the battle as best she could, then focused.

Nothing happened.

She tried again, picturing the blades sharpening in unison as the glowing flow of iron covered each one.

Again, nothing.

'Joan! Hurry!' James said. His eyes went wide. 'Behind you!'

She turned, withdrawing her handkerchief and shifting it to shield at the same time. The red cap clawing at her hissed in pain and pulled its hand back. Red-hot rage burned in Joan's chest, this time feeding Ogun's fire.

A distraction. Focus.

The last thing she needed now was such a disturbance. She clenched her fist, the iron threads wrapping around her hand and drove it through the creature's chest. She pulled free and turned back to her work as the body thudded to the ground behind her.

Do as I say.

She focused again and pushed. She felt ready to breathe fire, channelled that into her metalworking. Something shifted in her chest, a tangled knot of power where she always felt Ogun's presence rattling uncomfortably. She turned her attention to it, pictured it unravelling, bursting free in a cluster of flame.

Do as I say.

Her chest constricted and then unclenched with a pop. She tasted metal in her mouth as something bright and ethereal swept over her. She took a breath and felt light and blessed as the air flowed into her lungs. The scorching rush of power surged through her, blazing hot but without pain and with an uncanny ease.

Never had she felt more connected to her Orisha, Ogun's will and her own united as one.

It felt glorious, more beautiful than anything she'd ever experienced or ever would again. Tears sprang to her eyes.

Well done.

She smiled and pushed.

The comforting chill of iron surged down her arm, covering each blade in a liquid sheen. The gloss settled, leaving the blades sharpened to fine points and ready to hurt. She reached for them and they leapt into her grasp.

'Make sure you keep one of these,' she said to James, handing him the set and glaring until he shifted one into his right hand. She flicked her wrist, and Bia slithered down into her hand again. The sword vibrated excitedly. 'Stay safe.'

James frowned at her. 'You too. Just because you've a shiny new trick doesn't mean you can get cocky.'

She snorted a quick laugh and pulled him into a tight hug. Something cooed behind her, the sound half soothing her mind in a way she knew to be dangerous. She spun, thrusting her sword forwards as James did the same. The creature, with the upper body of a woman, stared down at where both swords impaled its chest. Its long eel-like tail thrashed at Joan and James weakly. They separated, both slipping out of the way of the slow blow that landed between them. James pulled his blade free as Joan shifted her weight and drove Bia up through the creature's centre, splitting it from waist to throat. It collapsed to one side and its tail gave a final twitch.

'God's teeth, Joan,' James said.

That familiar shame she'd thought she'd buried when she'd beheaded that first red cap crept back into her chest, clenching around her heart. She couldn't let it settle there, wouldn't let it immobilise her again. Not if she wanted them to survive this. Felling an opponent did not make her a monster.

Now was not the time for mercy. She looked at the creature she'd just split in half. She'd kill to save what she loved and not regret it. Not any of it.

She huffed out a breath and focused on the heat of Ogun's presence within her. She let that burn away anything else that might hold her back.

'"*Screw your courage to the sticking place,*"' she whispered. 'Isn't that what you said in the play?'

James snorted but smiled at her. 'Of course that's the Lady Macbeth line you remember. Lend me your mettle and I'll not fail.' Something in the air of the room shifted as his grin turned sharp. 'I follow your lead, then.'

Swirling clouds gathered against the high ceiling as a breeze tugged at Joan's clothes, first gently then growing stronger with each passing minute. She smiled too. This was James flexing his own power.

A hurricane was trouble enough. One inside the central room of the Banqueting House was chaos.

Perfect.

That last tense bit of her relaxed. She brought her sword up in a quick salute then turned to sprint across the stage. She spotted Nick slicing and stabbing at a red cap, Jack sprawled behind him clutching his bleeding arm. Nick swung high, and the red cap slipped under his guard, claws aimed to tear out his heart. A blow Joan couldn't hope to block.

No!

Focus blazed through her as she reached. Heat, like that day during *Troilus*, flared down her arm. She called to Nick's sword, felt it sing back, and pulled. His eyes widened as the blade swung down, forcing his arm to follow. It sliced through the red cap, splitting it from shoulder to waist. Joan sent it cutting through the creature again, slicing its legs away before she released her control.

Her hand shook and she struggled to draw breaths. She ignored it all as she ran to Nick. Their eyes met a moment before his lips crashed against hers in a desperate kiss. She melted into it, into him even as her senses screamed danger. She pulled away, flipped her sword in the slim space between their bodies and jabbed it into the eye of a frog-headed goblin. Nick's arm wrapped around her waist, tugging her back against him as she ripped Bia free in a spurt of blood.

'I can't keep letting you save me,' he whispered, his breath hot in her ear.

She closed her eyes and leaned into him. She felt dizzy. She needed to rest. 'Stop dropping your guard, then.' She gave herself this moment, let herself feel weak as he squeezed her close.

She turned and pressed her face into his chest, breathing in his scent before stepping out of his hold. 'Take Jack and get out of here.'

'I'll get him to safety,' he said, pulling the frightened man to his feet. He gazed at her, eyes fierce. 'But I won't leave until you do.'

Joan felt her heart swell with love and frustration. 'Don't be a fool.'

'Too late. I'm already in love.'

She kissed him again, ignoring Jack's shout as Nick dropped him to grasp Joan's face. But even now, her heart whispered another name, not in contrast but in tandem.

She leaned back. 'I have to find Rose.' She watched his face, waiting for the change at her words.

'Go,' he said softly, his heart still completely in his eyes, 'I'll get our other players out, then find you again.'

Love us both or neither, it won't change my feelings for you.

The words raced through her mind, wholly uncontrolled and completely inappropriate. She shook them away until later, when they weren't fighting for their lives, and smiled at Nick. He brushed his fingers against her cheek.

Yes, she'd return to that later.

Then she vaulted back into the stands.

She had a lady to find.

CHAPTER THIRTY-FOUR

A Great Reckoning in a Little Room

y the time Joan reached the royal dais, it was empty, thrones broken and scattered in splinters of gilded wood and fabric. She tried to feel something, some sliver of sadness as her gaze drifted over the bloody corpses of Goose Neck and Foul-Breath. But the sight evoked nothing.

Her mother still held Titanea's attention. She could see them trading blows over a cluster of fallen benches and bodies both human and Fae. Joan started to go to them but turned away. She needed to find Rose and the king.

'Witch . . .' someone croaked from nearby. 'You did this . . .'

Joan's head jerked towards the sound, the familiar voice breaking her heart. It came from behind a pile of splintered benches. She shoved them aside. Lord Fentoun lay beneath, his crimson uniform shredded and soaked through with blood. Joan kneeled beside him, knowing she could do nothing to save him. Tears burned her eyes.

'Witch . . .' His chest rattled with the effort of breathing, the pink of the meat beneath his flesh exposed through his bloody wounds.

He wouldn't live much longer.

'I'm no witch,' she said, wanting him to hear the truth even if he didn't believe her. 'Where is the king?'

He twitched, his eyes going wide and frightened. Joan heard a hiss behind her and spun, sword aimed to strike.

Something that looked like a pale old woman with pure black eyes and stringy white hair knelt at Fentoun's feet. Her long fingers tugged at his boot. 'He's already near dead. Let me drink the blood left and I'll leave you be, girl.'

Joan glanced at Fentoun. He gazed back, terror and pain twisting his face.

'Away.' She pressed Bia's sharp edge to the creature's throat. 'Or I'll be the last thing you ever see.'

It hissed again but scampered off, hand clutching where Joan's sword had pressed against its skin. Whatever the guard captain thought of her now, she'd not let his last moments be as this creature's meal.

'Lord Fentoun, please.' She looked at him again. 'Does the king yet live?'

He coughed, blood splattering across his lips as his eyes shifted in and out of focus. 'Aye, lass, aye. The king – and Montgomery and Cecil. They ran when the monsters attacked. I did my best to hold them off.'

'Were there others?' she asked desperately.

He groaned, his head lolling to one side as he spoke. 'His son and the queen's girl . . . she protected them.'

Hope flared in Joan's heart. That had to be Rose. She was alive, and Joan would find her.

She smiled at Fentoun. Each shallow breath struggled to sustain him. She grasped his hand. 'You've done your duty well. Rest now.'

His eyes locked on hers and he relaxed, his chest rising and falling twice more before he lay still. Gently, she dragged his eyes closed, then stood.

A gust of cold air whipped around her and she turned. There, in the darkness behind the dais, a heavy door creaked on its hinges. Its colour matched the wall so perfectly, she'd have never known it was there had it not been open. With one last glance at the fallen captain of the king's guard, Joan slipped through the door and down into the dark passage.

She could see the flickering candlelight far-off and ran towards it. The body of the Fae who'd been either Susan or Snort slumped across the floor, the remnants of its burst head leaned against the wall and surrounded by gore. A feat of strength that could've only been Rose's doing. Raised voices echoed through the hallway, followed by the sounds of a struggle. Someone cried out in pain – a woman – then more shouting.

Rose!

Joan lifted her skirts higher and sprinted as fast as she could. She dashed into a small stone room, feet slipping across the floor as she skidded to a sudden stop.

Rose stumbled back; hand pressed against her side as blood trickled through her fingers. Cecil stood in front of her, his dagger raised as if to strike again. A wide-eyed William crouched off to the side, shaking fiercely. Philip supported the king, who wavered on his feet, his head bleeding as his eyes fluttered and rolled.

'What are you doing, Salisbury?' Philip shouted. 'She was protecting us!'

Cecil swung his dagger at Rose again, and she stumbled out of the way. 'She's one of those creatures! That strength wasn't human. She's a monster like the rest.'

'You've gone mad!' Philip clutched the king as nearly collapsed.

Rose spotted her first, pain twisting her face, and rage filled Joan. The girl's wound bled sluggishly, and she swayed but stayed upright. Joan would pay Cecil back for the injury he'd done Rose once they were all safe.

'You thrice-damned girl . . .' the man growled as his eyes locked on Joan. He looked feral, his clothes dishevelled and torn and blood streaked along his pale face and hands. Crimson stained the dagger he gripped fiercely. 'This misfortune is long of you.'

Rose's blood.

Joan gritted her teeth, swallowing the words she wanted to scream. Calmed, she said, 'The palace has fallen. We need to get His Majesty to safety. Where does this passage lead?'

'Witch – you've caused this!' Cecil swung his dagger wildly in her direction. 'You swore you'd put down the Fae—'

Her grip tightened on Bia, but she relaxed her hand slightly as Cecil's eyes shot to her blade. 'I killed Auberon as you demanded, but the larger threat's been beneath your nose this whole time. Titanea—'

'No! No more lies! I will protect the king from you.'

Joan shook her head, glancing quickly at King James and Philip. Beside them, William watched her intently, his gaze shifting between Joan and his father.

'To the courtyard, Joan,' Philip called. 'The passage leads to the court-yard by that hall.'

Joan nodded to him gratefully and turned back to Cecil. She could disarm the raving man, but she had no idea how William would react to her attacking his father. He was the only other unencumbered person and capable of attacking her. In this moment, force could cause more harm than good. The risk was too great. She had to try to talk him down.

'We are of one mind, Lord Salisbury,' she said gently, hoping her use of his formal title would serve to calm him. 'We have a common enemy. And we need to get the king out of here.' She looked to Philip again. 'Go, before we're found.'

The man nodded, then whispered something to the king as they started for the hall.

'Don't move!' Cecil screamed, spit flying from his mouth. 'Don't listen to this demon.'

The king groaned and half collapsed in Philip's arms. Philip cried out and stumbled under the larger man's weight. Rose swayed again, her face growing paler by the moment.

Joan lost all patience. 'We have no time for this. We must move now.' She gestured at William, her gaze pleading. 'Help Lord Montgomery and the king.'

'Do not move, William.'

William half crouched, half stood against the wall, his gaze darting frantically between his father, his king and Joan.

Philip grunted as he struggled to get King James standing again. 'By heaven, Cecil, listen to her. Boy, William, come help me.'

'No! She's as dangerous as the rest. You can see it in that hellish stare of hers.' His gaze settled on Joan again. 'I'll kill her before I let her harm England or its crown.'

'You endanger the crown, you daft fool!' she shouted back.

She stepped towards Cecil, who flinched back, still brandishing his dagger. Fear, true fear, set his eyes wide as his chest rose and fell in rapid panting breaths. She took another step, and the hand holding his weapon began to tremble.

All the terror this man and his political strength invoked in her disappeared in an instant. She saw him for what he was: pitiful and weak and so blinded by hatred he'd rather they all die here than just listen to her.

Enough.

She dove forwards, catching the quillon of his dagger with the end of her sword and flicking it out of his hand. He shouted as his weapon flew beyond his reach, then glared at her. She sneered back, no longer afraid of his rage.

What was this small man to the might of the Fae that awaited them just outside?

'William, go with the king,' she said, keeping her eyes on Cecil. 'Your father and I will follow.'

She heard Rose's feet shuffling past her on the stone floor and Philip struggling after her with King James.

'Father . . .' William said weakly, his voice squeaking over the word, all his bravado gone in the face of real danger.

He's just a child, she thought.

Joan scowled at Cecil. 'Tell him to go.'

'No,' Cecil said.

She raised her blade, pressing the point to Cecil's throat hard enough to draw a drop of blood. 'Tell him to go.'

His hands clenched and unclenched but he jerked his head at his son. Joan heard quick footsteps and Philip's strained thanks. Relief flowed through her.

'I'll see you dead, girl,' he whispered. 'You'll regret ever crossing me when your soul burns in the eternal fires of hell.'

Joan snorted. 'Your threats mean nothing now. Your power is lost, stolen by the queen of the Fae.' She lowered her sword, letting every bit of disgust she felt for him curl over her face. 'Escape with your life. Surely that's worth more than your need to see me suffer.'

She turned to follow the others down the next hall, determined not to waste any more breath on the cowardly man. Rose was slowly making her way towards the door at its end first, William and Philip following gingerly behind, the king suspended limply between them. Rose stopped, catching her breath against the wall. She looked back at Joan and her face went stark with horror.

Joan spun just as Cecil leapt at her. She thrust her sword out but she'd given him easy aim directly at her heart, a blow she wouldn't survive.

'Burn in hell, witch,' he screamed as he plunged his blade into her chest.

Heat burst through her body as time seemed to slow. She felt the sharp point of the dagger press against her skin and focused there. It sang to her sweetly as she took control of the metal. She imagined it bending, curling away so it never pierced her body. She willed it so and felt the blade go soft.

Cecil's fist rammed into her chest. She blinked rapidly as time righted itself. She felt no pain, no rush of blood.

She looked down. Cecil's dagger bent sharply away from her, the cold smoothness of its flat side lying harmlessly against her chest. She met his gaze again, his eyes wide with shock and fear as the dagger clattered to the ground.

'You're going alone, I'm afraid,' she said.

They both looked down to Joan's blade, driven through his gut. He coughed, and blood bubbled over his thin lips. He grabbed for her wrist but she swatted him away. She placed her hand on his shoulder and then shoved him backwards as she pulled her sword free. He stumbled, falling to the ground with a wheeze as he clutched his belly. Joan didn't bother watching for him to rise again; she knew he wouldn't.

'Father,' William wailed. He rushed over, leaving Philip faltering with the king on his own. The boy's gaze met Joan's as he passed her, absolute devastation on his face. 'It's all right, Father, I'm here.' He dropped to the floor, clasping the dying man's hand in both of his. 'I'm here.'

Joan felt a pang of sadness then – not for Cecil but for his son. This didn't have to be his end, but she was happy to have given him what he wanted.

'William,' she said gently, 'we have to go.'

'No. I'm not leaving him.' He didn't even look at her, just focused on his father.

Joan understood and pushed him no further. She hurried over to Rose, who was struggling to help Philip get King James standing. Without another able body to help, their escape would be terribly slow. Joan was strong enough to help both Rose and the king but it would leave her unable to fight. They'd be vulnerable and stuck in a hall they could barely squeeze through.

Rose winced and grabbed her side with a moan.

There was no time for anything else.

Joan slipped between the two of them, tucking Rose's arm over one shoulder and the king's over the other. Philip looked at her gratefully as they managed to get them both moving.

'Come on,' she grunted, straining a bit but holding the weight of two injured people. 'I'm getting you all out of here.'

King James barely lifted his head to squint at her. 'You killed my secretary of state,' he slurred groggily.

'I did.' Joan glanced back at William one last time.

He was leaned over, whispering something to his father in the quiet room.

She looked away and started the slow trudge through the dark hall. 'Should we survive this, you can appoint another.'

She didn't turn back again.

CHAPTER THIRTY-FIVE

Like an Angry Hive of Bees

oan and her charges reached the door and burst out into the courtyard, leaving them all squinting in the bright sun. Behind them, the screams had quieted. The reality of why gave her no comfort. She left her three charges hidden in the shade of the palace clinging to one another. The king had regained his senses enough to stand on his own, though he still swayed a little if he moved quickly. Philip lingered close by his side, ready to catch him if he fell. Rose leaned against the wall and the king, her face a pale grey and dotted with sweat.

Joan pressed a hand against the girl's cheek, swallowing around the sudden lump in her throat as Rose pressed weakly into her touch.

'I'm getting you out of here,' she whispered, 'all of you. So hold on.' She kissed Rose and wished she could transfer some of her own warmth and vitality to the girl's chilled lips.

Joan slipped away, creeping along the wall in search of some escape as silently as she could. The sounds of fighting grew louder as she approached the wall before it exploded in a gust of wind. She threw herself back, readying Bia as she leaned around to glimpse into the gaping hole in the side of the Banqueting House. The building groaned and shifted, barely built to endure such stress.

James rushed out into the courtyard, followed by the King's Men. Burbage, Shakespeare, Nick and Phillips took up positions alongside James, blocking the way as Armin and Rob rushed survivors to safety. Sudden relief flooded through Joan at the sight of her friends. Nick turned then, shouting her name as he spotted her.

'I have Rose and the king,' she said quickly. 'They both need help.'

He nodded and ran over, tugging Master Burbage along as he passed the older man. They followed Joan back to where she'd left Rose and the rest near the secret hallway.

'Come with me, Your Majesty,' Burbage said as he slung the king's arm around his shoulders and Philip took up the other, grateful for the help.

Nick swept Rose up into his arms and Joan tried not to panic as her head fell limply against his shoulder.

'Stay with us, Rose.' Nick shook her gently until she opened her eyes again. 'Put your arms around me.' She did, and he met Joan's gaze, his expression gentle and reassuring. 'I've got her.'

Joan led them back out into the courtyard, trying to calm her racing heart. Now wasn't the time to make mistakes because she was shaken and frightened.

James swung at a long-armed red cap that leapt back away from the blow. He cut through the air again, this time slicing across the creature's eyes. It shrieked and fell away as he turned and spotted Joan.

'They're here,' he shouted. 'Now, Master Shakespeare!'

The tall man dropped his sword and reached out his hands, his face hard with focus. A jack-in-irons bounded for him from the other side. Joan raced forwards, Bia slicing through the air with a sharp whistle.

The creature collapsed, head rolling one way as its body fell in the other direction.

'Thanks, Joan,' Shakespeare said, his voice strained and his brow covered in sweat. 'This is taking longer than I—' His eyes widened as a grin spread across his face. 'There we go.'

A low rumbling, rushing sound grew louder and louder until huge columns of river water crested over the main palace and swept across the courtyard, washing away everything in their paths.

He swirled his hands, keeping the water churning around them in rapid circles that left the ground on which they stood clear. 'Now, Bess!'

Joan spun to see her mother marking a shape in the empty air. She flicked her knuckles in the centre and a knock echoed around them. A door swung open, revealing the rolling green hills of the countryside.

Suddenly her father stepped through from the other side. 'This way, hurry!'

Burbage and Philip stumbled through first with the king in a half run, half hop. Nick followed after, shooting her one last look over his shoulder before he stepped through with Rose.

Nick and Rose were safe now, as was the king. Some of the fear strangling Joan's heart unclenched. She could fight without worry now. She'd already defeated Cecil. If she ended Titanea now, that meant safety for everyone she loved.

Stopping the war before it began would make Baba Ben proud. She sharpened Bia's edge as her eyes swept the yard. She'd finish this today.

She could think of no better way to honour her godfather's memory.

Something split through the middle of Shakespeare's swirling waters, sending them crashing to either side in tall waves.

Titanea stood at the centre of the maelstrom, hands outstretched and face a mask of rage as the water flowed around her harmlessly and more Fae surged from the building behind her. Her eyes locked on Joan's mother and the door. With a roar, she sprinted towards it.

No!

Joan threw herself forwards, Bia tumbling from her grasp as she reached out for any metal she could sense between Titanea and their escape. She called desperately, not caring what answered just so that she could protect that doorway.

It sang back, not all iron but good enough, filling her head with a swirling harmony. A swirling river of gold and silver surged out of the gaping hole in the Banqueting House as sconces and candelabra turned liquid and danced towards Joan. She grabbed hold of their song, shaping them to her will and threw her hand up. A glittering wall shot into the air in front of Titanea. She smashed into it with a grunt and then screamed as it locked around her, closing her in a sphere of metal. Joan scrambled over. She pressed her hands against the ball to bolster it, using all of her will to keep it steady.

Titanea slammed against the inside, and it bowed but held fast. She shrieked, the sound muffled by her metal prison.

'Go!' Joan shouted. 'I'll hold her as long as I can!' Bia was the key to resealing the Pact. Once her loved ones were safe, she'd take on the Fae queen and see what the sword could do.

James stumbled towards her. 'Joan, no—'

'James, go,' their mother called. 'I can't hold this open for much longer.' Dark bruises covered one side of her face, which was twisted in a grimace of pain.

James cast a stricken look at Joan before he ran through the doorway. A creaking roar resounded as Phillips tore away one of the Banqueting

House's exterior support beams as if it were nothing. The building listed to one side, barely standing.

'I've got them, Will,' he said. He swung the heavy piece of wood in a wide arch, sending Fae flying this way and that.

Shakespeare released his control of the water, panting heavily. 'Thanks, Augustine.' He clutched his chest then limped quickly to the door.

Her mother stepped through behind him, holding it open from the other side. She caught Joan's eye, her arms shaking from the effort, the look she gave resolute.

Her mother would hold the doorway until Joan came through or she died from the strain of it. Joan looked at the metal ball that held the Fae queen then back at her mother. Those same instincts that drove her to protect everyone she loved at any cost flowed through her mother, through her father and through her brother too. Joan knew if she stayed in that moment they'd all return to fight with her or to die beside her.

She couldn't risk that. She needed to retreat.

'We'll go together, Master Phillips,' Joan shouted, the words cutting her pride as she said them. She grunted as Titanea struck her prison again. 'On three. One, two—'

Titanea's hand burst through the metal, fingers wrapping around Joan's wrist. Joan jerked back but Titanea held fast as she pulled herself free. Several people shouted her name at once but none seemed louder than Titanea's growled whisper.

Joan slipped her toes under Bia where the sword lay on the ground and flipped it up into her hand. She swung wildly for Titanea's head, missing as she leaned back under the blow. She jerked Joan forwards and caught her wrist on the sword's backswing, stopping the attack. Joan let iron flow down her arm, shooting out in a sharp spike. Titanea screamed as it impaled her palm. Her grip loosened, and Phillips slammed his entire body into hers. The three of them tumbled sideways but Titanea lost her hold on Joan, rolling across the yard until she slammed into the side of the Banqueting House.

'Run,' Phillips shouted as he dragged Joan to her feet.

They sprinted for the doorway, which was already starting to shrink closed.

'Traitor,' Titanea screamed. 'Traitor!' She appeared suddenly beside them, tangling her hands in Phillips's white hair and jerking him backwards.

Joan shouted as he fell, frantically swiping her blade at the Fae queen. Her first swings missed but the third hit, slicing across Titanea's ribs. She gasped as the blade connected, and Joan felt the zing of some energy shoot through the sword and up her arm. Bia's song burst out in a resounding ring that seemed to echo throughout the courtyard.

Titanea stumbled back, clutching her new wound as her eyes widened in fear. 'How did you get that blade?' Her face twisted into rage. 'How did you get that blade?'

Phillips slammed his body into Titanea's again, sending her tumbling away from them. Joan scrambled back. This was no good. She needed something stronger to stop the Fae queen to buy them time to escape. She glanced up and her eyes caught on the ornate iron gates down the long front pathway.

That would do.

She had a moment to mourn the loss of such beautiful craftsmanship before she reached out and called all the iron to her. It sprang to her will, slamming into the ground in a solid wall between them and Titanea, blocking her from following them. Joan's eyes met Master Phillips's, and they both ran for the door again.

Joan could see her mother on the other side, arms shaking hard as her father and brother supported her on either side. They'd barely make it, the opening so shrunken they could only cross one at a time.

Phillips suddenly shoved her in front of him, and she fell through into the soft grass. She staggered to her feet and spun. Blood splattered across her face as a hand burst through Phillips's chest. Joan cried out, reaching for him through the door as his eyes went wide.

How had Titanea broken through the iron wall to do this?

There was still time. Joan could go back again to grab the old man. If she pushed him through, she might be stuck, but someone could try to save him. He was Fae, he might survive such a wound.

'Close it,' he whispered.

The hand in his chest turned, another pushing through beside it as blood gushed down Phillips's doublet.

'Close the doorway,' Joan said, forcing the words from a throat tight with tears. 'Close it.'

Joan heard her mother gasp as she released the door, but Phillips gave her the barest nod before his body was split in two, pieces falling to either side and revealing the form of Goodfellow, their eyes cold and dark and their blood-covered hands outstretched. The doorway folded in on itself and was gone.

Then there was nothing but the quiet of the countryside and the smell of fresh blood and bright green grass.

CHAPTER THIRTY-SIX
Bright Metal on Sullen Ground

oan strode down the long corridor of Master Shakespeare's country home just as the morning sunlight blasted its way though the windows. She hadn't slept a wink – none of them had, as they'd spent the night caring for the injured and receiving more of the Orisha worshipping community as they escaped from London.

They were still arriving today, a steady stream of confused families knowing nothing more than to converge on Stratford-upon-Avon. Iya Anne – as Shakespeare's wife had asked to be called – seemed determined to house everyone here at New Place, and so far the estate had allowed for such generosity. Though, as more and more arrived, it became apparent that they'd need to look elsewhere for shelter.

Joan had never seen so many of their community gathered in one place beyond the ceremonies that brought them together in small groups. As their numbers in Stratford increased, she felt hope blooming in her.

Yes, they'd ceded London to Titanea and her followers, but perhaps they'd have the power to take it back.

She felt the phantom heat of Master Phillips's blood on her face, though she'd long cleaned away its stains. She clenched her hands as she tried to control her breathing, feeling the sharp pain of her nails pressing into her palms.

No. Even if Joan had to go alone, she'd make sure Titanea was sealed away again.

'I've bandaged his wound. If he begins to act erratically, come find me.'

Joan looked up to see three people standing further down the hallway. She recognised one as Philip Herbert, his usually immaculate posture slumped with exhaustion and worry. The others were Susanna, Shakespeare's oldest daughter, and Doctor Hall, Stratford's sole physician. Those two left together, and Joan hurried over to speak to Philip before he headed back into the room. He glanced up as she approached, giving her a small smile.

'I must say, this is the strangest day I've ever experienced,' he mumbled, rubbing his eyes.

Joan gave him what she hoped was a comforting look. 'How is the king?'

'Alive thanks to you and your friends.' He glanced at the door and sighed. 'Was that Susan . . .' He choked over the name, clearing his throat to start again. 'Was that my wife in the corridor?'

She took his hand. 'No.' She paused, unsure of how to deliver her next words gently enough not to break him. He seemed so fragile now. 'Your wife was gone long before today. I'm sorry.'

'Ah.' He laughed hollowly. 'I'll see to the king.' He stopped as Joan squeezed his hand but didn't turn to look at her. 'I . . .' He pulled out of her grip and disappeared into the room.

Joan watched the door close behind him. His heartbreak was palpable but she knew there was nothing she could say to help soothe it. She continued down the hall and spotted Iya Anne coming out of Rose's room. Joan broke into a run.

'Is she awake?' she panted as she reached the older woman.

Iya Anne smiled, the movement showcasing all the joyous wrinkles in her light brown face. 'She is. Your young man is there too.' Her grin shifted to something sly. 'Why don't you go see to them both?'

Joan flushed deeply but moved past her to enter the room. She'd sat by Rose's bedside from the moment they'd arrived in Stratford-upon-Avon. Her mother's doorway had dropped them just outside Shakespeare's home village where Iya Mary had been waiting. She'd led them to New Place where Joan's father had cleaned and bandaged Rose's wound and the king's. While they'd had Doctor Hall see to King James again, only Joan's father had cared for Rose. The girl had drifted in and out of sleep over the last several hours but was blessedly stable and alive. Joan had left the room for a moment to get some air and hated that she wasn't there when Rose finally woke up.

The door creaked as Joan slipped in. Nick sat beside Rose's bed, speaking softly to her. Joan felt some fear in her release as she saw the two of them together, but she refused to inspect its source. There'd be time for those questions later.

She moved over to stand behind Nick, placing her hands on his shoulders to massage the tense muscles. He leaned gratefully into her touch as he and Rose looked up at her.

'I'm glad you're awake,' Joan said, struggling to not let the words be overtaken by her fear and worry and affection.

Rose smiled, her expression showing she'd heard all Joan's secrets anyway. 'As am I.'

'And I too,' Nick said. He patted Rose's hand before reaching up to squeeze one of Joan's. 'Truly.'

Joan felt more of that fear leave her. Whatever shape this thing between them was taking, it was stable enough to leave unspoken for now.

It could wait until they'd all gotten sleep and the time to process what they'd lost.

Knock. Knock.

'Joan?' Susanna poked her head around the door, her hazel eyes looking as tired as Joan felt. 'Grandmother wants to speak to you.'

Joan glanced at over at Rose. She wanted to stay but knew she couldn't refuse Iya Mary's summons.

'Go,' Rose said, settling back into the pillows. 'I'm not going anywhere soon.'

Nick squeezed Joan's hand. 'I'll make sure of it.'

Rose snorted, and Joan smiled at them both before pressing a soft kiss to Nick's lips just because she could. His hand slipped around the back of her neck, caressing the skin there before he pulled away. She turned to Rose, leaned over to kiss her, because she could do that too. The girl melted at her touch and ran her fingers along Joan's cheek as she pulled away. Then, with one last glance at them both, she followed Susanna out of the room.

Downstairs, Iya Mary and several other community elders had gathered around the Shakespeares' dining table. In the hours following their flight from London, as the other Orisha-blessed people had fled the city and converged on Stratford, the elders had all come together. They'd set protections around the village, fortifying them as each new child of the Orisha arrived and making this the safest place in all of England.

For now.

Some of the younger adults, like Joan's parents and Iya Anne and Master Shakespeare, stood off to the side out of respect. Her mother looked terrible, bruised and exhausted. Shakespeare looked just as bad, his eyes sunken and dark. They'd both slept as soon as they'd arrived in Stratford and seemed barely awake now, leaving Joan wondering why stretching her powers hadn't drained her as it had them.

This would've been a question for her godfather, but he was gone. She swallowed around the lump in her throat and tried to focus on the present.

Iya Mary sat at the head of the table. Her curly, white-streaked black hair was pulled back into a sleek bun, and her brown skin was so pale it could've been mistaken for a tan. She gestured to the seat across from her, and Joan slowly sat down.

'Thank you, Susanna,' she said. 'You may go.'

Susanna glanced between Joan and her grandmother. 'I'd like to stay, if you don't mind.'

'I do.' Iya Mary said imperiously.

Susanna looked as if she wanted to ignore her grandmother's command before she sniffed and turned to leave the room. She cast a glance at Joan that clearly said she'd get answers from her later before she disappeared deeper into the house, slamming the door behind her. Iya Mary huffed out a breath once she'd gone then turned to Joan.

'We find ourselves at the start of a war,' She said, her voice quiet but not soft. 'Do you understand your role, Joan?'

Joan nodded. 'I have to seal Titanea and the rest of the Fae with a new Pact.'

'Did Benjamin tell you how?'

Joan glanced at her mother briefly, but looked back quickly when Iya Mary cleared her throat. 'No.'

'Damn,' Iya said as she glanced around at the other elders. 'Then it's up to us uncover the ritual.' She frowned as she addressed Joan again. 'You can go, child.'

'But, Iya—'

'But?' the woman said sharply, her glare fierce. 'Your meddling cost Benjamin his life. You have no idea what that loss has done to us. We will figure out the way and inform you of what we need. Do you understand?'

Joan flinched and looked away. 'Yes, Iya Mary,' she whispered even though she wanted to say more.

'That's all.'

Joan leapt up from the chair as soon as she was dismissed and bolted straight out into the back garden. She dropped down onto the grass, tucking her head between her knees, and tried to steady her breathing.

This was all too much. Baba was supposed to be the one protecting the Pact, he was prepared, his bond with Ogun was older and probably stronger for it. And Baba would still be alive if Cecil hadn't wanted to punish her.

I'm sorry, Baba. It's my fault you—

Her breath hitched, her mind not even letting her complete the thought as tears burned her eyes.

Joan was a fighter. She conquered her problems with her strength and her sword. She'd defeated Cecil in the end, but the blow he'd dealt her put their whole world in danger.

She felt someone crouch down beside her and turned her head to see James. He held out her sunflower handkerchief, the one Baba had made for her.

'I figured you'd need this,' he said. He took a breath and his lips trembled, his eyes red and surrounded by dark circles.

Seeing him and the last gift she'd received from her godfather broke through her steeled nerves. She dissolved into tears, curling in on herself. James wrapped his arms around her, hugging her close as he sobbed too.

'I'm sorry I couldn't save Master Phillips,' she whispered, 'or Baba.'

He rubbed his hand along her back. 'I know you did your best. We all do.'

Not all.

Joan thought of Iya Mary and her harsh admonishment. She squeezed her brother tighter, wishing his words could outweigh the elder's.

But did Joan even need them to? She knew everything she'd done, all the people she'd saved and helped save. The beings she'd defeated with her own hands. Yes, the losses were heavy, but she was strong enough to carry them without buckling.

She took a deep breath, feeling her resolve even through her weeping.

'Things seem hopeless now,' she said, 'but who else amongst us beheaded a powerful Fae?'

James snorted and shook against her. 'That's cocky of you.'

'But true.' Joan squeezed him tighter.

Yes, Titanea was stronger than Auberon ever was, and her power was growing by the moment, but so was Joan's. She felt Ogun's easy pulse in her chest and Bia's thrum at her wrist.

James had blown out the Banqueting House wall with a gust of wind and Shakespeare had summoned and controlled the fury of the Thames. They were all growing stronger. Iya Mary had no idea what they were capable of, what they could accomplish in the face of this war.

'Remember,' Joan said. '"*Screw your courage to the sticking place*" when you fear we'll be overcome.'

James snorted out another watery laugh. 'Lady Macbeth dies before the end of the play, you know.'

'Well, it's not the most apt turn of phrase but it'll do for now.' She squeezed him one last time, then leaned away. 'We are at a disadvantage, I will admit, but I have the utmost faith in us.'

He pressed the handkerchief into her grip. 'And I you. Just as Baba did.' He hugged her again then squeezed her hands and stood to walk back into the house.

Joan watched him go before taking a deep breath. She felt her confidence lifted by the spirits within her and the faith of those around her. Those would be enough to carry her through the weight of things past and yet to come.

And she had her sword. She shifted her wrist, feeling the shrunken Bia humming against her skin. Ogun said the blade was the key, and she'd felt something, some power, when she'd used it to cut Titanea. Iya was wrong: They weren't starting from nothing, even with Baba Ben lost to them.

The handkerchief tumbled from her lap and fell into the dirt. She reached to grab it but paused. She held her hand in the air above the cloth and called to the metal within it. A beautiful harmony sang through her mind before it leapt up into her waiting hand.

The intense feel of Ogun's presence washed through her, comforting her with its warmth. Yes, she'd lost the man who was supposed to guide her in her relationship with the Orisha, but she'd discovered new strengths on her own.

'Meferefun, Ogun.' The words of gratitude falling easily from her lips as an answering flush of heat bloomed in her chest.

With Bia and the ones who believed in her by her side, she'd bring down Titanea once and for all.

Hope mingled with the bright burn of vengeance in her heart as Joan made her way back into the house.

The queen is dead, and a Fae imposter sits on her throne.

But not for long.

Titanea would pay for all she'd done, and Joan would collect the Fae queen's debts in blood.

A Note on History

While this novel is a work of historical fiction, it was born from a place of historical fact. Several of the characters we meet were real people alive in 1606, and while there were narrative liberties taken with the timeline, most of it is true to life. While the existence of the Fae in England at this time is debatable, the presence of non-white citizens and queer people is not.

Real People

MORE OF THE COURT OF KING JAMES I

Philip Herbert was the Earl of Pembroke and Montgomery as well as a gentleman of the bedchamber – the closest position to the king and responsible for things like dressing him and providing companionship. He was a favourite of King James I and was believed to have been one of the king's lovers despite their eighteen-year age difference. The king paid off many of Philip's gambling debts and played a pivotal role in Philip's marriage to Susan de Vere in 1604. The First Folio – a collection of Shakespeare's plays published posthumously in 1623 – was dedicated to Philip and his older brother, William.

Thomas Erskine was a childhood friend of King James I as well as captain of the guard and groom of the stool – in charge of helping the king with hygiene and using the toilet (or chamber pot as it was then). He was made Viscount Fentoun in 1606.

William Cecil was the son of Robert Cecil. He was granted the title of Viscount Cranborne in 1605 after his father was raised to the Earl of

Salisbury. He was raised by his maternal aunt, Frances Stourton, after his mother's death in 1597.

Frances Cecil was the daughter of Robert Cecil. She eventually married Henry Clifford, first cousin to Lady Anne Clifford. In real life, she was two years younger than William but, for dramatic purposes, she is two years his elder in the Forge & Fracture Saga.

Susan de Vere was the wife of Philip Herbert and niece of Robert Cecil as well as a lady-in-waiting to Queen Anne. Susan and Philip were married at the royal court in 1604, and she was given away by Queen Anne and King James.

Aemilia Lanier (née Bassano) was the daughter of famous court musicians and the lover of Henry Carey – Baron Hunsdon, Lord Chamberlain to Queen Elizabeth and the first patron for William Shakespeare's acting company (then known as the Lord Chamberlain's Men). After Carey's death, she was married to Alfonso Lanier, another court musician. She is thought to be the 'Dark Lady' referred to in Shakespeare's sonnets and have inspired the characters of Bassanio in *The Merchant of Venice* and Emilia in *Othello*. She herself published a book of poetry called *Salve Deus Rex Judaeorum* (*Hail, God, King of the Jews*) in 1611, making her the fourth Englishwoman to publish poetry and the first to write an entire original book of her own poems.

Mary Shakespeare (née Arden) was William Shakespeare's mother and the youngest member of the prominent Arden family in the county of Warwickshire. She married John Shakespeare in 1557, and they had eight children.

Real Events

REAL EVENTS OF 1605/6

The Gunpowder Plot was an unsuccessful assassination attempt that was planned for the morning of 5th November 1605. The detonation of thirty-six barrels of gunpowder placed beneath the House of Lords was planned to coincide with King James I and VI opening the session of Parliament. The ensuing explosion would've killed the king, Queen Anne, Prince Henry and all the members of Parliament. It also would've levelled a large portion of London, including Westminster Abbey. The plot was discovered on the evening of 4th November when Robert Cecil and his soldiers raided the undercroft beneath the House of Lords and found Guy Fawkes and the gunpowder. His fellow conspirators were either arrested or killed in a firefight in the north of England. The date is marked now as Bonfire Night or Guy Fawkes Night and by the rhyme 'Remember, remember the fifth of November.'

  Twelfth Night occurs every year on 6th January. It's also known as Three Kings' Day or Epiphany Eve and is a Christian holiday that marks the end of the Christmas season. It was a day of great celebration at the royal court and usually involved performances of plays or masques – more pageant-like spectacles full of elaborate costumes and performed by the royals and courtiers. Shakespeare's play *Twelfth Night* is so called because it was written for performance on this holiday and to celebrate the visit of Italian dignitary the Duke of Orsino.

The Execution of the Traitors responsible for the Gunpowder Plot happened on 30th and 31st January in 1606 and were just as gruesome as described in the book. The first day of executions were held at St Paul's Churchyard, but it was believed to be a desecration of such a holy site so the following day's hangings and such were held at the Old Palace Yard at Westminster.

The First Performance of the Play *Macbeth* is believed to have happened at court sometime around the end of 1606, although the first recorded performance was at the Globe in April 1611. We don't know exactly when the play was written, though many scholars believe it was written as a tribute to King James, who ascended the English throne in 1603. The most agreed-upon date is 1606 given that it deals with the assassination of a Scottish king and might've been inspired by the failed Gunpowder Plot of November 1605. I've taken my own liberties here and moved its writing and first performance to suit my plot. I'm sure Shakespeare – who gave the landlocked Bohemia a coast for dramatic effect in *The Winter's Tale* – would be proud.

The Orisha

This novel contains a fictionalised version of the very real tradition, Orisha veneration or worship – which was born in West Africa, mainly in the area we now know as Nigeria. While certain aspects may be familiar to practitioners, this is not a true reflection of the religion and should be taken as fantastical.

My personal knowledge of the Orisha is through Lucumí (commonly known as Santería) – a branch of the practice from Cuba. It was born when enslaved African people blended their traditional religion with the Catholic practices forced on them by the Spanish. The cover of Catholicism helped them worship as they wanted without punishment.

For the religion as Joan and her family practice it, I asked myself, what would things look like if the religion came to England without being shaped by the cruelties of the slave trade? I also added the idea that the Orisha give you magical powers. If you'd like to know more about the Santería religion or the Orisha, I recommend *Black Gods: Orisa Studies in the New World* by John Mason and *Finding Soul on the Path of Orisa: A West African Spiritual Tradition* by Tobe Melora Correal, but ultimately the best resource is an actual practitioner or priest.

Acknowledgements

Book 2, baby! We're here, we did it! Thank you to myself to completing my second ever novel and my first ever sequel. I won't even lie to y'all, it was not easy but it's done and in your lovely hands, all thanks to the help of some truly incredible people.

Maggie Lehrman, my wonderful US editor, thank you for helping me whip the chaotic first draft I sent you into a sequel worthy of Joan and her fight. Thank you for deadline extensions and being both kind and honest in your feedback. Thank you for seeing all the gaps in the story and helping me flesh them out and for your eye for coordinating the most gorgeous covers. One more to go and I couldn't ask for a better partner to take this ride with!

Ama Badu, my incredible UK editor, thank you for your clear vision and for loving Joan as much as I do! Having you on my team is such a blessing. Thank you for bringing Joan and her crew home.

To my fantastic team at Faber: Natasha Brown, Sarah Connell, Carmella Lowkis, Bethany Carter, Barbara Mignocchi, Jack Bartram and the whole sales team. Y'all got my book into the gift shop at

Shakespeare's Globe, a blue sky dream that you made a reality. Thank you for all your hard work and care for this series.

Thank you to my copy editor Shasta Clinch, proofreaders Margo Winton Parodi and Diane Aronson, and my angliciser, Nate Rae, for polishing the manuscript of a chaotic writer who never paid attention to the rules part of English class and saving my UK readers from my American spellings. It's wonderful to have y'all's eyes to help get my vibes into a reasonable order and up to a universal standard.

To my cover illustrator Manzi Jackson, thank you for another great cover! Your detail work is incredible, I love it so much. To my art director Emma Eldridge, thank you for bringing it all together once again! The bar was already high but clearing it was nothing for y'all.

To my map artist Jamie Zollars, I already thanked you for giving me the map of my dreams for *That Self-Same Metal* but I'm going to say it again because this new map is even better! Thank you for your patience with all my notes. I might have struggled with visualising this but you never did. Your art and detail continue to astound me. I'm in awe.

Thank you to my beloved Carrie McClain for being my beta reader and giving me such wonderful and thorough notes. I couldn't have gotten this book to the finish line without your help. I love you, sis!

Thank you to everyone at my lit agency, Writers House. Special thanks to the foreign rights team: Cecilia de la Campa, Alessandra Birch and Sofia Bolido for doing your best to sell this niche series with ferocity and passion. Y'all rock!

Thank you to Burton Tedesco and the cast of *Henry IV, Part 1* for cheering me on as I drafted this book, swung a giant sword as Hotspur and took care of an infant. Thank you to Matt, Monica and the cast of *A*

Midsummer Night's Dream for cheering me on as I promoted *That Self-Same Metal*, directed our wild night outdoors while dodging the termite swarms and wrangled a toddler. Thank you to the cast of *Twelfth Night* for cheering me on while I edited this book, pranced around Illyria, and, again, wrangled a toddler.

To incredible agent and friend Alexandra Levick, thank you for talking me through the process of getting this book from my imagination to shelves. Thank you for your notes, for never letting me panic or spiral in isolation, for advocating for me when my anxiety holds my tongue, for always responding to my 8 million email questions and for being the perfect collaborator and business partner. Most importantly, thank you for making me write the summary of this book before we even took the series out to sell. Drafting it in the middle of life chaos might've broken me. I could not have done any of this without you, Allie!

Thank you to my wonderful friends who supported me through this process. To Tracy; Ayana; Amy & Paul; Leigh; Jalisa; Clinton; Ron & Leslie; Jonathan, Resse, Ashley and my Arena Players family; Nicole, Leslie, Izetta and Carrie, my Taco Tuesday, Womanism Everyday group chat; Will, Omar and the rest of my Black Nerd Problems family; all my beautiful, chaotic geniuses in the Black Nerd Problems Discord; my hilarious and supportive D&D squad; to my 2023 debut babes Jade, Danielle and Hannah; and Soni, Zoulfa and the rest of my Agent Siblings. Thank you for making all the hard work a little bit easier on my heart and mind, for keeping me laughing, and for reminding me of my brilliance.

Thank you to my wonderful family. Thank you to the whole Williams/ Johnson/Cook clan for always being my biggest cheerleaders even when you only halfway know what I'm talking about; the love I have for you all knows no bounds. To my brother, Eric, and his beautiful family – I love y'all so much! To my baby sister, Ericka, for being a cooler teenager than I could've ever hoped to have been – you're who I write for and I hope you feel seen. To Mom & Dad Older for supporting me in person and from afar; I literally could not have done this without y'all. To Malka, Lou & the kids, thank you for loving me and welcoming me into the family with such warmth and generosity. To Grandma for being my mom and grandma in one, my biggest cheerleader, and for supporting every wild and unusual thing I ever wanted to wade into. I wouldn't be her without your love.

To my love, Daniel, thank you for being a wonderful husband, partner and dad. Thank you for pushing me with love and kindness. Thank you for changing diapers and breaking story with me and helping me tug myself out of writer's block. Nothing I write on this page could capture the full breadth of my love and gratitude or how much I admire you both as a person and an artist, so I'll continue to show you in person.

To my brilliant, chaotic son, Tito, thank you for helping me grow and learn alongside you. Thank you for making me take breaks and be more loving with myself. Thank you for being a loving, curious little guy with a huge personality. I love you more than words could ever express, my little bun.

Finally, thank you to every single one of you who bought, requested, read, shared or talked up this book. Thank you to everyone who invited me to an event. Thank you to every bookseller who stocked this series, to every reviewer who took the time to write such lovely things, to every writer who put these books on a list and got it in front of new readers. Thank you to everyone who came out to see me on tour; I loved meeting each one of you. Thank you to all the authors and moderators I talked with on tour for your generosity and community.

Like I said before, the writing was solitary but the publishing is a group effort. Every single person here helped me along this this journey and I thank you all from the bottom of my heart.

ABOUT THE AUTHOR

Brittany N. Williams is a classically trained actress who studied musical theatre at Howard University and Shakespearean performance at the Royal Central School of Speech and Drama in London. Previously, she has been a principal vocalist at Hong Kong Disneyland, a theatre professor at Coppin State University, and has made appearances in *Queen Sugar* and *Leverage: Redemption*. Her short stories have been published in the *Gambit Weekly*, *Fireside Magazine*, and the *Star Wars* anthology *From a Certain Point of View: The Empire Strikes Back*. Learn more at brittanynwilliams.com.